DRY BONES

*A Selection of Recent Titles by Sally Spencer
from Severn House*

The Jennie Redhead Mysteries

THE SHIVERING TURN
DRY BONES

The Monika Paniatowski Mysteries

ECHOES OF THE DEAD
BACKLASH
LAMBS TO THE SLAUGHTER
A WALK WITH THE DEAD
DEATH'S DARK SHADOW
SUPPING WITH THE DEVIL
BEST SERVED COLD
THICKER THAN WATER
DEATH IN DISGUISE
THE HIDDEN

The Inspector Woodend Mysteries

DANGEROUS GAMES
DEATH WATCH
A DYING FALL
FATAL QUEST

The Inspector Sam Blackstone Series

BLACKSTONE AND THE NEW WORLD
BLACKSTONE AND THE WOLF OF WALL STREET
BLACKSTONE AND THE GREAT WAR
BLACKSTONE AND THE ENDGAME

DRY BONES

Sally Spencer

This first world edition published 2017
in Great Britain and the USA by
SEVERN HOUSE PUBLISHERS LTD of
Eardley House, 4 Uxbridge Street, London W8 7SY.
Trade paperback edition first published
in Great Britain and the USA 2019 by
SEVERN HOUSE PUBLISHERS LTD.

British Library Cataloguing in Publication Data
A CIP catalogue record for this title is available from the British Library.

ISBN-13: 978-0-7278-8754-2 (cased)
ISBN-13: 978-1-84751-870-5 (trade paper)
ISBN-13: 978-1-78010-933-6 (e-book)

This is a work of fiction. Names, characters, places and incidents
are either the product of the author's imagination or are used fictitiously.
Except where actual historical events and characters are being described
for the storyline of this novel, all situations in this publication are
fictitious and any resemblance to actual persons, living or dead,
business establishments, events or locales is purely coincidental.

Typeset by Palimpsest Book Production Ltd.,
Falkirk, Stirlingshire, Scotland.

PROLOGUE

5 October 1974

The cellar, which lay beneath the De Courcey Quad, was dark and damp. It was also cold – not cold enough to cause problems for brass monkeys, it must be admitted, but chilly enough.

But it was not the damp, nor the dark, nor even the cold, that anyone entering the cellar noticed first – it was the smell.

It was difficult to isolate quite what kind of smell it was. The odour of rotting eggs was certainly present, and there was also a delicate hint of untreated sewage, with perhaps a soupçon of decayed vegetation added for good measure. But whatever the constituent parts, there could be no arguing that it was both nauseating and overpowering.

The college porters should, by rights, have been the first ones to notice it, but they claimed not have been down to the cellars for weeks – so it was left to the superintendent of buildings, out on a bi-annual tour of inspection, to walk into the olfactory ambush. The superintendent took decisive action, first tracing the smell to what he thought was its source, and then summoning one of the stonemasons to do something about it, while he went off and had a substantial lunch on expenses.

There were two men (or, perhaps more accurately, a man and a youth) standing in the cellar and looking at the brick structure, which could best be described as a semi-circular chute, built flush to the cellar wall and running from floor to ceiling.

'What is it?' asked the youth, whose name was Tony Roberts.

'It's an experimental ventilation shaft, designed by Hubert of Ashby, way back before Adam was a lad,' said the man, Jim Withnell, who was a qualified stonemason, but knew quite a lot about bricks as well, so understood these things. 'As far as I know, it's the only one of its kind in the world. Now, why do you think that might be, young Tony?' he asked his apprentice.

'I don't know,' Roberts admitted.

'What possible reason could there be for other people not to have copied it?' Withnell asked, still patient, but with a warning edge to his voice that this patience had its limits.

'Is it because it didn't work properly?' Tony Roberts asked.

'Nearly right,' Withnell conceded. 'The truth of the matter is that, while it might have looked good on paper – or parchment as it must have been in them days – it didn't work *at all*.'

'So why didn't they take it down again?'

'Ah, the impetuousness of youth,' Withnell said, in a voice which managed to combine philosophical acceptance of the novice's naiveté, with a teacher's natural exasperation that his pupil was not making more rapid progress.

'You what?' Tony Roberts asked.

'"It's not right, so why not just take it down again?" Isn't that what you just said?'

'More or less.'

'Well, for a start, young Tony, the men who built this knew what they were doing and took pride in their work, so demolishing it would probably have been a real bugger of a job. Besides, for all they knew then (or we know now), Hubert might have integrated it into the stress structure. In other words, if we take it away, the whole bloody place might fall down.'

'I don't see any ventilation holes in it,' Roberts said, seeking to divert the conversation away from his failure to spot the bleeding obvious.

'That's right, you don't see any ventilation holes,' Withnell agreed. 'That's because there aren't any. They've been blocked up for as long as anyone can remember.'

'Then it's virtually a sealed unit.'

'Exactly.'

'So why do we think that it's the source of the stink?' Tony Roberts wondered.

'*We* don't – but Mr Crock, our superintendent of buildings, *does*,' Withnell said. 'And it doesn't matter that Mr Crock has no real experience of buildings like this, because he has *paper* qualifications. That's why his word is law, as far as us mere mortals are concerned, and why he has the right to sleep with our fiancées the night before the wedding.'

'You what?' Roberts said.

'I'm only joking,' Withnell assured him.

'Good, because . . .'

'He's usually willing to wait until they come back from the honeymoons before he does them.'

'But that's . . .'

'I'm still joking,' Withnell said. 'Listen, lad, we'll be working together until you finish your apprenticeship, which, God knows, is years and years away, so one of two things has got to happen – either I've got to lose my sense of humour or you've got to find one – and, given that I'm the stonemason and you're only the apprentice, which one do you think it should be?'

'I've got to find a sense of humour,' Roberts said. He paused. 'Should I laugh now?'

'No, the moment's gone,' Withnell said. 'Maybe, to make it easier for you, I should tap myself gently on the head with a hammer before I say anything remotely funny.'

'That would help,' Roberts agreed.

Withnell sighed. 'It's going to be a long few years,' he said. He turned to face the shaft again. 'Now, shall we set about the job, so we can get out of this stinky place?'

'All right,' Roberts agreed.

'What I propose to do,' Withnell said, 'is to take a few bricks out of the centre of the column – just enough for you to be able to stick your head and shoulders inside, and establish what we already know – which is that wherever the smell is coming from, it isn't coming from there. Once we've done that, we can bring the almighty superintendent of buildings back down here, let him see it for himself, and then close things up again.'

'There wasn't anything funny in that, was there?' Tony Roberts asked tentatively.

Withnell sighed again. 'No, there wasn't,' he admitted. He walked over to the wall and pointed to one of the bricks. 'You can start by chipping away the mortar on that one,' he continued.

'Won't you be doing it?' Tony asked.

'I will not,' Withnell told him. 'You're the apprentice, you need the practice. I'll nip upstairs to have a quiet smoke outside, where the air isn't quite so poisonous, and then I'll come back and supervise you.'

'You're too kind,' Tony said, very much under his breath.

It was not an easy task to chip away the mortar and ease out the bricks, and Tony Roberts told himself he would be heartily glad when the job was over. Even so, he was quite surprised when, having only removed less than a dozen bricks, he heard his boss – who had recently returned from his smoke – say, 'That's enough.'

Tony Roberts stepped back to look at the hole he'd created.

'I'll never get my head and shoulders through that, Mr Withnell,' he protested.

'I know that, lad, but I'm sick to my back teeth of being down here, and I reckon that hole's big enough for you to just about squeeze your head through,' Withnell replied.

'It'll be dark in there, so I'll need a torch, and how can I hold a torch if I can't get my hand through?' Tony wondered. And then, because he really was very pissed off at having been left to do *all* the donkeywork, he added (though he knew he shouldn't have), 'You hadn't thought about that, had you, Mr Withnell?'

'As a matter of fact, I had,' Withnell countered, 'and it seems to me that if that mouth of yours is big enough to cheek me, it should be big enough to hold a small torch.'

He held out the torch.

Tony hesitated, then switched it on, put it into his mouth, and turned towards the opening.

The hole was wide enough for a man with a torch in his mouth to get his head through, but there was not much clearance at the sides, and Tony Roberts eased himself in gingerly.

Withnell watched him with something almost bordering on affection. The lad was not the sharpest pencil in the box, he thought, but he had a feeling for stone and, given time, would make a fair mason.

It was once Tony's head was completely inside that something seemed to go wrong. The first sign was that his body started to twitch, the second that he made the sort of gagging noise that any man who wanted to scream – but was prevented by having a torch in his mouth – might make. Not that the torch remained in his mouth for long. Withnell heard the sound of it falling at the same moment as Tony – his former regard for caution now completely abandoned – pulled his head rapidly out of the hole.

'What's the matter, lad?' Withnell asked. 'What's in there?'

But Tony was too busy throwing up his lunch to give any clear answer.

ONE

7 October 1974

Since the only window in my office looks straight onto a
window in the building on the opposite side of the alley, it
would seem reasonable to assume that my lack of a view is
compensated for by the fact that I am at least sheltered from most
of the elements. After all, the wind likes to have a clear run at
things, doesn't it – hence the phrase 'wind tunnel'.

All well and good, except that the normal laws of meteorology
don't seem to apply here, and my current client and I are being
periodically distracted by this particular wind – a harbinger of the
chill winter to come – rattling away at the window frame.

I dread a cold winter, as would anyone having to run – and heat
– a business *and* an apartment in the historic city of Oxford.

I turn to my client and . . .

Actually, before we go any further, a few words of clarification
might be necessary. When I say an 'apartment', what I mean is a
bedsit with an attached bathroom which is so small that even the
mice are starting to feel hemmed in. And when I say a 'business',
I mean a one-roomed office (upstairs from a company with a flashy
purple logo, which imports dubious exotic goods from the Far East)
located at the unfashionable end of the Iffley Road – an office,
furthermore, which is being warmed this October by a paraffin
heater, because, as expensive as heating oil is, it is nothing like as
ruinous as the amount the robber baron who owns this building
would charge me for access to his central heating system.

I'm not complaining about my lot in life, you must understand.
I like living in Oxford, and I generally enjoy my work – when I
have any work to enjoy. I'm even *almost* reconciled to the fact
that I'm a redhead called Jennie Redhead (my late father always
insisted it was genetics, rather than malice on his part, which was
responsible for that particular predicament).

But that's all by-the-by. What's bothering me more than the

wind and the fuel bills – and this really *is* bothering me – is the man sitting on the opposite side of my second-hand desk. And the *reason* that he bothers me is that he wouldn't be here if he wasn't in deep trouble.

Of course, all the people who come to see me are in trouble – tear-stained women who suspect their husbands of unfaithfulness, anxious shopkeepers who have no idea which of their 'trusted' employees is stealing the stock – but what makes him different to the rest is that he is no stranger to me.

His name is Charles Edward George Withington Danby Swift. He is a genuine peer of the realm, the greatly respected bursar of St Luke's College, and absolutely my best friend in the whole wide world.

We met during my first week as a student at St Luke's, at a reception in the Master's Garden. I was standing in the middle of the throng – but I was not a part of it. How could I be? They (the rest) were predominantly southern and expensively educated, and when they spoke, it was with an almost lazy – and very confident – drawl. I was northern, state-educated, and with an only semi-refined regional accent.

And then there was the way we were dressed. We were all wearing subfusc (a strict requirement whenever the Master is present), which meant that I had on a dark jacket, white blouse, black bow tie, dark skirt, dark stockings, black shoes and commoners' gown. In other words, I was in the same uniform as every other girl there, and so should have blended in.

Right?

Wrong!

Because all the other girls' outfits had been *purchased* from top London stores (and no doubt charged to Daddy's account), whereas mine had only been *bought* from a discount warehouse in Whitebridge, for cash.

Standing there, I felt like a white nag of doubtful lineage which had been painted with black stripes, but didn't fool any of the surrounding thoroughbred zebras for a minute. I felt lonely and alone, and was just about to slip away when someone tapped me lightly on the right shoulder and I heard a plummy voice say,

'Hello, you seem to be a little down in the mouth. What's the matter, my dear – won't the other children play with you?'

I swung around, furious at being so openly ridiculed, and prepared to address the posh boy in language that I assumed he would never have heard before – an assumption which, I was to learn later, was about as far from the truth as it is possible to be.

Charlie was in his early forties then – a tall, stately-looking man with hair the colour of pale straw – and what struck me immediately was that despite his words, the expression on his face was completely free of malice.

'I'd ignore them, if I were you,' he continued. 'They're so terribly cliquish. But then, the *nouveau riche* always are.'

'The *nouveau riche*!' I'd repeated incredulously.

'That's right,' Charlie had confirmed. 'Take that chap over there.' He pointed to a typical Hooray Henry. 'I happen to know that only a couple of centuries ago, his family hadn't even got a pot to piss in.'

'Only a couple of centuries ago!' I'd repeated. 'Is that meant to be some kind of joke that only people already in the know would really understand?'

Charlie had assured me it was not a joke, then looked down at the glass of white wine he was holding in his hand.

'This Pinot Gris is perhaps a little too fussy for my taste. What do you think of it?'

What *I'd* thought was that it was only the third glass of wine I'd ever drunk in my life, and I was in no position to judge.

'I've tasted better,' I'd said, casually.

Charlie had just grinned.

'Have I said something funny?' I'd asked.

'No. I'm smiling because I'm embarrassed.'

'Embarrassed? What about?'

'About putting you in a rather difficult position.'

'I don't understand.'

'I said the wine was a Pinot Gris, but now I realise it's a Chablis, and you – having known from the first sip what it really was – have been wondering whether to correct me or let it pass.'

My rage returned. 'Just what kind of a sick bastard are you—?' I'd begun.

'There's no shame in not knowing about wines, you know,' Charlie had interrupted me.

'There might not be in most places, but it certainly looks like there is here,' I'd replied.

Charlie had looked around him.

'Perhaps you're right,' he'd agreed. 'What I'm really in the mood for now is a pint of best bitter in the Eagle and Child. Would you care to join me?'

'I would,' I'd told him, still in my pre-gin and tonic days. 'I'd like that very much.'

We've been best friends ever since, because despite our different backgrounds and experiences, we have plenty to talk about and can make each other laugh. And OK, it could be said that I find something in Charlie that I never found in my icy, non-communicative dad.

And yes – damn it! – I know that some women are drawn to gays because they know there's no danger with them of being sucked down into the pit of jealousy, dominance and recrimination. But none of that matters, because I love the man, and his worries and problems are my worries and problems.

He's smiling at me awkwardly, as if he doesn't quite know how to state the purpose of his visit.

'I take it that this isn't a social call, Charlie,' I say, in an attempt to kick the conversation into gear.

'No, no, it isn't social,' he says, shaking his head rather too emphatically. 'I'm here to purchase your professional services.'

Professional services! That makes me seem less like a gumshoe and more like a rather high-class call girl, I think.

What I *actually say* is, 'And what exactly is the nature of the task which requires these special services of mine?'

'Have you ever been down to the cellars under the college?' he says, going off at what – it seems to me – is a tangent.

But Charlie has as sharp and analytical a mind as you're ever likely to come across. He never goes off at tangents! I know *that*, and he *knows* I know it. So just what kind of a game is he playing?

'No, I can't say I have been to the cellars,' I say, noncommittally, biding my time.

'Most people automatically assume that there is nothing at all aesthetically pleasing about them – and very often they're quite right in that assumption,' Charlie says. 'But there are exceptions to the rule, and St Luke's cellars are a case in point. The one under the De Courcey Quad is particularly splendid. It was designed by Hubert of Ashby, the late-Medieval theologian. I expect you've read his rather important *"Ex Natura Deï"*.'

'No, I nearly bought the paperback when it first came out, but now I'm waiting for the film to be released,' I say.

'Paperback?' Charlie repeats. 'Film?' Then enlightenment dawns. 'Oh, I see, you're making a joke.'

'That's right.'

And it's even more worrying that he didn't realise I was joking immediately, because the Charlie I know would have.

'Anyway, Hubert was not only a learned theologian, but also an architect and, by the standards of the time, an engineer of some merit.'

'I'll be honest with you, Charlie,' I say, 'just listening to all this stuff is enough to make me lose the will to live.'

But what I'm thinking is: why can't he be straight with his best friend? Why can't he just tell me exactly what it is that's on his mind?

'Recently, there was the problem of a smell – probably linked to sewage – which seemed to have its source in that particular cellar,' Charlie says, speeding up because he's afraid he'll lose his audience before he gets to the punchline. 'The superintendent of buildings – whose judgement on architecture and engineering I'd trust about as much as I'd trust Attila the Hun's judgement on market gardening – decided it came from a sealed medieval ventilation shaft, and ordered the stonemason to open it up, in order to find out what was going on.'

'I see,' I tell him, dramatically tilting my head to one side, as if I've just hanged myself.

You get the point? It's a comic gesture designed to disguise how concerned I'm becoming that my Charlie might have got himself into a real mess.

'The smell wasn't coming from the shaft at all – as the mason found out the moment he'd made a hole large enough to stick his head through – but what he did discover in the hollow behind the wall was some bones,' Charlie says.

Oh Jesus, I think, as the room suddenly grows colder and darker.

'Some bones,' I repeat neutrally.

'That's right,' Charlie agrees.

Is he being evasive? You could say that. I've heard rolling drunks – who could hardly remember their own names – get to the point quicker than he is.

What he's doing, of course, is employing the standard police technique of breaking bad news in stages.

'Your husband has been in an accident, Mrs Jones.'

'Oh my God, was he hurt?'

'Yes, I'm afraid he was.'

'Badly hurt?'

'Yes.'

'He's not . . . is he?'

'Yes, I regret to inform you that he's dead.'

'They are human bones, aren't they?' I ask Charlie.

I'm hoping he'll say they were chicken bones, but if that were the case, he wouldn't be here now, would he?

'Yes, they were human,' he admits.

'Have you reported this to the police?'

'Not yet.'

'You must – and as soon as possible!'

'I will report it to the police, I promise you that – but first I need to talk to you,' Charlie says.

'I'm sorry, but I'm not prepared to . . .'

'Please, Jennie,' Charlie says, in the voice of a four-year-old who has badly scraped his knees.

'How many bones did he find?' I ask, against what I already know is my better judgement.

'Quite a lot,' he replies, and then he sees the look of growing disapproval on my face and adds, 'Enough for two skeletons, in fact.'

And this last piece of deliberately specific quantification makes my stomach go into freefall – because I now see what he is doing. He is manoeuvring me into a position in which I *have* to ask questions that I don't want to ask and would probably prefer not to know the answer to.

And beyond that, by making me ask the questions, he is attempting to transform me into some kind of accomplice in his conspiracy – to drag me, in other words, into the swamp where he himself is just about treading water.

If it was anyone else but Charlie, I would ask him to leave

immediately – but it *is* my beloved Charlie, and so I sigh and say, 'Are you telling me there were two bodies behind the wall?'

'Yes.'

'Two complete bodies?'

'Yes.'

'How can you be so sure?'

'I asked one of the college proctors – Patrick Harland Gray – to take a look at them.'

'You asked a man who invigilates examinations and handles complaints to look at these bones of yours.'

'He's not just a proctor; he's also an anatomist of some considerable international standing.'

It just gets worse and worse, doesn't it?

'By what twisted logic did you reach the conclusion that you had to consult me before you informed the police?' I ask.

'Among my many duties and responsibilities, one of the most important is to protect St Luke's,' Charlie says.

'Against what?'

'Against whatever happens to threaten it. In this particular case, it is to protect it against excessive claims for compensation that might be made by the greedy relatives of the two dead men.'

'Is that likely?'

'It's *very* likely. Everyone knows the college is rich – and therefore fair game – and since we failed to prevent the interment on college ground of men who died under suspicious circumstances – and were possibly even murdered . . .'

'Possibly?' I interrupt.

'Given that both their skulls had been stove in from behind, it's more than likely,' Charlie admits.

'Their skulls had been stove in!'

'Didn't I mention that at the start?'

'No, you bloody well didn't!'

'Well, anyway, that's exactly what happened,' Charlie says glibly, 'and, as I was explaining, there is a good case for arguing that we have been, *at the very least*, negligent. That is why I need to know the victims' identity even before the police do – because it will give me time to look into their respective backgrounds and, based on their domestic circumstances, plan out the nature and extent of our pre-emptive financial offer.'

'So all you want me to do is find out who they were?' I ask, in a tone which is probably a mixture of sarcasm and incredulity.

'That's right,' Charlie agrees.

'And what clues will you be providing me with to assist me in this relatively simple task?'

'Clues?' Charlie says, as if he's never heard the word before, and is repeating it so he'll be sure to remember it the next time someone uses it.

'Clues,' I agree. 'An envelope with an address on it would be a great help, but I'm willing to settle for a clothes label, or a ring with the jeweller's identifying mark inside it.'

'I'm afraid there's nothing like that,' Charlie admits. 'All we have is the bones themselves.'

'Then why have you been wasting my time?' I demand angrily. 'You talk as if the bones have only been there for a short while, but without other evidence, you've no idea how long they've been there. How old is the cellar?'

'It was constructed in 1214.'

'So these bones of yours could actually have lain there for over eight hundred years!'

'No, they couldn't,' Charlie says quietly. 'And I know that for a fact, because I took the left radius from each skeleton over to the science labs.'

The swirling fog thickens; the nightmare tightens up a notch!

'So you've not only messed with the bones at the crime scene, you took some of them away to be experimented on,' I say, just to make certain that – however ridiculous it seems – I've got it right.

'Our labs are better than the police labs,' Charlie says, almost sulkily. 'Our labs are some of the finest in the world.'

In the movies, the scriptwriter or director (or whoever else it is who takes the decision) always portrays the men as calm and collected in situations like this one, while the women – obviously more prone to attacks of hysteria (bastard scriptwriters, bastard directors!) – rummage around helplessly in their handbags for a packet of cigarettes. And as my fingers tunnel through a morass of compacts, perfume, and God knows what else, I am annoyed to realise how closely I am shadowing the stereotype.

I extract my cigarette packet, place a B&H firmly between my lips, click my lighter, inhale, and let the calming, deadly smoke snake its way poisonously around my lungs.

'So what have your labs discovered?' I ask, because, since the damage has already been done, we might as well reap the benefit.

'Both men were middle twenties to middle thirties,' Charlie says, 'but they were interred at different times.'

'Different times?'

'The first one – let's call him Body A – was dumped there somewhere between fifty-five and sixty-five years ago, and Body B joined him between thirty and forty years ago.'

Two bodies = two completely distinct crimes?

Now that was something I hadn't seen coming.

I do a rapid calculation. Body A was put there between 1909 and 1919, Body B between 1934 and 1944.

'Your scientists are sure about this, are they?' I ask.

'They wouldn't bet their mothers' lives on it, if that's what you mean,' Charlie replies. 'They're working with new techniques here, so they may well be wrong – but they're convinced that if they are, they're not *that* wrong.'

I slide the phone across the desk to him.

'Call the police now, while I'm here to advise you,' I say.

He pushes the phone back.

'I can't – not until I've identified the two dead men.' Charlie pauses. 'Look, if I'm in trouble with the police . . .'

'Believe me, there's no "if" about it.'

'Then I'm not likely to be in any more trouble in three or four days from now, than I am at the moment, am I?'

'They could charge you with obstructing justice . . .'

'Say one of the men was murdered in 1909 and the other in 1939. What difference is a few days going to make to anybody's investigation, after all those years?'

I sigh. 'I'm not going to help you identify them, Charlie,' I say. 'And if you don't ring the police, then I will, because after what I've just heard, I don't have any choice.'

Charlie is very fit for a man of his age, and he springs from his chair like a young gazelle. But then he falls to his knees, and the moment those knees make contact with the hard office floor, his hands come together as if in prayer.

'Please, Jennie,' he says, in a strangled voice.

'Oh, for goodness' sake get up,' I hear myself say, as if I were the heroine of a Victorian melodrama, and he my unsuccessful suitor.

'I'd die for you,' he says. 'I'd lay down my life for you.'

And I know he would – as I would for him.

I walk around the desk, grab him by the upper arms, and attempt to hoist him to his feet.

He suddenly weighs three tons, and cannot be moved an inch.

'Promise me,' he says.

In the end, my resolve breaks down, as both of us have always known it would.

'I'll give you three days,' I tell him. 'Three days – but not a minute more than that.'

He's back on his feet in an instant, and hugging me tightly to him.

It feels good!

It feels great!

But still my mind will not stop sorting and sifting what I know – and what I can merely guess at.

'When did you come up to Oxford, Charlie?' I ask.

First he stiffens, then he relinquishes the hold he has on me, and steps away.

'Why would you want to know that?' he asks – and he has suddenly grown rather pale.

'Given your age, you must have taken your entrance examinations in 1938,' I say.

'1937,' he replies, and then adds, perhaps a little arrogantly, 'I was way ahead of the rest of the boys in my year.'

'And when did you join the army?'

'1943.'

'So you were here for six of the years during which the second murder could have been committed.'

'I suppose so.'

Why is he doing this? I wonder. He was the man who wanted me to take on the case – begged me to take on the case – so why is he so unwilling to divulge any new information he might have?

And then it comes to me!

'You know who one of the victims is, don't you?'

He shakes his head, violently.

'Don't lie to me, Charlie,' I say sternly.

'I think I might have the vaguest hint of a suspicion who it *might* be,' he admits.

'Then give me a name!'

'I don't want to prejudice your investigation by feeding you any preconceived notions,' he says.

And then, quick as a superhero, he turns and dashes from my office.

TWO

3 October 1914

The morning had looked far from promising for a parade, with thick grey clouds hanging over the whole of Oxford. But then, just before midday, the sky had started to clear, and by the time the parade itself actually set off, most of the pothole puddles – unavoidable to anyone marching in step with others – had either evaporated or seeped quietly away.

The parade had a pre-arranged route that had been widely publicised, and by the time it reached Broad Street, a substantial crowd – in which all of the children and most of the adults were waving small paper Union Jack flags – had gathered along both sides of the street.

The parade was led by the WRM Motors Brass Band, and as the unusually bright autumn sun reflected off the golden instruments, the band played a melody of patriotic tunes which included 'Keep the Home Fires Burning', 'Pack Up Your Troubles in Your Old Kit Bag', and 'It's a Long Way to Tipperary.'

The crowd cheered enthusiastically, and when, halfway down the Broad, the band had exhausted their jingoistic repertoire and switched instead to old favourites like 'Down at the Old Bull and Bush' and 'Has Anybody Here Seen Kelly?,' the applause was in no way diminished.

Behind the brass band were the most recent volunteers. They

were still struggling to come to terms with the fact that once they
had signed on – and even before the ink had had time to dry – the
kindly recruitment sergeants with the twinkling eyes (who had
guided them gently through the paperwork) were suddenly trans-
formed into the screaming ogres who had occasionally haunted
sweaty childhood dreams.

The recruits had another problem – they were unused to
marching and found it something of a strain. They did the best
they were able – as the sergeants' barrage of invective poured
down on them like an unexpected rainstorm, and the crowds which
lined their route offered them uncritical encouragement – but they
succeeded only in moving in an even more haphazard fashion,
sometimes crashing into one another and sometimes tripping over
their own boots.

Behind this group came a much smaller one. These men were
much better dressed than the recruits who had just preceded them,
and – as even the least experienced observer would be bound to
admit – much better trained. They marched without the assistance
or interference of any of the recruiting sergeants – and their march
combined an almost mathematical military precision with a sort
of languid arrogance. These men (or perhaps it might be more
accurate to call them boys, since most of them fell two or three
years short of voting age) had been bred on their country estates
and in their public schools for just this moment in history. They
had no doubts, no uncertainties, and when they read the Sermon
on the Mount they mentally edited out the promise that the meek
would inherit the earth, and substituted 'the British upper class.'
They would later die in their thousands, in the process of leading
hundreds of thousands of less-privileged men to their own deaths,
and they would do it willingly and without flinching – but for the
moment, with death still a distant possibility, they were revelling
in the cheers of the crowd just as much as the common working
men who they were following had.

The dean of St Luke's College, Horatio Cornwallis Pierson, was
standing in the college's main archway, and recognised a number
of the young men marching by, which was hardly surprising since,
until a few hours earlier, they had been members of the college,
and hence, nominally at least, in his care.

He noticed, too, that he was not alone – that at the other end of the archway stood a very tall, very thin man with an aquiline nose and a broad mouth.

Gough, the head porter!

Pierson felt a momentary shiver run down his spine.

It wasn't that he was in any way intimidated by Gough.

Of course not!

He was, after all, the dean, and Gough was merely a college servant – but he still felt a certain amount of unease at being in the man's presence, an experience which he was not sure other Oxford deans shared when dealing with their own head porters.

Pierson crossed the archway, and as he drew level with the porter, Gough touched the peak of his cap in what *should* have been an act of submission, yet somehow didn't quite feel like it had been.

'Just watching our young gentlemen leave,' Gough explained. 'I have to say that they're a credit to the college, sir.'

'I'm glad you approve,' the dean said, then found himself hoping – though he wasn't sure quite why – that Gough hadn't read the comment as sarcastic. 'Have we lost many of our college servants to the war effort yet?'

'Two of them joined up today, sir,' the head porter replied. 'One of their early morning jobs was blacking up, so it looks as if the gentlemen are going to have to learn to polish their own boots.' He laughed, though it was one of the least humorous laughs the dean could ever remember hearing. 'Only joking, sir,' he continued. 'We can't have our gentlemen doing anything as common as that, can we? They'd probably end up getting more polish on their faces than they got on their boots. No, don't you worry, I'll find someone – maybe a retired servant – to fill the gap.'

'Actually, there might not be too much of a need for that,' the dean said. 'Nearly all our students have either joined up or seem to be on the point of joining up – and quite rightly so!'

'Will Mr Boulting be joining up, sir?' the head porter asked.

'Now why would you want to know that?' the dean asked suspiciously.

Gough shrugged. 'I was just curious, sir.'

It occurred to the dean that no subordinate had ever shrugged in his presence before – it was something that subordinates simply did not do – and he wondered how he should react.

He could, of course, tackle the problem head on – 'You will

not make casual bodily gestures in front of me' – but somehow even acknowledging that anything had occurred only seemed to make matters worse. And it had to be admitted that in a vague, undefined way, Gough was different to other head porters and certain allowances must be made.

Still, he was damned if he was going to let the blighter get away with it completely.

'It is not your place to be curious about your betters, Gough,' he said, harshly.

Gough should, by rights, have reacted to the rebuke by gazing at the ground and mumbling an apology – but if he *had* done that, then he wouldn't have been Gough.

'You're probably right that it's not my place, as an individual, to be curious, sir,' he said, 'but as the head porter, I have a responsibility for the college as a whole, and I have to tell you, sir, that there's a general feeling in St Luke's – a feeling which extends from most superior members of the college right down to the lowest class of servant – that we'd be better off without Mr Boulting.'

'Which superior . . .?' the dean began. Then, realising his *own* curiosity was on the point of dragging him down to the gutter, he continued, 'That's enough of that – I was telling you what will happen after the students have gone.'

'Were you, sir?' the head porter asked, recognising a diversion when he heard one, but content, for the moment, to go along with it. 'That's right, you were.'

'Once we know how many rooms we have available, we will be renting those rooms to the army, and the army, I assume, will provide itself with servants from within its own ranks,' the dean said.

The head porter made no reply.

'Do I take your silence to mean that you disapprove of the scheme, Gough?' the dean demanded, with just a hint of outrage in his voice at such a presumption. 'Because let me tell you, my good man, the college needs the money, and we can charge them two shillings a night each for accommodation, and add on extras such as the hot water they'll need if they are to take a bath twice a week. And then, of course, there is the electric lighting, which, I dare say, will be a novelty to some of them. That money, once collected, Gough, can be used for the maintenance and repair of the college, especially – as it happens – the repair of the master's roof.'

Oh, why am I justifying myself to a mere porter, the dean found himself wondering, as he reflected on his speech.

'Forgive me if I've given that impression, sir, but I wasn't complaining in any way, shape or form about billeting soldiers here – or about charging them for the privilege, sir,' the head porter said, his own level approach to their discussion clearly unchanged by the dean's display of mild petulance.

'Good,' Pierson said, 'I'm glad you clarified that, because, to be honest with you, Gough, I was starting to wonder which of us was dean.'

'Oh, you are, sir,' Gough said, as if the sarcasm had gone completely over his head. 'You're better educated, better trained, and – if I may be permitted to say so – a more natural, more inspirational leader.'

'Yes, well . . .' the dean said, somewhat flustered by the comment.

'But what I *was* wondering was which *particular* soldiers we'll be billeting in the college,' Gough said.

'We expect several regiments to pass through the city before the war finally comes to an end, and I believe that, initially, it's likely to be the Oxfordshire Light Infantry which is billeted with us.'

'I see,' Gough said, with a slight sniff.

'Do you have any objections to that, Gough?' the dean asked.

'Me, sir?' the head porter replied, as if truly astounded to be even asked the question. 'No, sir! Certainly not, sir. It's not my place to have opinions on such matters, as you've so recently pointed out in such an erudite way. If I were allowed an opinion, however, I'd probably say that I'm sure that the Oxfordshire Light Infantry are a very fine body of men, but . . .'

Don't play his game, the dean told himself – just don't play it.

'But what?' he heard himself say.

'The college isn't used to having men from the more minor regiments sheltering under its roof,' Gough said, 'and, to be honest with you, sir, I doubt it will enjoy the experience. If St Luke's men are intent on following a military career they usually join a regiment of some reputation, like the Coldstream Guards or the Blues and Royals.'

'You doubt the college will enjoy the experience,' the dean repeated, chuckling at the weird ideas which the lower orders sometimes seemed to entertain. 'You talk as if the college were actually a living, breathing thing. Did you realise that?'

'Yes, sir,' Gough said, deadpan. 'And if I talk about it that way, it's only because that's what it is – a living thing.'

Yes, it probably was a living thing to him, the dean suddenly realised.

Fellows and Dons tended to think of the college as theirs – 'I'm a St Luke's man through and through, and will be until the day I die,' they'd say – but few of them spent their whole careers at their beloved institution. (The draw of American universities, which might sometimes lack a mature academic ambience, but made up for it by being awash with cash, proved irresistible for many; while others chose to accept a chair in a provincial university, rather than gamble on one becoming available in their alma mater). And even the ones whose whole academic life was lived entirely in the city of dreaming spires still did not invest as much of their time in the college as did some of the servants, who started work at the age of twelve and sometimes continued into their seventies.

And that, of course, was probably only the tip of the iceberg of mystical attachment that some college servants seemed to have.

'Did your father work for this college, Gough?' the dean asked, testing the validity of his new thesis.

'Yes, sir, he did.'

'And what was his position?'

'Ultimately, he was the head porter.'

'And what about your grandfather?'

'He was the head porter, as well.'

'Was your great-grandfather the head porter, too?'

'No, sir.'

'Then what was he?'

'He was the college's head blacksmith, sir.'

The dean smiled. 'What a disappointment,' he said patronisingly. 'It's almost a blot on your family history, isn't it?'

'You seem to regard it as a trivial post, sir, but it wasn't,' Gough said. 'Back in those days, every student owned a horse – some owned more than one – and they depended on the blacksmith quite as much as our students now depend on the skills of a motor vehicle mechanic.'

'Yes, I can see that,' the dean said, with the vague feeling that he had just been put in his place. 'I suppose you're hoping that one day, your son will maintain the tradition and take over from you as head porter.'

'My wife and I haven't been blessed with a son, sir,' the porter said coldly. 'Nor a daughter, neither.'

'Oh, I'm sorry,' the dean said.

'Nothing to do with you, sir, so you've no cause to be sorry about it,' Gough said, matter-of-factly. 'As regards the next head porter, there's no doubt that Hugh Jenkins would be a fine and worthy replacement for me, but if anything happens to him while he's over in France, fighting the Germans, well, even though his son Harold is only four, there'll be plenty of time to mould him before I retire.'

'Good heavens, you're talking as if you had the right to nominate your own successor, Gough!' the dean said, shocked. 'Don't you know that appointments of that nature can only be made by the Maintenance and Enhancement Committee, of which I happen to be a member?'

'Yes, I did know, sir, but I seem to have forgotten it,' Gough said. 'I'm not very intelligent, you see.'

Dean Pierson was about to say that simply wasn't true, but then he suddenly realised that he ran the risk of getting far too friendly – almost intimate – with a college servant.

'Right, Gough, carry on,' he said, turning and striding rapidly across the Forshaw Quad.

He was still not sure whether or not talking to Gough had been a good idea, but he was starting to suspect it had been a very bad one. Had the head porter been making fun of him or hadn't he? And if he had, what was he, the dean, going to do about it?

It really would be advisable to take an interpreter with him when he intended to talk to the lower orders, he thought.

Or perhaps, as in the army, you should only communicate with them through a transitional figure like a non-commissioned officer.

'Ask him why his boots are dirty, sergeant.'

'Why are your boots dirty, private?'

'*I've just come off manoeuvres and I haven't had time to clean them yet, sergeant.*'

'*He says he's just come off manoeuvres and he hasn't had time to clean them yet, sir.*'

Yes, that would certainly make things easier, but unfortunately there was really no equivalent to NCOs in a university.

The dean had crossed the Forshaw Quad, and was passing under the archway that led into the Gothic Quad.

Gough had been right about one thing, though, he thought – if Albert Boulting could be persuaded to join the army, the college would be well shut of him.

THREE

7 October 1974

Jim Withnell, the stonemason, is quite broad, but would only ever be likely to win the prize of tallest man in the room at a Snow White convention. He has a nice smile and a twinkle in his eye. He's the kindly uncle type, I decide – that particular breed of uncle who has the gift of being able to pat you on the bottom at a wedding reception, without you wanting to reciprocate by slapping him hard across the face.

When he takes me down to the cellar, I'm surprised at the size of the hole in the ancient air vent.

'I thought it was just big enough for you to be able to put your head through,' I say.

'Big enough for my *apprentice* to put his head through,' he corrects me. 'There have to be some perks to being a master craftsman, because – Lord knows – the job brings enough aggravation with it.' He pauses and grins at me. 'You're right, it was just large enough for Tony to get his noggin through, but we had to make it bigger in order to remove all the bones.'

'In order to do *what*?' I shriek – and that shriek, of banshee intensity, bounces right back at me from the wall, a reminder (if I needed one) that I will never be an asset at a posh dinner party.

'We had to make it bigger in order to remove all the bones,' Jim Withnell repeats.

I take a step forward and shine my torch into the hole.

He's right – there are no bones there.

'So what have they done with the bones?' I ask, fearing the worst.

'They've taken them across the University Park to the medical department,' Jim says. 'They said something about having to store them under conditions that would prevent them turning to dust.'

So now Charlie has not just tampered with the evidence, he has dismantled the *entire crime scene*, I think.

Great!

The Thames Valley police will undoubtedly be totally over the moon about that . . .

The hole starts maybe three feet off the ground. It is not large – just wide enough to post a body through.

'So what can you tell me, Jim?' I ask.

'What can *you* tell *me*?' he challenges, flashing his torch up and down the brickwork, as if this was some television game show, with me the eager contestant and him the smug host.

'The brickwork around the edge of the hole looks a lot less professionally laid than the bricks further away,' I say.

'Exactly,' Jim agrees. 'The bricks that are further away were laid and mortared into place by real craftsman. The closer ones are the work – if you want to justify what he's done with that title – of a complete bungler. That's why we took out bricks from the area he was responsible for – because they were a lot easier to remove.'

'Maybe he was a bungler,' I agree, 'or maybe it was just the work of a craftsman in a hurry.'

As anyone might be in a hurry when he was concealing a dead body, I add mentally.

Jim laughs. 'Even in a blind hurry, a craftsman still wouldn't have produced this. With work of this nature, the correct way to do things is almost always the quickest way, too.'

'I see,' I say.

Jim frowns, then licks the pad of his index finger, rubs it against the exposed mortar, then pops it into his mouth, where he proceeds to probe delicately with his tongue, as he might have done if he suddenly thought he'd discovered a new erogenous zone.

'What's happening?' I ask – because it really does seem like the obvious question, given the circumstances.

'He used lime mortar,' Jim says. 'The bugger only went and used lime mortar!'

'Is that some new kind of mortar?'

Inhibition not being one of his strong suits, Jim laughs at my obvious stupidity.

'Some new kind of mortar?' he repeats, just to ram home the point that I really am dumb. 'No, it's definitely not that. The ancient Egyptians are known to have used it 6000 years ago.'

I don't quite see where he's going with this.

'So is that a bad thing?' I wonder.

'No, for a building of this nature, it's a very good thing,' Jim says. 'You see, what's mostly used today is OPC, and . . .'

'OPC?'

'Ordinary Portland cement. It's been around since the 1790s. It's quicker and easier to use than lime mortar, but one of its drawbacks is that it's a hard, rigid mortar, if you see what I mean.'

'I'm not sure I do see,' I admit, since I've not got a bleeding clue what he's talking about.

'An old building like this shifts slightly from time to time. Now when it does that, something has to give, doesn't it?'

'I suppose so,' I say, dubiously.

'And there's only two things that can give, aren't there – the bricks and the mortar. But Portland cement doesn't want to give, and so it's the bricks that get damaged, whereas lime mortar is so yielding and flexible that sometimes it doesn't even crack. And even when it does crack, they're small cracks which often heal themselves in time.'

I have a sudden vision of myself as an Agatha Christie-type detective, addressing all the possible suspects in the library.

'It was when I realised that the killer had used lime mortar rather than Portland that I understood why the horse had refused the third jump and what the mysterious Mongolian had been doing in the jam factory.'

I do my best to suppress a rising giggle, in case Jim thinks that I'm laughing at him.

'And then there's the moisture,' he says.

'What about it?'

'Lime mortar will absorb water, but Portland mortar won't. So if you've used Portland mortar, salts start to form on the bricks, which eventually lead to them crumbling.'

'So you're saying that the murderer used the best mortar in terms of the health of the building?'

'Yes, but as I hinted earlier, it's much harder to mix and work with – and it's unlikely the murderer was also a conservationist, isn't it?'

Highly unlikely, I think – near bloody inconceivable, if truth be told.

Whenever a fictional detective, on-screen or in a novel, starts talking about his need to examine the motive, the means and the opportunity as it relates to this particular crime, you can pretty much guarantee that a fair percentage of readers or viewers will yawn and start to lose interest. It's such a tired old cliché, they'll tell each other, and if an author (or scriptwriter) feels the need to embrace it, then that must be because the fountain of his imagination has sprung a serious leak, and all he is left with is a patch of uninspired mud.

But do you know something – it may be a cliché, but that doesn't automatically mean that it's a load of bollocks! In fact, saying a case should be tackled in this way is the best single piece of advice, in less than twelve words, that has ever been available to the members of *any* profession. And when you're drowning in the mysteries of an investigation (as I suspect I already am) it sometimes provides a handy life raft to cling onto – although often that life raft can turn out to be no more than the proverbial drowning man's straw.

So then, let's grab hold of the life raft and see where it gets us.

Means: In this case, anything from a hammer to a large frozen custard pie would have served as the murder weapon, so there's absolutely no point in worrying about that at the moment.

Motive: When you don't even know who the victims are, it's rather difficult to work out who would have wanted to kill them.

So what we're left with is – you've guessed it – opportunity!

Whoever bricked the two victims up in the air vent needed

access to the cellars (obviously!) and had to be reasonably confident that he wouldn't be disturbed while practicing his bit of home
improvement.

And who do I need to talk to, in order to find out which people
might have had that opportunity? Mr Jenkins, the head porter, of
course!

He is standing outside the porters' lodge, and when he sees me
approaching, a welcoming smile comes to his lips.

'And how are you, today, Miss Redhead?'

'I'm fine, Mr Jenkins,' I assure him.

Have you noted the 'Mr'?

None of the dons or students would ever have dreamed of
calling the head porter anything but simply 'Jenkins'. I have never
done that myself, not because I have a wild, egalitarian streak
running through me (though I do), but simply because I could
never think of calling a man of around the same age as my late
father solely by his surname.

And, in a way, this one little idiosyncrasy on my part has become
the basis of our relationship. It's not that Mr Jenkins minds being
called 'Jenkins' by lads who've only just learned to wipe their
own arses – like all the other St Luke's servants, he accepts this
is one of those college traditions that has refused to bend its knee
to the arrival of the second half of the twentieth century.
Nonetheless, my inability to overcome my background and adopt
some of these traditions myself clearly amuses him, and he feels
at ease in my company.

'I'm working for the college at the moment, Mr Jenkins, and I
need to talk to you about something,' I say, glancing at the ground
to indicate to him exactly what that 'something' is.

Mr Jenkins nods, and says, 'Well, you'd better step inside then.'

I have never been into the porters' lodge before, and the first
things I notice as I step over the threshold – perhaps because
of their positioning, perhaps because of the unanticipated incon-
gruity – are the two glass display cases mounted on the opposite
wall.

'May I?' I ask, forgetting, for a moment, why I'm here.

'Of course you may,' Mr Jenkins replies.

Both the cabinets are works of art in themselves – the dark
wood polished until it positively dazzles; the joints invisible, so

that it seems as if they are held together by magic – but it is their content which takes my breath away.

In one sits a model of a sailing ship.

'It's an exact copy of the Cutty Sark,' Mr Jenkins says from behind me. 'In its day, it was the fastest tea clipper in the world.'

I marvel at the intricacy of the detail – the infinite care that has gone into the construction.

'And in the other cabinet we've got soldiers of the Napoleonic War,' Mr Jenkins continues.

The soldiers are – in their own way – as impressive as the sailing ship, and I catch myself making up very short stories about this very distinctive infantryman and that clearly haughty cavalry officer.

'Did you paint them yourself?' I ask, 'because if you did, I'm very impressed.'

'I did more than just paint them – I cast them and moulded them,' he says.

'You're an artist,' I tell him, admiringly.

The air is instantly chillier.

'I'm not an artist,' he says, 'I'm a head porter who dabbles in handicraft. I never forget that – and I'd be grateful if you didn't.'

I get it (I think). He defines himself by his role as head porter, and nothing can be allowed to detract from that.

'I'm sorry,' I say, 'I never meant to offend you.'

'Nor did you,' he says, as the warmth starts to return to his voice. 'Now you sit down, and I'll make us both a nice cup of cocoa.'

'I don't want to put you to any trouble,' I protest – because I really *don't* like cocoa.

'It's no trouble at all,' he says firmly, which leaves me with the choice of possibly insulting him a second time or submitting myself to ordeal by cocoa.

'That would be lovely,' I lie.

I sit, as instructed, in one of the room's two armchairs – an overstuffed monstrosity which was probably way past its best when dinosaurs roamed the earth.

I look around me. The lodge is a bit like Dr Who's Tardis, in that it's much larger inside than you think it could possibly be from the outside. As well as the armchairs, there is a desk, and the table on which (I assume) the mail is sorted. There is also a large paraffin heater, which looks like it should be included in the next NATO-Warsaw Pact arms reduction treaty, and a black-and-white portable television which sits atop an old orange crate. And, of course, there is a sink, a kettle, and several pottery coffee mugs.

Mr Jenkins returns with two of the mugs – one for each of us – in his hands.

The message on mine reads, 'Jesus saves – but Moses invests!'

It's mildly sacrilegious, and I suspect that though Mr Jenkins would never have considered buying it himself, it doesn't offend him enough to warrant being thrown out.

As I force myself to take a sip of the cocoa, I try to imagine I'm actually drinking a gin and tonic.

It doesn't work!

'This is very nice cocoa, Mr Jenkins,' I lie again. 'Can I ask you about the bodies, now?'

'Of course. That's what we're here for.'

'I need to know who would have had the opportunity to brick the dead men up,' I say.

Mr Jenkins smiles. 'Well, there's me, for a start – but not if they were walled up before 1926, which is when I started working for Mr Gough – or between the twenty-third of April 1943 and the fifth of March 1948, which was when I was in the army.' He pauses. 'Actually, I suppose I could just have squeezed it in between the twelfth and the sixteenth of October 1943, because before the powers-that-be sent me off across the water to defeat Hitler, they did generously grant me a few days leave with my wife.'

I smile back at him. 'You're very precise on the dates,' I say.

'They're very important dates to me – all of them,' he replies, suddenly more serious. 'I don't begrudge the time I spent in the army – it had to be done, and I did it gladly – but there was never a moment when I didn't wish I was back here.'

'Tell me about Mr Gough,' I suggest.

'In the twentieth century, this college has so far had five masters, six deans and seven bursars,' Mr Jenkins says, 'but it's only had three head porters – me, Mr Gough and Mr Gough's dad.' He pauses to brush an invisible piece of dust off his jacket shoulder pad. 'You'd like me to tell you what kind of man he was, wouldn't you?'

'Yes, please.'

'Do you remember that we once had a conversation in which I told you how I felt about St Luke's?' he asks.

Indeed I do. It was during my investigation of the Shivering Turn, and it had such an effect on me that I think I can repeat it almost word for word *'I'm loyal to the buildings, I'm loyal to the traditions, and I'm loyal to the master,'* he'd said. And then he'd gone on to talk about Sir Hope Stanley – who was master a hundred and fifty years ago – as if he'd known him personally.

'Now, there was a man who combined principle with ability if there ever was one,' the head porter had told me, with absolute assurance, *'Sir Hope could have been prime minister if he'd wanted to be, but instead he chose to devote his mind to a much more worthwhile cause.'*

Have you got that? From Mr Jenkins' perspective, being master of St Luke's was more worthwhile than being prime minister! But I'm sure that if I'd asked him if that also applied to being the master of any of the other Oxford colleges, he'd have looked at me as if I was mad, because – as far as he was concerned – none of the other colleges even began to measure up to St Luke's.

'I know you care a great deal about the college,' I say, inadequately.

'I'm lukewarm in comparison to Mr Gough,' Mr Jenkins said. 'I'm not sure I'd actually lay down my life for St Luke's, but he did.'

'Did he? How?'

'In 1954, he announced that he was retiring, which came as a surprise, because though he was in his early seventies by then, there was no one who didn't believe that he was fit enough to have carried on for at least another ten years. The college asked what he wanted as a retirement present, and he said he wanted to see me made up to head porter. That was another surprise. "He's not got the experience," everybody said. "He's only been back from the war for six years."'

'Bastards!' I hear myself say.

'No, no, they were quite right, by their own lights,' Mr Jenkins tells me. 'But Mr Gough wasn't having any of that. "Not got the experience?" he says. "I've been training this lad up since he was four years old."'

'And had he?'

'Oh yes, he had. My dad was killed towards the end of the First World War. Well, the widow's pension wasn't that much, and what you did if you lost a husband in those days was to try and find another one as quick as you could. But mum wasn't the remarrying kind, which meant that times were hard – and they would have been harder if Mr Gough hadn't decided to take me under his wing.' Mr Jenkins pauses, as if he's just realised he's somehow gone off track. 'What was it I was I telling you about?' he asks.

'You were telling me about how you took over from Mr Gough.'

'That's right. Normally, when people retire from a job they've had all their lives, they find it impossible to completely let go. Sometimes, they hang around hoping something will go wrong, so other people will say, "That would never have happened in X's day – he was too canny to have made a mistake like that." Then again, there are those who hang around because they want to be useful, and . . .'

'I'd bet Mr Gough was one of the latter,' I interrupted.

'Well, if you did, you'd lose your shirt,' Mr Jenkins says. 'You know, Miss Redhead, anticipation's a very useful quality to have in some jobs, but in your particular line of work I would have thought you might be better advised to concentrate on listening.'

He says it all with a kindly smile, but it's a rebuke nonetheless – and, I decide, a thoroughly justified one.

'I'm sorry,' I say.

'Think nothing of it,' he tells me. 'Anyway, Mr Gough didn't hang around at all. In fact, he left Oxford immediately, probably to avoid just that temptation. He was dead within three months, of course, but then we all thought he would be.'

'What!' I say.

'You heard.'

'But I thought you told me, not five minutes ago, that he was strong enough to last another ten years.'

'So he was – as long as he was head porter of St Luke's. But the job had been his life, and once he'd given it up, he had no real reason to carry on.'

'Do you ever feel . . .' I begin, before I can stop myself.

'A little bit guilty?' he asks.

'Well, yes,' I admit.

'Not at all!' Mr Jenkins says, and he sounds completely sincere. 'Mr Gough was like a father to me, but getting me this job was no paternal act – if he hadn't thought I was up to it, he'd never have proposed me.'

'No?'

'No! He knew it would kill him to leave the college, but he cared more about St Luke's than he did about himself, and he was terrified that if he suddenly grew weak and feeble – if he had a stroke, or started going senile – someone else would choose his successor, and would make the *wrong* choice.'

I remind myself why I'm here – and why I'm forcing myself to drink this cocoa.

'Did Mr Gough control the access to all the cellars?' I ask, and the moment the words are out of my mouth, I realise that I've said them just a little *too* casually.

Mr Jenkins' eyes harden – as if he senses his hero is about to come under attack.

'Yes, he did have keys – but so did the master, the dean, and the bursar,' he says.

He seems to be suggesting that there were only four keys – in which case this might turn out to be easier than I'd thought it would.

'Even though the other people had keys, I imagine that Mr Gough, from what you've told me about him, would have been the kind of man to know exactly who used the cellar and when,' I say.

'You're suggesting that those bodies couldn't have been bricked up without his knowledge, aren't you?' Mr Jenkins demands angrily.

'It's a question I have to ask, and a possibility I have to look into, Mr Jenkins,' I say.

He sighs. 'Yes, I suppose it is. But what you have to understand is that, as good as he was at his job, Mr Gough wasn't a super-human. He spent most of his time in the college, but he didn't *live* here, and sometimes he had to go home. The master, the bursar and the dean, on the other hand, *do* live here – but maybe you've already ruled them out, because they're so educated.'

No, I haven't ruled them out, but it's true I'd placed Mr Gough at the top of the mental list – which is dumb because having little formal education isn't even a small step towards being a killer, and having enough academic qualifications to stuff a large pillow with is no debarment to indulging in a little part-time murder.

'Besides, if you don't mind me pointing it out, Miss Redhead, you're forgetting the two world wars,' Mr Jenkins says.

'Am I?'

'You most certainly are. During both World War One and World War Two, a number of soldiers were billeted here, and though I don't know it for a fact, I wouldn't be surprised if they used the cellars to store their equipment.'

I wouldn't be surprised either, I think, reflecting that it has only taken a few well-chosen words from Mr Jenkins to expand my suspect list into the tens, or – more likely – into the hundreds.

Charlie didn't mention this possibility, did he?

And I know *why* he didn't mention it – because if he had, I'd never have agreed to take on this investigation, however much he'd begged me.

Not that I can blame him, I suppose – though in his shoes I'm not sure I'd have been equally tricky and disingenuous with my best mate.

There's just one more thing I need to run by Mr Jenkins.

'The stonemason thinks that whoever bricked up the bodies – or at least, bricked up the *second* of the bodies – made a pretty botched job of it,' I say.

'I think I have to agree with him,' Mr Jenkins says.

'So you noticed it yourself?'

'Yes.'

'When?'

'Just before I became head porter. I took my annual two-week holiday, and I spent those two weeks going through the college until I knew every brick and stone in it.'

I like Mr Jenkins a lot, and I certainly don't want to find a way to implicate him in the second murder (he must have been somewhere between minus four and plus three when the first one occurred, so we can safely rule him out for that), but like him or not, I have an unpleasant job to do, and unfriendly questions to ask, and that's just the way it is.

'Did you report this botched job when you noticed it?' I ask.

'No, I didn't.'

'Why not?'

'It was ugly, but it seemed safe and solid enough.'

'And you weren't surprised that the bursar had passed it as acceptable work, despite it being far below the standards of anything else in this college?'

'No, what I thought was that there'd been a war going on.'

'What do you mean?' I ask.

'As the war progressed, all the college servants of a suitable age were called up. So what was Mr Gough to do? He brought in retired servants, doddering old men, bow-legged with age, who spilt much more wine at table than they poured.'

'I'm not sure I see the point,' I admit.

'It was the same across the board. Most of the bricklayers and carpenters either joined the army or were given work directly related to the war effort. So when the bursar needed a builder, he'd have had to call on a retired brickie or chippy – old men whose hands shook, and who'd forgotten half the skills they once had.'

'So you thought that was who had worked on the air vent – a man well past his prime?'

'Exactly. For a while, I expected the bursar to have the vent re-done, now there were better men around to do it – but he wasn't one for spending money, so I wasn't entirely amazed when he didn't.'

'So you noticed it, but you didn't report it because you thought it was an official piece of work, authorised while you were away, which had been badly finished?'

'That's what I'm saying.'

'But Mr Gough would have known about the work that been authorised in that cellar, so when he noticed the botched job, why didn't *he* report it?' Even as I ask the question, I'm holding up my hands, ready to ward off a verbal attack, and when one doesn't come, I add, 'I'm not trying to fit him up for it, Mr Jenkins – really I'm not. I just think that it's curious.'

'Maybe he didn't notice it,' Mr Jenkins says. 'That vent is in the darkest part of that particular cellar, which is probably why the murderer chose it, and Mr Gough wouldn't have carried out the same detailed inspection I did, because he'd been head porter for a long time, and he already knew every brick and stone.'

It would be really convenient if the murderer did turn out to be Mr Gough, I think to myself.

And the circumstantial evidence does seem to be pointing in his direction.

Fact One: He is likely to have been the only man on the scene when both the murders occurred.

Fact Two: Even given Mr Jenkins' point that Gough couldn't be in the college all the time, it is hard to see how anyone could knock down part of the medieval air vent, cram his victim inside, and then rebuild the air vent, all within the limited period when the head porter was absent, which would surely suggest that he was at least complicit.

But unmasking the killer – and if it was Gough, then producing a rock-solid argument is almost impossible now that he's dead – is not the job I was hired to do. What Charlie wants to know is the names of the victims, and I seem to be no closer to that now than I've ever been.

'You wouldn't have any idea who the dead men in the air vent were, have you, Mr Jenkins?' I ask.

'No,' the head porter replies, 'I haven't.'

I was afraid he'd say that.

FOUR

2 October 1943

Charlie Swift stood on the doorstep of St Luke's senior common room, gazing out into the night at the historic city of Oxford. Or perhaps it would be more accurate to say he *would have* been gazing at the city – its majestic domes and dreaming spires – if those domes and spires had been at all visible. But they weren't visible, because there had been a government-imposed night-time blackout since the autumn of 1939, and all he could actually see (as there wasn't any moon that night) was the darkness. Still, he mused, as with so many things in life, it was nice to know they were there, even if – at that particular moment or under those particular conditions – you couldn't take advantage of them yourself.

He had only been a baby when the last war had been declared. Everybody – from the government and press magnates at the top, right down to the humblest labourer and his wife in the lowliest village in England – had believed that *that* conflict was nothing less than 'the War to End All Wars.'

But it hadn't been, had it? Charlie thought.

In the light of recent events, it was clear that it had been no more than a dress rehearsal for this war – though, granted, it had been a particularly bloody one.

Although it had been waged during his infancy, he knew all about the First World War. His father, the Old Lord, had made certain of that by going to endless pains to fill him on all the details (whether he wanted those details or not!)

'That war swallowed up working men the way a meat grinder swallows up meat, Charles,' Lord Roderick had told him. 'I stopped the army taking away the men working on our farms – got onto my friends in the government and pointed out that they were necessary for war-time food production – but there was nothing I could do about the rest of the staff. We were left with only one gamekeeper – *one* – and people called him Blind Jack, so you can guess just how effective he was. With him in charge, the poachers could have a heyday, but fortunately most of them were in the army, too.'

'Then obviously, the poachers had no influence with the government,' Charles had said.

'Well, of course they had no influence with the government – they were poachers,' the Old Lord had replied, missing the point. 'There were the gardeners, too. The only ones I was allowed to keep were three old men who were too creaky to wield a hoe, let alone a bayonet. And as for the footmen and grooms – don't even ask me about them. It was a nightmare.'

The Old Lord had painted a convincing picture of heartless government officials, like slavers of yore, swooping down on the estate and dragging away the helpless men, whilst their distraught wives beat their bosoms in agony, and their unhappy children begged the slavers not to take their daddies away.

It hadn't been like that at all, of course. Between August 4th and

September 12th 1914, four hundred and seventy-eight thousand, eight hundred and ninety-three men had *volunteered* to join the army, and by the time conscription was introduced in January 1916, the figure had risen to two million, four hundred and sixty-six thousand, seven hundred and nineteen – among them, Charlie was more than willing to wager, all those gardeners, footmen and grooms who his father claimed the government had stolen.

This time, it was different. This time, every man between the ages of twenty and forty-one (and not involved in a reserved occupation like coal mining) would be required to fight eventually, but unlike the last war, they weren't all leaving their homes in a sudden flood to be washed up on the shores of France a few days later. Rather, they were being drawn away in slow streams to join disparate units which would eventually all coalesce when the time came to invade Europe.

Charlie opened the Senior Common Room door for just a second, allowing so little light to spill out into the darkness that it would have taken a very alert German pilot or navigator to spot it.

Once inside, he looked around him. There was the dean, there was the bursar, and there were three young commoners. It was a long-standing tradition in St Luke's that on Thursday nights, the bursar and the dean would invite several undergraduates for drinks (nature unspecified on the invitation, but usually a very dry sherry, produced exclusively for the college at one of the better bodegas in Jerez de la Frontera), and thence to a lavish dinner at the high table.

The three selected for the honour on Thursday were Thomas Hadley, Gideon Trollop and James Makepeace. The trio shared a common background. They were of similar build (athletic but stocky) and similar colouring (English pale, with a slightly weather-beaten overlay, as a result of days spent out on the grouse moors). It would have been unfair to call them a clique – or even worse, a tribe – because although they had all attended Eton, and now were all studying at St Luke's, they had been in different houses at Eton (and no two houses had the same ethos, as they would be at pains to tell you) and now lived on different staircases in the college (where the ethos was generally the same, but the plumbing varied).

Yet it would equally be a mistake to fail to spot the distinct differences which swam quietly through their sea of conformity, thought Charlie Swift who, as a junior lecturer in English, had been invited along because – he assumed – the dean and the bursar, being old out-of-touch conservatives, felt they needed some kind of bridge between them and Hadley, Trollop and Makepeace, who represented *young*, out-of-touch conservatism.

Yes, Charlie thought, examining them again, it would certainly be a mistake to regard them as pretty-much-of-a-muchness – for while they had all been through a system designed to turn them not just into English gentlemen but into identical, *interchangeable* English gentlemen, there were still differences which could be spotted by a confirmed cynic who happened to be an Old Etonian himself.

Hadley, for example, was one of life's optimists – the sort of chap who, when his rugby team was thirty-five points down at half time (and to a clearly superior team), could still believe – and get the other members of his side to believe – that victory was possible.

Trollop, on the other hand, would assume they were heading for a defeat the moment he arrived at the venue and saw the size of the oppositions' full-back – and would, furthermore, gain a morbid satisfaction from such knowledge.

And Makepeace? Makepeace was the chap who would always think that victory was in his grasp, if only he could devise a clever (and undetectable) way of cheating. He was also – and Charles was virtually certain of this – a homosexual. So, to sum him up – he was a rogue, there was no doubt about that, but hopefully, he would turn out to be a loveable rogue (which was to say, fun to take to bed).

It was the dean who was doing most of the talking over sherry – that was the way it normally went, the dean talked and you listened – and *what* he was talking about was the effects of the last war.

'In many ways, the Germans could be said to have won, because they seriously damaged the way of life we had so come to cherish. Believe me when I say this, it was a different world after 1918.'

'This is all most interesting, sir. In what way was it different?' asked James Makepeace. So the man was a bit of a crawler, too, Charlie Swift noted – but he would only crawl as long as he could see it was to his advantage.

'In what way was it different?' the dean replied. 'It was different in that so many of our young men died,'

'Yes, they did,' the bursar said, sounding genuinely regretful, because he truly hated waste, whether it was butter squandered at the refectory table or young men's blood squandered on the battlefield. 'They were slaughtered like cattle. There's no other way to describe it. At one point, the life expectancy of a young officer was little more than a week.'

'Yes, a great number of them never came back,' the dean agreed, and though the bursar was supporting his argument, his face showed his displeasure at being interrupted in his flow. 'And so, after the war, with much of the best of our young manhood dead, we were forced to accept students who fell far below the gentlemanly standards we had come to expect.'

The dean sounded just like his father could, though with much less justification, Charlie Swift thought. He wondered why it was that those with the least reason to be snobbish were often the most snobbish of all – then realised he had answered his own question.

'When I talk about falling below the gentlemanly standard, I don't mean you men, of course,' the dean continued. 'We're more than delighted to have chaps like you – but I think we all know the kind of chancers and interlopers that I'm referring to.'

'He's referring to the sons of brewers, builders, solicitors, civic engineers, surgeons and people of that ilk,' Charlie Swift said, just to stir matters up.

'I don't think there's any need to be as specific as that, Lord Charles,' the dean said. He turned his attention back to his guests of the evening. 'How old are you three young men?'

'We're all nineteen, sir,' Hadley said.

'Then I expect you'll all be called up soon.'

'Yes, sir, we were all in the Officer Training Corps at school, and we're all as keen as mustard to do our bit in the armed forces.'

'I'm expecting to be called up soon, too,' Charlie Swift said, 'and I'm also as keen as mustard.'

'You, Charles?' the dean asked, amazed.

'Me,' Swift confirmed.

'I should have thought that, as the only son of a grandee of England, you'd have found it quite easy to obtain an exemption.'

'Yes, I think I probably would have,' Charlie Swift replied, 'but I chose not to.'

The dean considered the prospect for a moment, then said, 'Well, I expect an organised chap like you will be a very useful addition to one of the ministries of supply.'

You've finally worked out that I'm a homo, haven't you, you snobbish, brandy-soaked old bastard? Swift thought. And if I *am* a homo, then that means, at least in your mind, that I'd be bloody useless as a soldier.

'I'm hoping to avoid working in a ministry,' he said aloud. 'What I've actually asked for is a place in one of the front-line regiments – and given that two of my uncles are generals, I think my request is likely to be granted.'

'Really!' the dean exclaimed.

'Why the surprise?' Charlie asked. 'Do you think that *because of what I am*, I would be incapable of killing if the need arose?'

The dean, realising he had been driven into a verbal corner, reddened. 'I don't . . . I mean to say . . .' he began.

'Is it perhaps because I'm so sensitive – maybe even over-sensitive – that you don't believe I could ever be a rough, tough soldier?' Charlie Swift ploughed on relentlessly.

'Really, Lord Charles, this is neither the time nor the place . . .' the dean spluttered.

'Because there must surely have been other men like me – I mean, of course, graduates in Middle English poetry – who've turned out to be effective warriors,' Charlie said.

'Well, yes,' the dean said weakly.

Further embarrassment for the dean – which Charlie Swift was more than ready to inflict – was prevented by the arrival of the head porter.

'Yes, Gough?' the bursar said.

'I wonder if I could possibly have a word with you in private, sir?' the porter said.

'What's it about?' the dean asked imperiously.

'It's about the catering arrangements, sir.'

'Oh, very well then, if I must,' the bursar said, with a heavy sigh as he rose to his feet.

Charlie saw the three commoners exchange puzzled glances, and laughed inwardly. Why had the catering arrangements anything to do with the head porter, they were asking themselves? Surely it was more a matter of concern for the butler – or possibly even the chef.

But what they hadn't realised at this point – but would eventually, if they stayed in St Luke's long enough – was that the head porter was like a spider whose web reached all corners of college life.

The previous bursar had resented this, and having spent a year at Harvard University, where he had studied the works of Max Weber, he had found no difficulty at all in constructing an organisational chart.

'Now this being a new concept to you, it might seem quite complex at first,' he'd explained to all the staff, 'but in essence, it's very simple.' He'd held it up for them to see. 'Think of it as a railway line map. The dean, the master and I are all mainline stations, and you are all branch lines connected to one of us. The kitchen, for example, is on my branch line, whereas the bulldogs are on the dean's branch line.'

And there, at the very edge of the page – at the very end of the line – were the porters in what might as well have been called Way-Out-On-A-Limb Halt.

But it hadn't worked out like that at all, Charlie Swift thought. The porters' office was not, to use the bursar's own terminology, the end of the line – it was the junction which the big stations had to feed trains into if they ever wanted anything done.

Mr Gough did nothing to fight off this attempt to exclude him from the mainstream life of the college. He knew that he did not need to, and contented himself with simply following the bursar's strict instructions as to his role and function and waiting for things to fall apart.

It did not take long. The chef, having an artistic nature, was the first person to have a nervous breakdown, but the bursar was not far behind, and the new bursar – *this* bursar – had rapidly decided that since things seemed to have worked quite well in the past, it would be best to revert to the old system (whatever *that* was!)

The bursar returned to the table looking grave, with an even graver Gough by his side.

'I'm afraid that, for this evening at least, the waiters will, in fact, be waitresses,' the bursar said.

'What!' the dean exploded. 'But that's unheard of in the entire history of the college.'

'Yes, it is,' the bursar agreed, 'but as Gough has just pointed out to me, most of the college servants have now been called up by the army.'

'And what about all the old college servants who you employed to replace them, Gough?' the dean demanded.

'They are, as you have just so eloquently pointed out, sir, *old*,' the porter said. 'Jeremiah Dorkins' lumbago has flared up, and Seth Halcrombe is down with the influenza.'

'But *waitresses* . . .' the dean said, helplessly.

'I know, dean, it is most regrettable,' the porter agreed.

'Is there no one else who can do it?'

'Well, there's always Lennie Moon,' Gough said.

The dean felt a shiver run through him. There were good reasons – very good *economic* reasons – why the college employed Lennie Moon, but the man was a dribbling cretin, and there was no way that he could be let loose near a civilised dining table.

'These women,' he said, 'who are they, Gough?'

'One of them is Lucy Jenkins, sir.'

'Jenkins? Jenkins?' the dean mused.

'She's the wife of one of the junior porters – Harold Jenkins,' Gough said. 'He was called up a few months ago.'

'And who's the other one?'

'She's Harold Jenkins' cousin, Mildred Drew – the wife of one of the groundsmen. Of course, neither of the women has ever been in college service themselves, but they will have heard their husbands talk about their duties and responsibilities, and so will already know what is expected of them.'

The dean sighed. 'Very well then, I suppose we all have to make sacrifices in wartime, and in that spirit we will consent, on this occasion, to be served by women – but I trust that such a situation will not occur again, Gough.'

'I'll do my best to see that it doesn't, sir,' the head porter promised.

St Luke's refectory had been constructed at a time when Gothic architecture was *de rigueur* in Oxford, and in consequence, it had an impressively tall (and impressively sharply arched) ceiling. The

high table was located at one end of the refectory, and was, as its
name suggested, a table on a raised platform, from where it was
possible to look down on the other tables, at which (normally) sat
young, slightly-bloated backwoods aristocrats struggling with (or
more often, ignoring) the demands of their courses, and young,
sharp-faced and ambitious law students, with their thoughts firmly
set on a future judge's bench and horsehair wig.

But there weren't many aristocrats or lawyers at the moment,
the bursar thought, because, over the last couple of years, most of
them had been sent off to prepare for the task of confronting that
jumped up little Austrian who the normally sensible Germans had
allowed to take over their country.

Now, thanks to Hitler, most of the accommodation – and hence
most of the tables in the refectory – were occupied by military
men. Thus far, the college had housed a Senior Officers' School,
then a Liaison Officers' School, a Signallers' School and finally
a Junior Officers' School.

From the very start, the bursar had been well aware of the
mistakes made by the previous bursar in the last war.

That bursar had been wise enough to negotiate an agreement
on the price to be paid for food and accommodation, but had
neglected to include clauses covering damages, missing items and
general wear-and-tear – including the loss of chamber pots, which,
in moments of high spirits, the young officers had removed from
their rightful place under the beds (where they performed an
invaluable bladder-relieving service in the middle of the night)
and placed on the heads of the nearest convenient statues.

This bursar, keeping in mind normal rents, floor space costings,
loss of income from other sources, and the value of some of the
furnishings, had hammered out an agreement with the War Office
which kept the latter pretty damned tightly nailed down.

Even so, he had still miscalculated *some* things, as had soon
become evident when the officers in charge of the soldiers started
demanding the same quality and quantity of food they had been
getting on army rations, from a college which was only supplied
with per capita civilian rationing. Still, even this difficulty had
gone away when the army had agreed to feed its own staff
and – though the bursar had had to swallow hard before accepting
the downward adjustment to the deal he had signed with the

War Office – he could, at least, have a secret chuckle over the fact that the army was still paying for all the hot water, which meant that members of the college got their baths for free.

The two to-be-dreaded women arrived at the table, one carrying the wine, the other with the basket of bread. The one with the wine decanter – Lucy Jenkins – was ever-so-slightly plump, and Charlie Swift, who could quite picture her as a medieval serving wench, thought she would probably seem quite attractive to most men. That was, however, mere guesswork on his part, because she did nothing at all for him. The other woman was much thinner, and whilst her face showed character, it also suggested a sour view of life.

'Are you Mrs Jenkins?' the dean asked the pleasantly plump one, in an I-don't-have-to-be-polite-to-this-woman-but-because-I'm-a-jolly-fine-chap-I-will-be-just-that voice.

'Yes, sir, that's me,' the woman replied nervously, as she started to fill his glass.

'And how is your husband doing in the army?' the dean asked, in much the same tone.

'He writes he's doing very well, sir,' Mrs Jenkins replied.

'Where's he posted at the moment?' James Makepeace asked, completely out of the blue.

'Oh, good heavens, sir,' said Lucy Jenkins, who had finished pouring the dean's wine, and was now filling Makepeace's glass, 'my Harold's not allowed to tell me where he is.'

'Well, I expect to be posted myself in the next couple of weeks, and wherever I'm sent to, I'll make it my business to find out if your husband is there. And if he *is* there, I'll be sure to tell him that the last time I saw you, you were looking *really* marvellous.'

'It won't be necessary to go to all that trouble, sir, because cousin Harold will be home for a short leave in a few days' time, and then he'll be able to see for himself, won't he?' said the sour-faced woman handing out the bread. Her name was Mildred Drew, Charlie Swift recalled – mildew would been closer to the mark.

'Thank you for your offer anyway, sir,' Mrs Jenkins, red in the face, said to James Makepeace. And then she put down the decanter, and turned and fled, leaving everyone else to serve themselves.

'You really shouldn't have talked to her like that,' Charlie Swift told Makepeace.

'And why is that?' Makepeace responded, with a total lack of concern in his voice. 'I didn't damage her, did I?'

Yes, in a way, you did, Charlie Swift thought, but not wishing to give the other man the satisfaction, he said, 'You shouldn't have done it because you sounded like a fool.'

'What!'

'You heard me.'

'I'm not sure I like your tone.'

'I couldn't care less what you think about my tone. All I'm doing is stating an obvious fact. But you shouldn't be too hard on yourself,' he continued, shifting gear and adding to the general confusion. 'It's not your fault that you don't have the dean's gift of being able to talk to the common people – there are very few people who are blessed with it.'

The dean heard the exchange, and was not sure whether Lord Swift had complimented him or insulted him. Unable to decide, he turned his attention to the menu.

Before the war – or even a year or two into it – they would have read something like '*truite aux amandes*' or '*ris de veau à la reine*' but now what he saw was '*saucisse, purée de pommes de terre et petits pois.*'

Even in French, bangers and mashed potato and processed peas sounded disgusting. The American military didn't have to eat this muck, he thought angrily. He had been invited out to their nearby base, and had dined on steaks which were crudely cooked, but at least had more than a passing acquaintanceship with a cow. It simply wasn't fair that the soldiers – even the ordinary GIs – were living better than he was, he thought.

'The problem with the Americans is that they're overpaid, oversexed and over here,' he said aloud.

The assembled company laughed, because although they had heard the joke before – many, many times, before – they had never, as far as they could recall, heard it from the *dean* before.

But Charlie Swift did not laugh for long, because he had his own *bon mot* to add to the conversation.

'And what the Americans say about us is that we are underpaid, undersexed and under General Eisenhower,' he told them. 'Well, I for one don't consider myself underpaid *or* undersexed – but as for being under General Eisenhower, well, given the fact that he's past fifty and starting to wrinkle in a most unattractive manner, I certainly wouldn't fancy that. Mind you, he's got an *aide-de-camp* whose weight I think I could bear happily enough.'

If I could have you drummed out of the college I would, the dean's eyes said. And if, by chance, you survive the war and come back to St Luke's, I'll labour night and day to ensure that you never rise above the rank of junior fellow.

Charlie Swift, for his part, favoured everyone with a happy smile, since he was convinced he had done more than enough to ensure that he would never again be invited to be a bridge between the old fogeys and the young fogeys.

Then he frowned as he saw James Makepeace so obviously flirting with the now-returned Lucy Jenkins. What was more, Lucy Jenkins herself seemed to be rapidly getting used to it.

Charlie's first impulse was to be annoyed with Lucy, because in order to defend her, he had queered the pitch (now there was a Freudian slip if there ever was one!) as far as his own seduction of Makepeace went.

His second thought was that none of this was making sense anyway, because there was no reason at all why a homo like Makepeace – and he was convinced now that Makepeace was a homosexual – should even *want* to chat up Lucy Jenkins.

FIVE

7 October 1974 – Late Morning

There are so many ways in which I differ from the private eyes who are so beloved of pulp fiction.

For a start, I'm not a man – and have the substantial bumps on my chest to prove it.

And while we might all wake up with hangovers, I do not greet the arrival of the morning with a strong cup of black coffee and a slug of old Kentucky bourbon. I prefer to start my day with a nice reviving cup of Twinings English Breakfast tea and a slice of white toast, spread thinly with Frank Cooper's Vintage Oxford marmalade.

Then there are our respective backgrounds. If, for example, any of these fictional gumshoes has an upper second in English from St Luke's College (it should have been a first, damn it!) or from any other institution of higher education for that matter, then all I can say is that they keep very quiet about it. On the other hand, I have a singular lack of experience of fighting in the Korean War and being physically (or mentally) scarred by it, and I haven't had a mysterious blonde die in my arms (though, I suppose, there's still time for that).

I've never shot anybody, either and, since I have absolutely no intention of owning a gun between now and the moment I kick off this mortal coil, I think it highly unlikely that I will ever ventilate an opponent with my .44 Magnum.

That said, there are a few ways in which I *do* conform to the image of the hard-boiled detective.

I do swear quite a lot.

Well, shit, that must have taken you completely by surprise!

I play poker for more than I can afford to lose – if you're interested, the game is held on Friday nights, and is run by Dr Roddy McCloud, the current holder of the Pascal Chair of Probability Theory, out of his office in St Jude's.

What else? Oh yes, I have a shitbox office at the top of a set of squeaky stairs, and also a buddy in the police force.

The buddy, in my case, is called Detective Inspector George Hobson (the 'inspector' is a recent addition). He did not save my life in South-east Asia (he's probably never got any closer to that hot and exotic continent than Dover), and, equally unsurprisingly, I did not take a bullet for him in a seedy warehouse on the Jersey Shore.

We are friends, and we were – for the briefest of periods – lovers, but we're far too mature to let that latter fact affect the relationship we have now in any way (hah!).

We agree to meet in the Bulldog, which is located on St Aldate's, just opposite Christ Church College. It is one of my favourite pubs in the whole of Oxford, and given how much I like pubs in general, that's no mean achievement.

After we've met and exchanged chaste kisses, I buy George a

pint of best bitter (pretty much the standard sweetener when I'm trying to squeeze information out of him) and we take our drinks over to a dinky little corner table with a beaten copper top.

'So what is it that you want this time, Jennie?' he asks, gulping down his drink with all the abandon of a man who knows that, the second he's finished it, the beautiful, flame-haired woman who is sitting opposite him will quickly offer to buy another.

'So what is it that I want this time?' I ask, trying to sound mystified. 'So what is it that I want *this time*? Hasn't it ever occurred to you, George Hobson, that I might just fancy the idea of spending a couple of hours with an old friend?'

'No,' he says bluntly.

OK, so there's no point in pretending that he's not got my number when he so obviously has. In fact, this is exactly what I want, because I'm like a magician, trying to ensure that of all the cards I offer him, he takes the one I *intend* him to take, and for that to work, I need him to feel in charge – to imagine he's controlling the whole conversation.

'All right, I do want a small favour,' I concede. 'If you could possibly manage it, I'd like to know the names of any and all the people who went missing in Oxford between 1909 and 1944.'

'What exactly do you mean by missing?' he asks.

I sigh. 'Don't be difficult with me, George,' I reply.

'What *exactly* do you mean by missing?' he repeats, unbending.

'I suppose I haven't really thought it through,' I lie. 'Let's just say I'm interested in people who were here, and then suddenly – with no explanation – were gone.'

George leans back in his chair.

'Are you mad, Jennie?' he asks, conversationally. 'Are you completely off your head?'

'Yes, I think I am – but probably not certifiably so,' I reply – making my little joke, you see, to show that I'm perfectly relaxed, and that no one is trying to manipulate anyone into doing something they might (with hindsight) wish that they hadn't done.

I smile sweetly. 'Is there any particular reason that you think I may have gone loopy?' I ask.

'None at all – except that you seem to be confusing me with James Phelps,' George says.

James Phelps?

Ah, yes!

'That's the name of the character Peter Graves plays on Mission Impossible,' I say.

'"Your mission, should you choose to accept it, is to list the names of all the people who went missing between 1909 and 1944",' George parodies. 'You do realise, Jennie, that that period includes two bloody world wars and the Great Depression, don't you?'

'So?' I counter, as if I can't see why incidents like those could be in any way relevant to my request.

'So they were all times of change and general disruption. Just take the thirties as an example. You had men who drifted into the city from all over the place, looking for work in the motor factory. Except there was *no* work to be had, and when they eventually realised that however long they stayed, there would *never* be any work they drifted out again. Are any of these men – or their movements – on record, for any reason? Well, it's possible that a few might be, I suppose, but that's all it will be – a very few.'

'I know all that, but . . .'

'Then we get to 1939. The government thinks that Adolf Hitler is about to send his Luftwaffe over to bomb our cities – which is exactly what he does do – so it decides to evacuate three hundred and fifty thousand people. *Three hundred and fifty thousand people!* Count them, Jennie!'

'That's a lot of people,' I agree.

'But they're city dwellers, through and through, and a great many of them don't like living in the countryside and the small towns at all. In fact, they bloody loathe it. So, after the Battle of Britain is finally over in May '41, and it becomes obvious to them that the Blitz has come to an end, they start to drift back home – and a good many of them don't even take the time to advise the authorities that they've gone.'

'I don't need a history lesson,' I say.

'I beg to differ,' George replies. 'I very much beg to differ. Then there's the Second World War itself to take into consideration. According to the authorities, everyone in the country was fully documented, and so the government knew where each and every person was at every minute of the war.'

'And isn't that true?' I ask, ever the helpful dupe.

'It's about as true as the statement that the government always intended the London Underground to serve as a gigantic bomb shelter.'

'Didn't it?'

'No, it bloody didn't. At the start of the war, the government posted soldiers and policemen at the entrances to the Underground, specifically to stop people getting in. But then the mob grew so big that it overwhelmed the army, and suddenly, using the underground railway stations as shelters had *always* been the caring government's idea – and a jolly good one, too.'

George is occasionally subject to these rants. It is, I suspect, because deep inside the middle-aged guardian of the law, there lurks a tousle-haired youth longing to be standing on a barricade somewhere, with one hand raised in a gesture of contempt and other clutching a handy brick.

'So not everyone here was documented,' I say, bringing him back to the topic in hand.

'You're damn right,' George agrees. 'There were American soldiers and camp followers, British and American deserters, crooks from the big cities making their grand robbery tour of the under-policed smaller ones, refugees from Poland, Greece, Latvia . . .'

It's time to produce my pack of cards and mesmerize him into taking the right one.

'Perhaps we'd better narrow the scope down, then,' I suggest.

'Narrow it down to what?'

I purse my brow – I'm pretty good at that – as if I'm trying really hard to find a way out of the dilemma.

'How about if . . . I don't know . . . how about if we concentrate only on the people who have some kind of connection to St Luke's College?' I ask, as innocently as I can.

'Here's another idea – how about if we concentrate only on the people who have some kind of connection with Morris Motors?' George says, suspiciously.

You're about to take the totally wrong card, George – but I really can't tell you that.

'Yes, let's look at Morris, if you'd prefer it,' I say, trying to sound casual.

'So it doesn't really matter to you which of the two – St Luke's College or Morris Motors – I choose?' he asks, the suspicion still there.

'I'd rather you chose St Luke's, if only because I'm more familiar with it,' I say, like it doesn't *really* matter, 'but if it's easier for you to get the information on Morris . . .'

Take my card! Take my card!

'Why do you want this information?' George asks.

'I need it in order to be able to carry out the work that my client wishes me to carry out,' I say, with just the right amount of prim stiffness.

'Who is he?' George asks.

I wag my finger playfully at him. 'Now you know I can't tell you that, George.'

'Is he a journalist?'

'Not exactly.'

Although Charlie has written a number of articles.

'Then is he an academic?'

'In a way.'

And that's true (in a way!) because as the bursar he does no teaching, and his research is now more of a hobby than a disciplined journey of discovery.

I glance down at my gin and tonic, and can feel George's eyes boring relentlessly into my skull.

'Should the thing you're investigating – whatever it is – have already been reported to the police?' he asks.

Damn it, George – that's just too good a guess!

I look up, and stare him straight in the eye.

'Are you asking me if there's been some criminal act committed that I should have told you about?' I say, choosing my words as carefully as I'd choose my steps if I was walking across a minefield.

'Yes, that's exactly what I'm asking,' George says.

I hold my gaze steady.

'If there has been any sort of criminal act committed, George, then I promise you that I've seen no evidence of it,' I say firmly.

Nor have I, because by the time I got to examine the medieval ventilation shaft, both the bodies had been removed by university scientists and were residing in the labs across the park.

George holds his pint pot up to the light. 'There seems to have been quite a lot of evaporating going on,' he says.

Translation: if you buy me another beer, I'll do what you want.

I take the glass off him, and as I do, I try to hide the fact that I have just released a gasp of relief.

It is later that the guilt starts to set in. Though I have not actually lied to George, I have gone out of my way to avoid telling him the truth, and I hate myself for it because he is both a friend and an ex-lover. But Charlie Swift needs me to do this, and he is not just *a* friend, he is *the* friend I have been searching for all my life.

I would lie for Charlie, I would cheat for Charlie, I would prostitute myself with the entire Oxford United Supporters' Club for him.

I can't say with absolute certainty that I would kill for him – but I hope that I would.

SIX

7 October 1974 – Afternoon

It occurs to me, as I'm walking back from the Bulldog to St Luke's, that Britain is a clearly divided nation, and that division is not between north and south, nor east and west. Neither is it the division between men and women, or the rich and poor, though both these things have been important in the past (the Suffragette Movement and the Jarrow Crusade, to quote just two examples) and will almost certainly be important in the future.

The real division at this particular moment in time, it seems to me, places middle-aged southern farmers and Midlands coal miners (not to mention Scottish ship builders and London city clerks!) on one side of the great divide – and my generation squarely on the other. And what is this Grand Canyon of attitudes and philosophies? It is a six-year period in our national history known simply as the Second World War.

The war, as I see it, was the most traumatic event that ever occurred in most people's lives. It called for bravery and sacrifice, and sometimes brought forth greed and cowardice instead. It was a glorious time and a terrible time. And we – my generation – missed out on it by being stupid enough not to be born until it was nearly over!

And so we see the tears in the eyes of people watching old newsreel film of VE night in Trafalgar Square, and we sort of understand why they are crying and wish that we could cry over ancient history, too.

I'm not sure what's set me off up this particularly twisted alley of speculation. Maybe it's a gut feeling that the two stiffs in the air vent would never have been there, had it not been for the two outbreaks of madness across the Channel.

Whatever the impetus, when I see Mr Jenkins standing outside the porters' lodge, the first words that come to my mind (and are allowed, by a lack of self-discipline, to escape through my mouth), are, 'What kind of war did you have, Mr Jenkins?'

He thinks about it for a while, then says, 'It was twelve months of boredom while we were training in England, three hours of absolute terror when we landed on the beaches in France, and then nearly four years of disgust and despair as I saw first-hand what war can do to innocent people.'

I find his words simple and sincere, and feel both touched and humbled by them.

'I hope you didn't mind me asking,' I say.

'I don't mind at all,' Mr Jenkins assures me. 'If you don't ask, you'll never know, will you?'

'Mr Jenkins is a hero – and he's has got a medal to prove it,' says a voice from somewhere behind me.

I turn to look. The speaker is a big man in his fifties with pale yellow hair. He has large eyes which are not exactly blank, but certainly suggest a lack of any real awareness, and these eyes are set in a podgy face with several double chins. His porter's cap is at an angle which is awkward, rather than jaunty – and he wears the rest of his uniform as it were a potato sack tied in the middle with string. I know his name is Lennie Moon, but it suddenly occurs to me that in all the years I've been coming to the college, I've never got this close to him before.

'Tell her, Mr Jenkins,' Moon says excitedly. 'Tell her that you've got a medal.'

'There doesn't seem to be much need for me to tell her now you've told her yourself, Lennie,' Mr Jenkins says, and though his words are firm – and perhaps a little censorious – they are not unkind. He looks down at the other man's hands and says, 'What have you done with our boat, Lennie?'

The big man looks down at his hands, too.

'I don't know,' he mumbles. 'Honest, Mr Jenkins, I don't know.'

'You *do* know, Lennie – you've just forgotten,' Mr Jenkins says. 'Let's see if we can get you to remember, shall we?'

'All right,' Lennie says reluctantly.

'When we were talking this morning, we both thought it would be a good idea to take the boat down to the river for a test run. Did you do that?'

'Yes.'

'And did you get as far as putting it into the water?'

'Yes.'

'And did you take the remote control out of your pocket, so you could make the boat do what you wanted it to?'

'Yes.'

'Are you sure of that?'

Lennie puts his hand in his pocket, and it's obvious that his fingers are touching the boat's remote control. The look which crosses his face could be one of indecision, but then again, it might simply be confusion.

'There were these two lovely little puppies playing on the riverbank,' he says, and as he's speaking, a happy smile is slowly replacing his disturbed expression. 'They were chasing one another. It was so funny.'

'And when you looked around again, the boat had gone?' Mr Jenkins suggests.

'Yes.'

'That would be the current, wouldn't it, Lennie – carrying the boat down the river? We've talked about the current before, if you remember.'

'I'm sorry, Mr Jenkins,' the big porter replies, almost in tears. 'I'm really so sorry.'

'It's partly my fault,' Mr Jenkins says soothingly. 'I shouldn't have let you do it on your own.'

'I lost our boat,' Lennie wails.

'Don't worry about it,' Mr Jenkins tells him. 'I can always build us another one.'

'But it took you weeks to make!'

'And I had fun making it – just as I'll have fun making the next one,' Mr Jenkins says. He checks his watch. 'And now, Lennie, I really think it's time you went home and had a rest.'

'I can't go yet,' Moon says worriedly. 'It's not time. I have to wait until it's time for me to put my card in the magic pinging clock.'

'Give me your clocking-in card, and I'll do it for you, Lennie,' Mr Jenkins tells him.

'And . . . and I have to wait for Mrs Lucy,' Moon says, agitatedly.

'Ah, I'd forgotten that,' Mr Jenkins admits. 'You see, you're not the only one who can forget things, Lennie, I can, too.'

'You can, too . . .' Lennie repeats, obviously overawed at the thought that the Great Man shares his failings.

'Why don't you go into the lodge, Lennie, and see if you can find anything nice on the television,' Mr Jenkins suggests.

Lennie nods, then seems to have remembered something he wanted to say earlier, and turns to me.

'Mr Jenkins isn't the only man to have a medal from the war,' he says proudly. 'I've got one, too.'

'Is that right?' I reply, feeling, even as I speak, that of all the possible replies I could have made, this is probably the worst, yet still unable to come up with anything better.

'Yes,' Lennie says. 'I got it . . .'

'Lennie!' Mr Jenkins says, in a voice which, it seems to me, is uncharacteristically loud and sharp.

'Yes, Mr Jenkins?' Lennie says – and it's obvious he has picked up on the dissonance, too.

'Do you remember what we agreed when we talked about that medal, Lennie?' Mr Jenkins asks.

The big porter frowns, but I can tell he is only imitating the outwards signs of thinking he has observed in others, without even beginning to initiate the inner mental process himself.

'No, I don't remember, Mr Jenkins,' he says finally.

'Think about it,' Mr Jenkins urges him.

'I can't . . . I . . .'

'We . . . said . . . that . . . you . . . shouldn't . . . talk . . . about . . . the . . . medal . . . to . . . people . . . because . . . it . . . might . . .?'

'I don't know.'

'Because . . . it . . . might . . . *what*?'

'Because it might make them angry!' Moon says, in a sudden burst of revelation.

Mr Jenkins smiles encouragingly.

'That's right, Lennie, it might make them angry.'

'Sorry, Mr Jenkins, I forgot.'

'It doesn't matter,' Mr Jenkins says, his voice soothing now. 'You go inside and watch television until Mrs Lucy comes. And if anybody turns up and wants something doing, tell them to call back later. Got that?'

Moon nods. 'Yes, Mr Jenkins.'

'Good,' the head porter says. 'I'm about to make my daily rounds, Miss Redhead. Would you care to walk with me?'

'I'd be delighted,' I tell him.

As we walk across the quad, Mr Jenkins says, 'I hope I didn't sound too harsh back there, but people who actually have been awarded medals for displaying great courage can get quite offended when they hear Lennie pretend that he has one. I don't know why they should – they can see what he's like as well as you and I can, but the plain fact is that they do – and so, in order to avoid any unpleasant scenes, I've told him never to talk about it.'

'He was right about *you* having being awarded a medal in the war, though, wasn't he?'

'Yes, he was right about that,' Mr Jenkins agrees, with some show of reluctance.

'Can I ask what medal it is?'

We go under the archway and into the Fellows' Quad, where Charlie Swift has his rooms.

'The war has been over for nearly thirty years now,' Mr Jenkins says. 'There are some veterans of it who still like to refight their old battles, but I'm not one of them. As far as I'm concerned, it doesn't really matter what medal I was awarded – or even if I was awarded a medal at all.'

'If I had been awarded the Distinguished Service Medal, you certainly wouldn't catch me being so quiet about it,' I say.

'How do you know it was the Distinguished . . .?' Mr Jenkins begins. Then he smiles and says, 'That was a trick, wasn't it?'

'In a way,' I admit.

'Tell me how it works.'

'It's really just a case of applying what you know about a person to any given situation,' I tell him. 'Now, from observing you over the years, I've reached the conclusion that you're a rather modest man. That doesn't mean you don't take your talents seriously – I'm sure you do – but you don't particularly like being in the spotlight. Am I right?'

'I suppose so,' he concedes.

'Now if you'd been awarded a minor medal – for example, the Military Medal – I don't think it would have bothered you to say so. But to admit that you hold the DSM – the second highest medal you *can* hold – would seem a little like bragging to you.'

Mr Jenkins's smile has become a grin.

'I see now why you're in so much demand as a private detective, Miss Redhead,' he says.

If only I was!

'So how did you earn your medal?' I ask.

'Does it matter?'

'I'd really like to know.'

Mr Jenkins shrugs. 'It was during the Battle of the Bulge,' he said. 'We thought we'd have a pretty clean run through the Ardennes, but the Germans suddenly launched a counteroffensive which took us completely by surprise. My platoon was ambushed and pinned down by some German infantrymen, I killed them and my platoon got away. And that was it.'

'You make it sound like nothing.'

'I wouldn't exactly say that, but it was certainly ordinary enough. Things like that were always happening, and I thought no more about it until word came down the line I was to be awarded the DSM. I didn't want it, because it would involve going back to England and having my photograph taken for the papers, but my company commander said I should accept it on behalf of all our fallen comrades, so that's what I did.'

We are in the Master's Garden now, and I can see Mr Jenkins running his eyes carefully over every bush and plant in the garden.

'That one needs replacing, that could use more fertilizer, that just needs a bit of love and care,' he says, pointing out various plants to me.

This isn't, strictly speaking, his job, but I'm not going to be the one to tell him that.

'I didn't realise that Lennie Moon was . . . was a bit . . .' I begin, branching out into a new subject.

'You didn't realise he was a bit *backward*?' Mr Jenkins says, apparently unwilling to leave me floundering there.

'Yes, that is what I suppose I meant,' I agree.

'He's *not* backward in the sense you might think – which is that he was born that way.'

'That was what I was thinking,' I admit.

'Lennie was taken on as a porter shortly after I was,' Mr Jenkins says. 'He wasn't the sharpest knife in the drawer – that was obvious to Mr Gough at the time – but back then, running the college involved a lot more manual work than it does now. We needed someone who was big and strong to do things like stoke the heating boilers with coke every morning, and Lennie was more than happy to do any job Mr Gough chose to give him.'

'Go on,' I say – because there is obviously more.

'The bursar who we had at that time wasn't . . . how shall I put this? . . . he wasn't very keen on spending money,' Mr Jenkins says.

I laugh.

'Has there ever been a bursar who was keen on it?' I ask.

'Probably not,' Mr Jenkins concedes, 'but he was worse than most. We called him Mr Scrooge, behind his back. Anyway, there was quite a lot of equipment that needed replacing, but he always said that times were hard and we'd just have to make do and mend.' He pauses. 'One of those pieces of equipment that needed replacing was a long ladder.'

'And Lennie fell off it?'

'It was more a case of it collapsing below him. It was a longish fall, and when he hit the ground, he landed head first.'

'He sustained brain damage?' I guess.

Mr Jenkins nods.

'That's right. He was like a child again, and the specialist who examined him said it was permanent. Mrs Moon, his mother, went to see a solicitor, to ask what compensation she was entitled to, and the solicitor had a meeting with the bursar. Together, they came up with a deal. Actually, they only *thought* they came up with it – the original idea was Mr Gough's.'

'What kind of deal was it?'

'Lennie had two choices: he could either take a lump sum then and there – and if he did that, the college had no more responsibility for him – or St Luke's would guarantee to employ him until he reached pensionable age.'

'And he decided on the latter?'

'It was his mother who did the deciding. And don't go pulling a face, Miss Redhead—'

'I wasn't,' I say – and realise that I probably was.

'. . . because seen from her point of view – and from Lennie's – it was exactly the right thing to do.'

'Are you sure about that?'

'I am. People were crying out for a job – any job at all – back in the thirties, and here he was being offered a job for life. Besides, the compensation seemed quite a lot of money at the time, but it would all be long gone by now – and then what would Lennie do? And though he sometimes isn't able to pull his weight around the college, he can still be quite useful.'

'So useful that you send him down to the river to play with boats you've made together?' I ask, not without a trace of mischief in my voice.

'Some days, the only work that needs doing is the sort he *can't* handle,' Mr Jenkins says in such a serious voice that I start to feel guilty about my temporary frivolity. 'But he's a good lad, and none of the porters object to carrying him, by doing a little more than their fair share.'

'Does he still live with his mother?' I ask.

'No, she died a few years ago. After her funeral, we found him a nice little bedsit on the Banbury Road.'

'We?'

'We were all on the lookout for a place, but it was my missus who found it and helped him move in.'

'How does he manage, living on his own?'

Mr Jenkins shrugs. 'He gets by well enough. He can perform most simple operations, as long as they're carefully explained to him – and we're all prepared to chip in and help when things get too difficult, just like we are with his job.' He pauses for a moment. 'There are some of us who remember him before the accident, you see – and a more willing, helpful and unselfish lad you'd never hope to find.'

We wheel around, and walk back to the porters' lodge. Looking in through the door, I can see that Lennie Moon is sitting down, and a woman is bending over and talking to him.

Mr Jenkins notices I've seen her, and says, 'I don't think you've ever met my wife, have you, Miss Redhead?'

'No,' I agree, 'I don't think I have.'

'Then let's rectify that right now,' he says.

As we enter the lodge, I can see that Mrs Jenkins is not just bending over Lennie, but is handing him a covered basin.

'How hot do you heat the oven, Lennie?' she is asking.

'I turn the knob until the three is at the top,' Moon says.

'Excellent,' Mrs Jenkins tells him. 'And how long do you put it in the oven for?'

'Thirty minutes.'

'And you must make sure you don't leave it in there any longer than that,' Mrs Jenkins cautions.

Lennie smiles, as if he's pleased with himself.

'I won't,' he says. 'I've got a system.'

'And what system is that?' Mrs Jenkins asks, and I detect a hint of anxiety in her voice which suggests she thinks it just might be a system for disaster.

'You know that programme that comes on the telly, where there's a man who tells you all about what's happening everywhere?'

'I'm not quite sure I know the one you're talking about,' Mrs Jenkins says dubiously.

'And then there's another man – or sometimes it's a pretty girl – who tells you what the weather's going to be like.'

'Do you mean the news?'

'Yes, I think that's what it's called. Anyway, I know it's exactly half an hour long, so I put the basin in the oven when it starts, and take it out again when it's finished.'

'Now that really is clever, Lennie,' Mrs Jenkins says – and sounds as if she means it.

She stands up. For the first time, I get a proper look at her, and it is only by a great effort of will that I avoid gasping with shock.

I had imagined her to be around the same age as her husband, and I think she probably is, but whilst he has weathered well, she looks very much battered by the storm. She is thin – almost skeletal – though there is evidence, from the odd flap of redundant skin, that she was once a much more sensible weight. Her face is filled with deep ugly ruts which are slashed across her forehead and plunge down at each side of her mouth, bringing to mind a field which has been used for motorcycle scrambling.

Her eyes are watery, her . . .

'Lucy, this is Miss Redhead, one of my favourite ex-students,' Mr Jenkins says. 'Miss Redhead, this is Lucy, my wife.'

We shake hands. Her skin feels like parchment, her fingers are like bony needles.

'One of his favourite ex-students, eh?' she says. 'That's quite an accolade, you know, Miss Redhead. I don't think there've been more than four or five students who've qualified for that title in all the time he's been working as a porter here. Isn't that right, Harold?'

And then she smiles fondly at her husband, and I catch a brief glimpse of the pretty woman she must once have been.

Mr Jenkins returns his wife's smile with one of his own, which is equally as affectionate.

'Yes, I'm certainly very particular about who my favourite students are,' he says.

I wonder what has reduced this woman to the physical wreck that she is now – what she has suffered that could have resulted in such a transformation. It is not Mr Jenkins who has crushed her – I can tell that, just by seeing them together – so what is it? Did she have to nurse one of her parents through a particularly prolonged and painful death? Did she lose a child?

I don't know, but what is troubling me more than her personal tragedy is the feeling that Mr Jenkins deliberately engineered this meeting – that he took his time walking me around the grounds, and only returned me to the porters' lodge when he knew (because Lennie had reminded him) that she would be there.

But why would he want to do that?

And more significantly – why would he want to do it just as I was starting an investigation into the college?

You're reading it all wrong, says a calming inner voice, which I sometimes think of (fancifully, I'll fully admit) as my mental pixie. *It wasn't contrived at all, Jennie. You both just happened to be there at the same time, and Mr Jenkins thought it would only be polite to introduce you.*

Well, that's at least one weight off my mind, I think.

But my inner voice hasn't finished with me yet.

So, you see, it's not him that's being devious, it's you that's seeing conspiracies everywhere – you stupid, paranoid bitch! it says.

Well, thanks a lot, mental pixie.

SEVEN

7 October 1974 – Evening

As I stand outside The Head of the River pub, I feel the chill rising up from the Isis and I remember those long-ago mornings when I would drag myself out of a warm cosy bed at five thirty, and (after slurping a hasty cup of tea), would cycle madly down to the boathouse on the opposite bank of the river from the pub, in order to subject myself to early morning rowing practice. I never cared much for the sport even in the warm weather – endlessly pulling on an oar always seemed a pretty pointless occupation – but in the winter, when the wind slashed at my face like a razor, I positively hated it.

So if it's all so unpleasant, why bother to row at all, you might ask? And if you *do* need to ask, then its more than likely you've never been an eighteen-year-old girl, hundreds of miles away from home, attending a posh university, and desperate to fit in.

Over time, Charlie Swift cured me of that. Over time, he taught me that the only chance you ever have of finding happiness is to be yourself – and even then it's only ever a pretty slim chance!

I check my watch and see that DI George Hobson is half an hour late, which is not like him at all. I feel a shiver run through me, and I am almost certain that is less to do with the cold than it is with the bad feeling that I have been doing my best to shake off.

I light up another cigarette. I'm smoking too many these days, but then, if you believe the medical reports (and there's no earthly reason why you shouldn't), *one* cigarette is one too many.

Another ten minutes have passed, and I'm almost on the point of giving up when I see George's green Cortina pull up on the car park.

When you want something from someone, you can't afford to be petulant. So instead of huffing over his tardiness, I walk over to his car, and as he gets out, say, 'Hi George,' as if he's not kept me waiting at all – and even if he has, I haven't noticed.

His eyes are hollow, as if he's been worrying about something.

'I nearly didn't come,' he says.

'Oh,' I reply.

'Don't you want to know why?' he asks.

'Why?' I say, because honestly, he's not really left me much room for manoeuvre here.

'I nearly didn't come because I'd decided that if you were digging yourself into a deep hole – and I really think you are, Jennie – then I didn't want to be any part of it.'

'So what changed your mind?' I say.

He shrugs. 'You're a fully paid-up adult, and if you want to bury yourself, then that's really nobody's business but your own.'

But that's not it at all. He's not here to assist me in digging my own grave – he's come to persuade me to throw away my bloody shovel.

'Shall we go inside?' I suggest.

Another shrug.

'Why not?'

We are sitting at yet another table with a beaten copper top, (what is it with breweries and beaten copper tops?), and George has a beige folder spread out in front of him, which, I assume, is the result of his day's labours on my behalf.

'I have two names that might be of use to you,' he says, all crisp and business-like. 'The first is Albert Boulting. He comes from a very old county family, and was educated at Harrow School. He disappeared one night in February 1916. His disappearance may or may not have something to do with the fact that the police were watching him.'

'Why were they watching him?' I ask.

George tells me, and as his tale unfolds, I feel myself getting sicker and sicker.

'So why hadn't the police *already* arrested him?' I demand, when George has finished his foul story.

'You're getting too emotional, Jennie,' he cautions.

'It's an emotional subject,' I say, in my defence.

'We're talking about crimes that happened over sixty years ago, and if you're upset about them, it can only be because you're *already* upset about the situation that you find yourself having to deal with now.'

He's probably right, though – aside from the fact I've failed to report a serious crime to the police, which could well mean I end up in prison – I can't think *what* might be upsetting me.

'So why hadn't the police *already* arrested him?' I repeat, this time more calmly.

'They didn't have enough proof,' George says.

'Oh, come on now, George, from what you've just sketched out for me, there must have been at least a dozen witnesses who could have placed him very near the scene of *at least* one of the crimes.'

'What you're forgetting, Jennie, is that it's 1916 we're talking about here,' George says.

'What's that got to do with it?'

'Back then, there were the wrong kind of witnesses and there were the right kind of witnesses.'

'Meaning . . .?'

'Meaning that if the magistrate had had to choose between taking the word of a man like Albert – someone with a background no doubt similar to his own – and taking the word of a washer-woman or a small shopkeeper, he'd take Albert's word because Albert was a gentleman.'

'That's outrageous,' I say.

'Yes,' George agreed, 'but that's the way of the world, and most magistrates would have been inclined to believe that the washerwoman was lying, probably for profit, while a gentleman would never stain his soul by uttering an untruth. It's all down in black and white, in the local inspector's official papers. He seems to have been a decent man who wanted to do his duty, and he wrote that, while he had enough evidence to arrest Albert Boulting, he had nowhere near enough to be certain he could make it stick.'

'Tell me about the other man who disappeared,' I say.

'His name was James Makepeace – funny name to have, "Makepeace," in the middle of a war, don't you think?'

'It's absolutely hilarious,' I say.

'He had a similar background to Boulting, but he went to Eton rather than Harrow, and there's no indication he was addicted to the same disgusting vice as Boulting was. Anyway, his disappearance . . .'

'Wait a minute,' I tell him. 'You say there's no indication he was addicted to the same disgusting vice?'

'Yes.'

'*Where* is there no indication?'

'In his police record.'

'He has a police record? What does it say?'

'I'm coming to that, if you just be a little patient,' George says.

'Sorry.'

'Makepeace disappeared in late October 1943, and just like Boulting, one minute he was there and the next he was gone. Neither took anything with him, and both had been called up by the army and were about to be posted, so it's possible they both deserted.'

'The police file,' I say, impatiently.

'James Makepeace does have a police file,' George says, 'but there's absolutely nothing in it.'

'And what does that mean?'

'I've no idea.'

'But there must be some way to find out,' I say.

'I don't think there is.'

'It's only thirty years ago. There must still be coppers at the station who were there when the file was opened.'

'It was opened in late 1942, by which time all the younger regular police officers were in the army, and the station was being run by blokes close to retirement, who were supplemented by other blokes who'd retired years before. So what do you think are the chances of any of them being alive today?'

'Slim,' I say.

'Well, that's all the information I've got for you,' George says. He sighs, heavily, and I realise that we've come to the point where – much as he might not like the idea – he simply has to say his piece.

'There's one thing that's been troubling me, Jennie,' he says, 'and it's this – why did you ask me to do your checking up for you?'

'I asked you because you're my friend, and friends are *always* asking friends for favours,' I reply. 'And you know, don't you, that if I can ever do you a favour in return, you've only to ask.'

'You see, it's not that you asked me to do you a favour that's got me worried, it's that you asked me to do *this* favour,' George says.

'What do you mean by that?' I ask, and I realise that I've started to tremble, because my gut is telling me that whatever he says next, I'm not going to like it one little bit.

'You see, I haven't found out anything that the bursar of St Luke's . . . his name's Swift, isn't it?'

'Yes.'

'I haven't found out anything that Swift couldn't have come up with a bloody sight quicker. Now, given that he's also a friend of yours . . . I'm right about that, too, aren't I?'

'Yes, you are.'

'Given that he's also a friend of yours, I've been wondering why you didn't ask him directly, and however much I think about it – and however many different angles I examine it from – there's only one explanation that seems to make any sense at all. Would you like to hear it?'

'Yes, all right,' I say. I don't sound enthusiastic, because I'm not. In fact, I don't want to listen to what he's about to tell me at all, but I know that I'll have to sooner or later, and it might as well be sooner.

'My explanation is that your client – whoever he is – specifically asked you not to go to the bursar for information. And if that is the case – if he wants Swift kept in the dark about what he's doing, then I've got serious reservations about him. And if I've got serious reservations about him, then I've got serious reservations about your whole investigation.'

I should already be preparing the snappy answer which will smooth over all his doubts – but I'm not doing that at all. And the reason I haven't produced a snappy answer is that I'm in a state of near shock, because what he's just said is perfectly logical.

My client *can't* be the bursar, because the bursar wouldn't need me to collect information that he already had. But my client *is* the bursar, and he is paying me to find out things he already knows, for reasons that I can't even begin to guess at.

I'm wondering why I didn't see all this before – and why it needed George Hobson (a solid copper, but not the brightest star in the firmament) to point it out to me. And what I soon realise is that my own logical thought processes have been numbed (or maybe just diverted) by the almost hysterical show of emotion that Charlie bombarded me with in my office.

George Hobson is still looking at me – waiting for me to say something to calm his fears for me.

'Relax,' I tell him.

'Relax?' he repeats incredulously. 'I can't relax – and after what I've just told you, you certainly shouldn't be able to, either.'

'But I can relax,' I say, 'because I know exactly why my client didn't want me to use the bursar as a source of information. It's a very good reason – though, for professional reasons, I obviously can't tell you what it is – but you can rest assured that there's absolutely nothing for either of us to worry about.'

And even as I'm saying the words, I'm thinking that because of Charlie I'm turning into a woman I have little choice but to despise.

I call in at Charlie's rooms in St Luke's, and he isn't there. I ask Mr Jenkins if he knows where he's gone, but the head porter is unable to enlighten me. Charlie's not in the Lamb and Flag or the Eagle and Child either, so, unless he's out on what he so elegantly (and so euphemistically) calls a 'hunt for fresh young buttocks' he's deliberately hiding from me.

I don't want to spend any more time in either of the pubs where I habitually drink with Charlie, so I go back to the old, reliable Bulldog, and just manage to order a G&T – a double – before the pub lights all flash dementedly and the barman throws the towel over the draught beer pumps.

It's when I'm half way down my drink that I realise that some part of my brain has already decided I'm going to carry on with the job Charlie gave me.

So just what kind of idiot does that make me?

EIGHT

12 February 1916

When Albert Boulting chose to become introspective, as he did occasionally, what he usually discovered at the very core of his being was a genuine hero, a man made of much the same mettle as Christopher Columbus and David Livingstone.

He, like them, was an explorer, he told himself, opening up trails that others dared not open, entering into the places which – by that very act of entering – put his life in danger. But it would not be like this forever. Eventually, the rest of the world – currently so backward in its thinking – would catch up with him. It would, in other words, overcome all its prejudices and understand that what all these small girls (the ones he'd been with) had ever wanted from their miserable little lives was the opportunity to serve him, whilst experiencing, for the first time, their own sexuality. Once that obvious truth had been universally accepted, he was quietly confident that there would be statues erected of him throughout all Europe and beyond.

That afternoon, his adventurous nature had led him to stand on a small pile of bricks, which made him just tall enough to see over the crumbling wall and across to the patch of waste ground, where the children – ignoring the cold – were playing a game of rounders, with a plank for a bat and a ball made of rags.

Though there were other sweet children there – so many juicy berries to pluck! – it was a little girl of about seven years old who he was focussing his attention on. She had long blonde hair, which was badly knotted through lack of care, and was dressed in a ratty red woollen cardigan, and a heavy grey flannel skirt that was much too big for her and trailed along the ground.

It was the little girl's turn to bat, and she stood on the first base, licking her lips in concentration. When the ball came, she took a tremendous swing at it, and then was off, running towards the second base.

It was her long skirt which let her down. She tripped over it, and went sprawling, accidentally revealing a pair of dirt-encrusted legs that Boulting considered just perfect.

Almost without realising it, his right hand was down his trousers, and he was imagining having the little girl to himself for the afternoon. First of all he would bathe her and wash her hair, then he would towel her down and comb the hair until the knots were gone. Naturally enough, she would be nervous, but he would be very, very gentle with her. And then he would realise that she didn't actually want him to be gentle – that she had a blazing passion which equalled his own – and that he could be as rough with her as he liked.

Hold back! He ordered himself.

Hold back!

Don't squander your pleasure all at once!

Think of something else!

The distraction that he settled on was the ambush – there really could be no other word for it – which had occurred the previous August, in front of St Luke's porters' lodge.

He had been approached by two men with serious expressions on their faces and the light of evangelism burning in their eyes. One of the men had been in his sixties. The other was in his late twenties – and was missing his right arm.

'My name's Tom Smith,' the older man told Boulting, 'and I am proud to say that all three of my fine strapping sons are fighting bravely for their king and country in France.'

'And my name's Hector Judd, formerly of the Oxford Light Infantry,' the one-armed man said.

'We're Parliamentary Recruitment Committee canvassers,' Smith said. 'If you want me to, I'll explain what that means.'

'I don't need you to explain it,' Boulting had said.

Nor did he. It all went back to the Derby Scheme, created by the Earl of Derby, Lord Kitchener's deputy in the War Office. The reason why Derby had come up with this scheme was that, by the middle of 1915, the rate at which men were enlisting in the army had slowed down quite considerably, and since soldiers were getting killed in ever larger numbers in France, it was obvious that – unless there was a sudden upsurge in volunteers – conscription (which would be bad politically) would have to be introduced.

In essence, the scheme was an attempt to encourage – or perhaps even manufacture – that necessary enthusiasm. In practical terms, this amounted to tracking down every man who was old enough to fight, and handing him a letter from the Earl of Derby that explained how much his country needed his help.

Boulting's first instinct was to refuse to take the letter that Smith was offering him, but then he changed his mind, and decided it might be quite amusing to go along with the game these two pathetic pieces of humanity were playing.

He read the letter from the Earl slowly, occasionally casting a quick, covert glance at the canvassers, who were waiting for him to finish like eager and impatient puppies.

'So what does it mean when it says that I should "attest to joining the armed forces"?' he asked, when he reached the end of the letter.

'It means that you promise us you will enlist within forty-eight hours,' Hector Judd said.

'Or, if you prefer it, we can take you to the recruiting centre now,' Tom Smith told him, 'and once you're sworn in, they'll give you a special signing-on bonus of two shillings and ninepence.'

'Two shillings and ninepence!' Boulting said in mock awe. 'I've never had that much money before. I don't know what I'd do with a whole *two shillings and ninepence*.'

Hector Judd scowled, recognising sarcasm when he heard it.

'Well, will you do it?' Smith asked, and it was plain that though he was the older of the pair, he was also the more naïve, so the sarcasm had gone right over his head. 'Will you come down to the recruitment office with us?'

'If you don't mind, I'd like time to think about it,' Boulting said.

'What is there to think about?' demanded Judd. He waved his stump angrily in Boulting's direction. 'I've already made my sacrifice for my country – now it's time that you made yours.'

Boulting recalled a song which had become very popular in the previous few months.

'"I gladly took my chance, Now my right arm's in France",' he sang, imitating the music hall artist he had seen perform the number, '"I'm one of England's broken dolls".'

By the time he'd finished, the other two men were glaring at him angrily, but he wasn't worried, because one of them was an old man and the other was a cripple, and neither of them posed a serious threat. He was not even bothered when he noticed Gough, the head porter, glaring at him with pure hatred from the lodge door. True, Gough was tall enough and strong enough to cause him problems, but, when all was said and done, he was still nothing but a servant – and the day when the quality started being afraid of their servants was the day the world would come to an end.

The little blonde girl was fielding now, which was much better – much less likely to overexcite him and bring to a sudden sticky end what should have been a much longer process. And yet, even out there – standing perfectly still – she was causing his heart to palpitate, and he knew that he needed to stop focussing on her for at least a couple of minutes.

This time, he did not turn his thoughts to events that had occurred months earlier, but instead recalled what had happened that very morning.

Reading between the lines of the newspapers, it had been obvious to Boulting for some time that far too many of the men approached by the Parliamentary Recruitment Committee canvassers had answered in a manner which, whilst probably not as crass and unfeeling as his own response, had nonetheless been equally as negative. As a result, conscription had finally been introduced, and Boulting himself had received a curt letter, informing him that he should report to the conscription office at the time indicated.

Boulting was pleased by neither the decision nor the letter. The first year and a half of the war had been a golden time for him, because so many married men had joined up, leaving behind them young daughters who were both unprotected and vulnerable to approaches by any man who reminded them, even a little, of their beloved daddies.

Oh yes, it had been wonderful, so why had the government, and the army, and the Germans, all conspired to spoil it for him? And why, if he must report to the conscription board, did he have to do it at the barbarically early time of ten o'clock in the morning?

He had not expected a warm welcome, so it was no great disappointment or shock when the captain glared at him from across the desk and said, 'Well, what have you got to say for yourself?'

Boulting looked back at the captain. He was still in his twenties, and had the sort of regional accent you did not normally hear coming from the lips of officers and gentlemen. So it was likely he had risen through a field promotion, and field promotions were, in Boulting's opinion, a big mistake, because you didn't make a king out of a turnip simply by putting a crown on its head.

'Well?' the captain demanded, impatiently.

'What have I got to say for myself?' Boulting mused. 'Well, there are many things I could say – and on such a wide range subjects, too – but I really don't have a clue what it is that *you'd* like me to say.'

'You could have joined up when war was declared,' the captain said, now it was clear that Boulting wasn't going to play by the rules the way that everyone else did. 'Millions did join up, you know. Or you could have attested under the Derby System, when you were approached by the canvassers, but you didn't do that either. What's the matter? Are you a coward?'

'I don't think so, no,' Boulting said, 'but neither do I see the need to deliberately expose myself to enemy bullets, when there seem to be so many other men eager to fill that role.'

'You disgust me,' the captain said.

'And am I supposed to be offended at being insulted by a man who, in peacetime, would probably be expected to enter my house by the back door?' Boulting wondered.

The captain smiled. 'Well, you had your chance,' he said, 'but you did nothing, and now the decision's been taken for you. As of this morning, you are a second lieutenant in the Welsh Engineers.'

'The Welsh Engineers?' Boulting repeated with disdain. 'Aren't they mainly those grubby little miners who dig their foul stinking tunnels right under the Hun's lines?'

'Sir,' the captain said, his smile broadening.

'What?' Boulting replied, mystified.

'You are now subject to King's Regulations, and even if I *would* be told to enter your house through the back door in peacetime, I am now your superior officer. So what you should have said is, "Aren't they mainly those grubby little miners who dig their foul stinking tunnels right under the Hun's lines, *sir*?" And yes, that's exactly what they are.'

'They're not really my style, you know,' Boulting said, then he caught the dangerous look in the corner of the captain's eye, and added a reluctant, 'sir.'

'No, I imagine they're not,' said the captain, who looked as if he'd really started enjoying himself.

'I doubt I'd even understand what they were saying . . . sir,' Boulting continued. 'I'd really be much more comfortable with a commission in one of the Guards regiments.'

'You sail for France next Wednesday,' the captain said. '*Bon voyage*, old chap!'

Boulting didn't argue. What would have been the point, when he had no intention of going to France and becoming just one more name on the 'killed in action' page of *The Times*? His family was rich – fabulously so – and had estates in the West Indies. He could slip away to one of those estates, and spend the rest of his war pleasuring himself with dusky prepubescent maidens.

A woman appeared on the waste ground. She was perhaps in her early thirties, and wore a turban on her head. Her breasts – great floppy things – hung pendulously over her big stomach. It was hard to believe that she could be the mother of the little blonde-haired angel, but that was probably exactly what she was. And if that *were* true, it was likely that by the time the angel was her age, she would look like that, too. But that was the advantage of doing things the way he did – because, long before they got to be fat and ugly, you had used them, squeezed them dry, and moved on.

The mother looked across in his direction, but before she had time to get a proper look at him, he stepped off the bricks and became invisible to her. Not that there was any real need to do that now, because the time element meant that her grubby little lamb was quite safe from Albert the big bad wolf.

As he walked away from the waste ground – with the winter

wind freezing his ears, and the frosty air nipping at his ankles like a demented ferret – he was whistling quite philosophically.

When he got back to his rooms, he would pack a few essential things in his Gladstone bag, and catch one of the morning trains to London. After that, it was just a question of going down to the East India Docks and bribing his way onto a suitably luxurious ship that would soon be setting off in the right direction.

He was half-way down Walton Street when he felt a sudden tingle at the back of his neck which made him come to an abrupt halt. He had the greatest respect for his instincts – they were highly tuned, as they had to be if he were to pursue his guilty pleasures without fear of apprehension. And what his instincts told him was that, at that moment, he was being watched.

It wasn't the police.

He was sure of that.

He knew that the police *had* been watching him from time to time, hoping, in their bumbling way, to be able to catch him in the act. But he always knew when they were there – his instincts picked up their presence as clearly as if they'd brought a brass band with them.

He looked up and down the street and could see nothing and no one the least suspicious-looking.

But it didn't matter – it didn't matter a *damn* – because he could still sense them out there.

He went back to St Luke's by a roundabout route, and employed any number of diversionary tactics – entering the Lamb and Flag by one door and leaving by another; taking a sudden turn down Turl Street, then turning left at the first cross street – but it made no difference, because when he finally reached St Luke's, he could still sense that the presence was with him.

Standing there, in the gateway, a dozen yards from the porters' lodge, his instinct told him that he should go straight down to the railway station and catch the first train to London, but though he recognised that this would be his wisest course, he could not bear the thought of leaving without the collection of erotic photographs he had hidden in his room.

It won't take a minute to pick them up, and then I'll go straight to the station, he told himself.

Gough appeared in the doorway of the porters' lodge.

'Good evening, sir,' he said.

'Has anybody been looking for me, Gough?' Boulting asked.

'Looking for you?' Gough replied. 'Now why would anybody have been looking for a yellow-bellied coward like you, sir?'

Hearing those words – from that man – was like plunging into ice-cold water, Boulting thought.

It took your breath away – it really did.

'How dare you?' he raged. 'How dare you!'

Before he knew it, he was striding furiously towards the head porter. He would thrash the man to within an inch of his life, he told himself, and he wouldn't even have to pay a fine, because by the time anyone found Gough, he himself would be long gone.

Gough watched his approach calmly, and when Boulting had covered about half the ground between them, the head porter held up his hand and said, 'If I was you, sir, I wouldn't come any further.'

Boulting realised he had come to a halt. He didn't understand how it had happened. He certainly hadn't consciously willed it – and yet some tiny controlling spot somewhere in the back of his head seemed to have thought it was a good idea not to take Gough on.

The head porter was still standing there, watching him through eyes that were filled with contempt.

'I'll have your job for this, Gough,' he blustered. 'I'll see you kicked out of this college for openers, and then I'll make sure you never work anywhere else, ever again.'

'You must do as your conscience dictates, sir, and I will do the same,' Gough said, before taking a step back into the lodge and closing the door firmly behind him.

Boulting took a deep breath in an attempt to calm down, and wondered what to do next.

There seemed to be no one else around – the army people were probably out on manoeuvres again – and it was a long walk from the archway to his staircase.

Should he risk it?

Gough had said that no one had been asking about him.

No, what Gough had actually done was wonder why anybody would ask for him, which was not the same thing at all.

And anyway, Gough had turned so strange that there was no point in paying attention to anything he said.

There would be no danger in collecting his precious pictures from his room, he told himself – no danger at all.

And even at that very moment, there was a part of him which knew that he was making the biggest mistake of his life.

NINE

8 October 1974

A
lbert Boulting went missing in 1916, and James Make-peace was last seen in 1943, and those disappearances corresponded – more or less – to the times the two (as-yet-unidentified) bodies were bricked up in the air vent in the cellar of St Luke's College. Therefore it follows that the dead men in the vent have to be Boulting and Makepeace, doesn't it?

No, it doesn't. Coincidence is not proof, which is why, when the police find a body that matches the description of a missing girl – right down to her shoes and the birthmark on her left arm – they will still not confirm it actually is the missing girl until the girl's parents have made a positive identification.

Having said that, I'll admit that I'd be very surprised indeed if the bodies don't turn out to be those of Boulting and Makepeace, but that's a long way from stating categorically that it has to be them, because the simple fact is that people who disappear often do 'pop up' again unexpectedly somewhere else, sometimes many years later.

So what I need to find out – doing the best job I can with my limited resources – is whether either Boulting or Makepeace ever actually 'popped up' again, and it is this mission which has brought me to the charming Northamptonshire village of Kneebury Thrubwell.

I have not come alone, but instead – in the back of the light blue Vauxhall six-hundredweight van, which I hire for such occasions – have brought with me all the costumes which comprise the wardrobe of what I like to think of as my one-woman repertory company.

When I arrived in the village – Norman church, thatched cottages, duck pond on the village green with real ducks bobbing complacently up and down on it – I still had no firm idea about who I would be. So, in order to assist me in reaching my decision, I headed straight for that repository of all local knowledge and wisdom: the village pub – which, in this particular case, was named (probably by the sharp-suited geniuses in the brewery's public relations' department) The Headless Rider of Kneebury Thrubwell.

The morning meeting of the village dipsomaniac society was already in session when I arrived, but it was no closed, insular society, and I found that my offering to buy a round of drinks was enough to ensure that I was treated like a long lost member.

My new friends were a retired postman, a retired shopkeeper, a retired garage mechanic, and a ne'er-do-well who was looking around for something not to retire from. When I asked them about the Boulting family I unleashed a positive flood of anecdotes, gossip and innuendo.

I claim no credit for getting them to talk, incidentally. There is little skill in getting men who have already started slurring their words to gabble on – though there is considerable skill in getting them to shut up.

After listening to my new pals talk for fifteen minutes or so, I began to mentally weed out some of the characters that I had brought with me in the back of the van.

The first to go was Betsey Weaver from Kansas City – calico dress, wide smile and an all fired-up enthusiasm – 'I knew I had to trace my ancestors right back to this cute little village of yours, or I'd just die.' She had served me well on several occasions, but I thought the Boulting family – or at least, the family member in residence at the moment – might not exactly take to her.

Next to fall by the wayside were Tania Taylor the estate agent – 'We have big plans for developing this area, and anyone who comes in with us on the ground floor could make himself a real killing,' – and Alice Blunt, the county council civil engineer and all-round bloody-minded bureaucrat – 'Granted, it seems a real pity that the road would run right through the middle of your living room, but that's what it says on the plans, and unless you've got a very good reason why it shouldn't, that *is* where it's going to run'. Again, they had been loyal foot soldiers and served my devious purposes well, but they would be of no use to me now because, quite simply, you should never try to bribe or threaten a family that has been in residence for over five hundred years.

Linda Moore and Elaine Eccles were also posted into the reject slot, which left me with Poppy James – all wide-brimmed hat, white dress patterned with big black spots, and conspicuous cleavage.

The costume donned, an easel and paint box tucked under my arm, I make my way up the country lane to Kneebury Manor.

It is an old Tudor manor house with a built-in moat and, though I hate myself for being impressed, I just can't help it.

I cross the drawbridge (how cute is that – and so practical if you're feeling anti-social!). I ring the bell in the massive oak door at the other side of the moat, and my ring is answered by a man in his late twenties. He is really rather attractive, in a schoolboy-ish, gauche sort of way, and if I had an afternoon to spare, and he wasn't involved in the investigation . . .

'I'm looking for the owner of this lovely house,' I say, gazing at him over the top of the huge glasses that I always wear with my Poppy outfit. 'It doesn't happen to be you, does it?'

'Gosh, no, it belongs to my parents, and they're off on a safari in Kenya at the moment, no doubt slaughtering some animals who never wished them any ill will at all,' he says. 'I'm Arthur, their younger son,' he holds out his hand to me, 'and I'm looking after the place while they're away.'

Full marks to the Headless Horseman Public Bar Intelligence Unit, I think, as I raise my hand to shake his.

The inevitable happens. My easel slips free, my paint-box follows. Microseconds later, they both hit the ground, the easel with a dull thud, the paint-box with a metallic chink and tinny bounce.

What a ditz I am!

Arthur and I crouch down almost simultaneously, and it is only by the narrowest of margins that we avoid our foreheads colliding.

'I'm so clumsy,' I say, reaching for my easel.

'It could have happened to anybody,' Arthur assures me, collecting up my paints.

As we stand up again, both of us recognise that things have changed. From being complete strangers a moment ago, we have now shared in a mildly amusing incident, and there has been some bonding.

I smile, to reward him for his efforts, and then allow my face to slowly fill with signs of nervous hope.

'If you're in charge of the house, that means you can give me the permission I need,' I bite my lower lip slightly – Oscar-winning stuff, this is – 'but I don't want you to do it against your will. I mean, I wouldn't like to think that I'm pressuring you in any way.'

His face quickly clouds over. Perhaps he's imagining that I'm going to ask him if I can bring fifty orphans here for the day, or maybe hold the annual conference of some nudist organisation in the great hall. Whatever he's thinking, he isn't exactly happy.

'What sort of permission would you be wanting?' he asks, looking really sad that he's going to have to turn a pretty girl like me down.

I hold up my easel to him as a sort of visual aid, even though – after our scramble on the floor – he's already very familiar with it.

'I'd like to paint a picture of the house,' I say.

He emits a gasp of relief and follows it with a lopsided grin.

'I don't think you need *anyone's* permission to do that,' he says.

'Maybe I didn't express myself very well,' I tell him. 'I know that in theory I don't need your permission, but I like to know how people will feel about it before I begin to paint their house, because if they wouldn't like it, well, I simply wouldn't feel comfortable doing it.'

He gives me a look that seems to say that he thinks I'm the most gorgeous butterfly that he's ever seen, and he would give anything in the world to have me in his collection.

'Would you like to come in for a drink, before you get started?' he suggests, trying his best to hide the eagerness that is starting to bubble up inside him. 'And maybe, if you have the time, I could show you around the place. Someone with your interests might find it . . . er . . .'

He is stuck here, because he doesn't want to repeat himself, but he can't think of another word to replace interesting.

I decide to rescue him.

'I might find it fascinating,' I suggest.

'Exactly,' he agrees, with some relief.

'Thank you, that would be really marvellous,' I say.

Do I feel guilty about exploiting a nice man like he so obviously is? No! As a reward for his kindness, he will get to spend an hour or so with a really nice girl (even if the girl he thinks he's spending his time with isn't actually me), so what's there to feel guilty about?

You would expect a house like this to be full-to-bursting with servants – serious-looking middle-aged men with side-whiskers and dressed in frock coats, young women with white starched aprons and white crochet caps.

Not here!

Here, we seem to have the whole place to ourselves.

'My parents are forced to rely on agency workers,' Arthur says, reading my puzzlement. 'It's been virtually impossible to get reliable, permanent servants since the war. There's just no respect for tradition, any more.'

'Well, I suppose that you don't feel like being a domestic servant when you've played your own small part in defeating Adolf Hitler.' I suggest.

'Oh, not that war,' he says dismissively. 'It's the Great War I'm talking about.'

'Do you mean the one that ended thirty years before you were even born?' I ask.

'That's right,' he agrees, his puzzled look suggesting that he can't even begin to guess at the point I'm trying to make.

I don't think I'll ever understand these people.

After drinks (a glass of dry sherry for Arthur, a demure iced grapefruit juice for me), we begin our tour in the banqueting hall with its minstrels' gallery. Under normal circumstances, I'd find this part of the house fascinating, but what I want to see now – what I'm positively *bursting* to see now – is the famous family portrait gallery, of which my late-morning drinking club in the public bar of the Headless Horseman spoke at some length.

Eventually, we do get to the gallery. It is a long, thin room. The paintings in it have been ordered chronologically, which means that, after we pass a few late Tudor portraits (all caps and ruffs), we are thrown into the world of the Stuarts and immediately surrounded by men in short unstiffened jackets and wide breeches hanging loose at the knee – men who strike heroic poses, but whose faces betray a disappointment (though this may just be me being fanciful) that they are not being immortalised by the great Van Dyck, but instead merely captured on canvas by some far less talented Dutchman.

As we move along the gallery, I can almost smell the powder on the wigs of the gentlemen painted by a number of would-be Joshua Reynolds. And then it is work in the style of David Wilkie – heroic men and beautiful women posing woodenly against backgrounds so depressingly detailed that I could almost count the dog hairs trapped in the carpet.

I know, I know, it's very hard to please me!

We have reached the beginning of the twentieth century and, though we have thus far been promenade viewing, I now come to a decided halt.

'Who are those two?' I ask, pointing to two portraits of young men set side-by-side.

'Ah, they are my great-uncle Albert and my great-uncle Oswald,' Arthur tells me.

I quickly assess the paintings. Oswald looks cautious and dry, Albert quixotic and selfish.

'It's easy to see where you inherited your good looks from, Arthur,' I say – shamelessly. 'What happened to these two?'

'Uncle Oswald studied law, and then joined the colonial service. He was a high court judge in several of the empire's most important possessions. Of course, once we lost the empire, he had to come home.'

'Where he died of a broken heart, brought on by thoughts that the good old days had gone forever?' I suggest, mischievously.

'No, actually, he got a job as professor of constitutional law in a provincial university, and now lives in a retirement home in Western-super-Mare. He's quite gaga, of course, but perfectly harmless.'

'And I bet Albert made a name for himself, too,' I say.

Arthur chuckles. 'I suppose he did, though probably not in the way you imagine.'

'What do you mean?'

'He was the black sheep of the family – altogether a bit too much of a ladies' man.'

He says the words with a certain amount of grudging (or do I mean guilty?) admiration.

Most men will tell you that womanising is wrong and irresponsible, but – by God – it cheers their spirits to know that there are at least *some* men out there who *can* be both wrong and irresponsible, and can get away with it!

He doesn't realise it, but this particular bit of family history had already been through the wash several times before it got anywhere near him.

A ladies' man! A bloody ladies' man!

He wasn't a ladies' man at all, I want to scream. *When girls got beyond the age of eight or nine, he lost interest in them.*

I *want* to scream it, but of course, I don't.

'So what happened to your great-uncle?' I ask Arthur. 'Did he sail away to America, and become a legendary lover in the silent pictures?'

'No, he didn't,' Arthur says. 'I rather wish he had, because that would have become a really good story. What *actually* happened was that, early in January 1916, he completely disappeared.'

'What do you mean – he completely disappeared?'

'That's just what happened. He was a student at Oxford at the time, and one morning, when his scout took him his cup of tea, there was no sign of him. The scout thought nothing of it, because all Uncle Albert's things still were there – his clothes, his banjo, etc. – so wherever he was, he couldn't have gone away for long. But he had. He was never seen again.'

'And what do you think happened to him?'

'There's a theory in the family that he was recruited by the secret service, and died somewhere overseas, while carrying out an important – and totally hush-hush – mission.'

'And do you believe that?'

'Well, I think it has to have been something of that nature, otherwise he would have contacted the family, especially when his father died, and he was entitled to a third of what was a very large estate. I mean, any man would naturally claim his birthright, wouldn't he?'

Yes, I think, but it's very difficult to claim it when you're walled up in the cellar of St Luke's with your skull bashed in.

I look at my watch. 'I have to go,' I say.

He looks disappointed. 'But what about your painting?' You haven't even made a start.'

'Maybe another day,' I lie.

And as I cross the drawbridge, I'm thinking, 'That's one down – and one to go.'

TEN

22 October 1943

T here was no moon that night, and the whole of the Oxford that Charlie Swift had learned to love was in darkness. It was not the same sort of darkness as had existed pre-war. Back then, even when the streetlights had been switched off, there were still sources of man-made illumination – chinks of light seeping through the drawn curtains of bedrooms and living rooms, bursts of light as a car or a motorcycle passed by. Now, the exclusion of the light was total and ruthless, because there *were* no car headlights, and the bedrooms and living rooms were tightly sealed with blackout blinds.

The blackout was all Germany's fault, Swift thought sardonically, as he made his way slowly and cautiously along the High, with only a pinprick light from the centre of an otherwise blacked-out flashlight glass to guide him.

It wasn't that he blamed the Germans for the Blitz – that heavy aerial bombing campaign against Britain's industrial cities, which had lasted from September 1940 to May 1941. That had been no more than an understandable retaliation for what the Royal Air Force had already done to Germany. No, what he blamed the Germans for was not sending the prime minister, Winston Churchill, a postcard to tell him the Blitz had been called off.

He composed such a postcard in his mind.

Dear Winston (you poor, confused, deluded old-age pensioner), This is just a quick line to let you know that you'll have to do without the excitement of air raids from now on, because we won't be bombing you anymore. This is a pity, after you've gone to the trouble of building all those air raid shelters, but you would insist on shooting down our beautiful shiny planes, so you only have yourselves to blame. We are now bombing Russia and they are not being half as unpleasant about it as you were. So now that we've stopped bombing you, why don't you end this ridiculous blackout of yours? All it does is make you look foolish.

 Yours
 Adolf.

 P.S. Wish I was there (in Buckingham Palace, of course!)

And yet, even if Hitler had been so whimsical as to send that sort of postcard (and he was more widely known for his ranting frothing-at-the-mouth speeches about annihilating his enemies than he was for his whimsicality), it wouldn't have made any difference, Charlie thought. The government already knew that the measure was no longer necessary, but the war effort – or at least that aspect of it involved with manipulating the civilian population – rested on the twin pillars of theatre and sacrifice, and the blackout was such a perfect embodiment of both these things that the war would have to have been almost won before Churchill and his cabinet would consent to abandon it.

Charlie grinned into the darkness, aware that his particular brand of cynicism was the very anathema of the patriotic spirit that Winston Churchill, with his bombastic and oratorical nightly radio speeches, had been doing his very best to engender.

Well, he, Lord Charles Swift, was a patriot, too – patriotic enough to sign up for front line duties, a personal decision which could well result in his being sent home in a box (and possibly in several pieces) – but his patriotism was no reason for him to drown his mind in the sludge of crude wartime propaganda.

He estimated he was almost at the corner arranged for his rendezvous, and whistled.

Another whistle – slightly more tuneful than his own – answered.

He took another cautious step forward, and felt a pair of hands rest on his shoulders. He cocked his head to one side, and kissed the man who had been waiting for him.

The blackout had its advantages after all!

He didn't like James Makepeace, he thought, as he felt the other man's tongue expertly exploring his mouth – he didn't like him *at all* – but it was beyond question that he was mad for him.

Makepeace broke away, so unexpectedly soon that it might almost have been called prematurely.

'What's the matter?' Charlie asked.

'What's the matter with you?' Makepeace countered. 'That was like kissing my grandmother – only not quite as exciting.'

'I'm sorry,' Charlie said, 'I'm just not really in the . . .'

'Do you have a problem with me?' Makepeace demanded.

In an attempt to avoid seeming petty, Charlie was about to say that no, he didn't have a problem with anything. Then he decided that the matter which had been bothering him, had been bothering him *so much* that it wasn't really petty at all.

'I don't like the way you've been sniffing around Lucy Jenkins,' he said. 'I *really* don't like it.'

'Ah, you're still her knight errant, are you, defending her just like you did that first night in the refectory?' Makepeace asked.

'No, that's not it,' Charlie replied.

Nor was it, because although James was right, and his aim on that particular occasion had been to defend Lucy Jenkins, this feeling he had now really wasn't about the woman at all.

'Well, are we going to stand here all night, or should we head for the pub?' Makepeace asked.

'We'll head for the pub,' Charlie said.

They set off, each with his own tiny pinprick of light to guide him. They could hear each other breathing, but if they occasionally caught a glimpse of a black shape, neither could be really sure whether it was the other man they were seeing or merely a lamppost.

They'd gone perhaps no more than fifty yards when Makepeace burst out laughing.

'What's so funny?' Charlie Swift demanded.

'Is that really what you think I've been doing?' Makepeace

asked. 'Can you possibly be imagining that I've been sniffing around Lucy Jenkins and doing my best to talk my way into her knickers?'

'Yes – and there's no *thinking* about it,' Charlie Swift said angrily. 'Every time I see you together, you're stuck in some corner, giggling away like children. I noticed that you had the sense to restrain yourselves a little while her husband was here on leave, but I think he sensed that something was going on anyway, and since he doesn't strike me as the kind of man you can mess with, I'd tread very carefully indeed the next time he comes home.'

Makepeace laughed again. 'Her husband's regiment is in lockdown,' he said. 'Jenkins won't be back in Oxford (if he ever *does* come back) until after the invasion of Europe.'

'How can you be so sure of that?' Charlie wondered.

'I happen to be on very good terms – if you understand what that means – with a captain in the same regiment,' Makepeace replied.

They could feel the camber of the road rising slightly, and then they heard the gentle swish of water far below them, so they knew they were crossing Magdalen Bridge.

'Still, even if he's not coming back, it was stupid of you both to be so obvious,' Charlie Swift said, but the wind had been somewhat blown out of his sails, and there was little conviction behind the words.

'Are you jealous of me and little Lucy?' Makepeace asked teasingly – almost, in fact, tauntingly.

'Of course I'm not jealous,' Charlie said.

'Do I need to remind you that we'd agreed that we could both sleep with whoever we wanted to?'

They *had* agreed that, Charlie thought, and it was the same sort of agreement he'd reached with most of his partners – yet somehow, the fact that Makepeace preferred a woman to him (if only occasionally) seemed like the blackest kind of betrayal.

'Well, *do* I need to remind you of our agreement, Charlie?' Makepeace prodded.

'No, of course not.'

Makepeace gave a throaty chuckle. 'You needn't worry your little self,' he said, and there was the tiniest hint of tenderness in his voice, which was about as close as he ever got to real affection. 'There's nothing going on between Lucy and me. What we have is a purely business relationship.'

'Do you mean she's *paying* you for sex?' Charlie Swift said, before he could stop himself.

Makepeace's chuckle became a full-throated roar.

'Oh yes,' he said. 'That's it, precisely. I couldn't possibly live as well as I do if it wasn't for the vast amounts of cash that that little serving maid can afford to pay me for screwing her.'

'So what other reason . . .'

'I'll give you a clue,' Makepeace interrupted. 'And the clue is . . . are you ready for this?'

'Yes.'

'The clue is – New York-London. Not New York and London, you note, or even London-New York, but New York-London.'

'I'm not in the mood for any stupid games, James,' Charlie Swift said – though Makepeace's clear assertion that he himself wasn't playing second fiddle to Lucy Jenkins was making him feel much better.

The pub that was their destination was located just the other side of Magdalen Bridge. It was run by an ex-wrestler called Billy Bones, and was one of those institutions that you went to if you cared more about good beer than you did about elegant surroundings.

The main bar had a brewery-installed piano at one end of it, though Billy did not usually encourage singing, since, as he pointed out, his business was to sell beer, and you couldn't sing and drink at the same time.

At the other end of the bar, sitting on a perch, was a blue-and-yellow macaw. Most people, seeing it for the first time, took its immobility as an indication that it was stuffed. Thus, they were naturally shocked when, once the landlord had rung the bell for closing time, the macaw suddenly came to life and proceeded to do its best – by way of haranguing the customers with novel suggestions on the uses they might make of their sexual organs – to encourage the more reluctant of them to leave.

There was the usual sort of crowd in there that night, Charlie Swift noted, once the heavy blackout door had swung closed behind them and they'd sat down at an empty table. There were students

– though, as more and more were called up, their number had markedly decreased. There were men too old for war – pensioners who had fought in the last war, and now found that no one was interested in hearing about the sheer hell they had gone through. There were labourers – big strapping men, many of them imported from neutral Ireland – whose job it was to prevent the country's infrastructure, on which the military so heavily depended, from crumbling away.

And there were the Yanks!

There were always the Yanks now.

These particular Americans – three of them – sat at the far table, with at least half a dozen local girls in attendance.

It was obvious why the girls were there, Charlie thought. And it wasn't sex they were after – it was something far more beautiful, more poetic, and (if handled right) more long lasting than sex.

It had been very early in the war that silk stockings had become unavailable, and girls were faced with the choice of wearing woollen stockings when they were out on the town (God no, never!) or of exposing their pale white English limbs to the world (God no, never!).

The solutions they had come up were ingenious. Some girls, for example, had dyed their legs with gravy browning and then drawn a seam down the middle of them with their eyebrow pencils.

And then, in 1940, the miracle had happened. Du Pont Chemicals, in the USA, had made it possible to produce nylon stockings, which were even better than silk ones.

Hallelujah! Legs could once more be displayed in public.

It should have been a perfect combination. The girls, working in war production industries, had more money in their pockets than ever before, and were almost desperate to spend it on beautifying themselves. The chemical company, on the other side of the pond, was eager to sell as much of its exciting new project as it possibly could.

The problem was that the British government was only allowing the importation of goods considered vital to the war effort and – look at it any way you wanted to – there was no argument that would allow nylon stockings to fit into that category.

One of the American soldiers, a big man with sergeant's stripes

– his pockets no doubt stuffed with the aforementioned nylon stockings – was laughing at something one of the girls had said. Then he noticed that Makepeace and Swift were sitting there, and the smile drained away, to be replaced by something which was close to black anger.

He'd recognised them as homosexuals, Charlie thought. It happened once in a while, because however carefully you dressed or behaved, some people were like truffle hounds, and had a knack for sniffing you out.

In his mind, he quickly examined the ways in which this situation might possibly play itself out.

One: the sergeant might be angry that two nancy boys had dared to breathe the same smoke-filled air that he was breathing, yet decide it was best to keep the anger to himself.

Two: he might tell his friends, and they might give the pair of queers hostile stares, and leave it at that.

Three: the sergeant might come over to their table and get abusive, and Billy Bones – who measured a man by how much he drank and not by what he did with his penis – would quickly throw the American out.

Four: the sergeant might turn violent before Billy Bones could get there, but this was no problem, because although the Yank was a big man, Charlie had boxed for the university, and had no doubts he could handle him.

What the sergeant actually did do was to walk across to their table and lay his hands flat on top of it.

'Well, hi there, James, you little faggot,' he said, in a low, growling voice. 'How are things with you?'

'Look, Hiram, this isn't the time or the place for us to be having a discussion,' Makepeace said uneasily.

'Really?' the sergeant asked. 'Then when *is* the time and place?'

'I don't know. I haven't thought about it. I'll call you and we'll arrange a time that is mutually convenient.'

'And would this mutually convenient time be before or *after* you've gone?' the sergeant wondered.

'I've no idea what you're talking about.'

'You're shipping out of here in two days, ain't you?'

Makepeace licked his lips, nervously.

'Yes, that's right, I am,' he admitted. He turned to Swift. 'I was going to tell you, Charlie. Honestly, I was.'

'*When* were you going to tell me?' Swift asked.

'Hey, don't talk to him, talk to me,' the sergeant said, and as his voice rose in volume, so the level of conversation at the other tables quickly decreased. 'We have some unfinished business to deal with, and I suggest we step outside and deal with it now.'

'I'd have to be completely mad to go out there with you, Comstock,' Makepeace said.

Everyone was looking at them now, including Sergeant Comstock's two friends.

'Last chance,' Comstock said.

'No,' James Makepeace replied, and the fear in his voice sounded genuine enough. 'No, I won't.'

Seemingly from nowhere, the knife appeared in the American sergeant's hand.

'Get up now, you little faggot,' he snarled. 'Do it before I stick you like a pig.'

It was then that Makepeace made his big mistake – a mistake that would have easily won him the first prize in any contest that aimed at finding the stupidest man around and crowning him King Idiot.

It was then, in other words, that he reached across the table and tried to take the knife away from the big sergeant.

The move was so unexpected – and so obviously insane – that it took Comstock by surprise. He jerked the knife away, and, in the process, unintentionally drew the blade across Makepeace's wrist. The blade left a thin, bloody track behind it, and as Makepeace gazed down at it in horror, the cut began to ooze blood.

Makepeace fell back in his seat. Comstock just stood there, perfectly still, in shock.

Charlie Swift stood up, and delivered what was probably one of the finest blows to the jaw in his pugilistic career. Certainly Comstock seemed to appreciate it, as his legs buckled and he crumpled to the ground.

Comstock's two mates were on their feet now, only to find their path blocked by the massive frame of Billy Bones.

'I want you two lads to take your pal out through the front door and never come back,' Bones said, in a voice which boomed as though it were coming from the bottom of a deep well. 'Do you have any problems with that?'

'No, sir,' one of the Americans said, earnestly.

'Good boy,' Bones said, and actually patted him on the head.

The two GIs dragged their sergeant clear. James Makepeace was huddled in his chair, moaning to himself.

'Let me take a look at that arm,' Bones said, grabbing it before Makepeace could object. He ran his eyes over the wound. 'It's no more than a scratch. I'll bind it for you, and within an hour you'll have forgotten all about it.'

He produced some bandages and a large glass of whisky, and whilst Makepeace sipped at the whisky, he bound the wound in a most professional-looking manner.

'Where did you get that?' he asked, when he'd finished.

'Where did I get what?' Makepeace asked.

'That cut.'

'You know damn well where I got it.'

'No, I don't,' Bones said, in a voice which was cold enough to chill the blood. 'I have no idea where you got it. The only thing I do know for certain is that it didn't happen here.'

'You're right,' Makepeace agreed, finally getting the picture. 'I . . . mm . . . I think I must have done it on a sharp piece of metal in the college boathouse.'

Bones nodded. 'Good,' he said, satisfied. 'Dangerous places, boathouses, if you're not careful.' He glanced at the front door, and then turned to Charlie Swift. 'And just in case the Yanks are still outside,' he continued, 'you'd better take your little pal out through the back door.'

That seemed like a very sensible idea, Charlie thought, picturing what the scene might be like if they left by the front door – three Americans trying to hurt two Englishmen, and none of them having any real idea who they were hitting out at in the darkness.

Once they were out on the street, Makepeace made a great show of needing assistance, but it was as uncomfortable for him as it was unconvincingly theatrical to his audience of one, and he soon gave it up.

'Do you want to tell me about it?' Charlie Swift asked.

'I'm not sure I know what you're talking about.'

'A man threatens you with a knife, which means – to all intents and purposes – that he threatens me with a knife, too. I'd rather like to know what you did to upset him.'

'Oh, that,' Makepeace said carelessly. 'I stood him up on a date. He doesn't seem to have liked it much.'

'I heard him call you "faggot",' Charlie Swift said. 'Isn't that what Yanks call queers?'

'Yes, but . . .'

'So if he's actually one of us, why would he be using the word as an insult?'

'I don't know,' Makepeace said exasperatedly. 'Maybe he said it so his mates would think he wasn't.'

'Wouldn't he be running a risk that you might scream back that he was a faggot himself?' Charlie Swift wondered. 'Mightn't his best course of action have been to simply say nothing?'

'I don't know,' Makepeace moaned. 'I've had a difficult night. I've been attacked, and I'm in pain, so I don't know the right answer to anything. Can't you leave it at that?'

'Were you really planning to tell me you were leaving Oxford?' Charlie asked.

'Of course I was,' Makepeace lied.

'I'm going to miss you,' Charlie said.

'Me, too,' Makepeace said – and for this last remark, at least, he was making an effort to sound sincere.

23 October 1943

Harold Jenkins was naked, and was bound to a metal chair by thin rope. At first, the rope had been no more than a minor irritation, but every time he made even the slightest movement, it would rub. He suspected that the skin on his wrists and ankles had been worn raw by now, but he could not check on that, because the room in which he was being held was in complete darkness, and had been for most of the time he'd spent in it.

He knew that he had been brought to the room on the 21st of October, and for the first few hours, he had been counting off the seconds – one elephant, two elephants, three elephants – but then either his concentration had slipped or he had fallen asleep, and when he became aware of things again, he had no idea whether he had only lost a few seconds or if it had been several hours. After that, there seemed little point in counting any longer.

The biggest danger he had to face was thinking too much, he warned himself. Think too much – about what Lucy was doing at that moment, about what Lucy would do if he never went home again – and he would undermine his sense of self, and hence destroy his will to resist.

Too much thinking was doing *their* work for them.

The light came on with no warning. It was aimed directly at his face, and it was very bright – brighter than any light should ever be.

He closed his eyes as tightly as he could, but it made no difference to the dazzle that was filling his brain.

He heard the door open, and footsteps cross the room.

'How are you feeling?' asked a solicitous voice.

'Go to hell,' Jenkins growled.

'You are cold and you are hungry and you are thirsty,' said the voice. 'That's right, isn't it?'

Jenkins said nothing.

'You have soiled yourself, you know,' the voice continued. 'You have probably got used to it by now, but let me tell you, for someone entering the room for the first time, the stink is almost overwhelming.'

'If you don't like the atmosphere in here, then why don't you just piss off?' Jenkins asked.

'And I am a little worried about your wrists and ankles. There is a very real danger, I'm afraid, of them becoming septic, and of gangrene setting in. I saw several victims of gangrene on the Russian campaign, and believe me, it was not a pretty sight.'

'*You're* not a pretty sight,' Jenkins said. 'I can tell that from the sound of your voice.'

'You are being very brave, and I commend you for it,' the invisible man said. 'But the simple truth is that all you are doing is causing yourself unnecessary suffering. We do not wish you to betray your country. Far from it! All we require from you is a few harmless facts. No, we require even less than that. We just need you to *confirm* some facts we already know. Once you have done that, you will be bathed and fed and your wounds will be taken care of. So what do you say?'

'My name is Harold Jenkins, I am a lance corporal, and my number is 5782305,' Jenkins said.

'And what is your regiment?' the voice said coaxingly. 'It will surely do you no harm to tell us that.'

'My name is Harold Jenkins, I am a lance corporal, and my number is 5782305,' Jenkins said.

Despite the fact that he was anticipating the blow to the face, it still came as a shock, catching him, as it did, just under his left cheekbone and throwing his neck into whiplash.

'I did not like doing that, but you left me very little choice,' the voice said. 'Please be sensible, Harold.'

'My name is Harold Jenkins, I am a lance corporal, and my number is 5782305,' Jenkins said.

He braced himself for a second blow, but it never came. Instead, there was the sound of retreating footsteps and the door closing.

The light went out again, but he knew from recent experience that its golden glow, which had imprinted itself on his retina, would take some time to fade.

What would Lucy be doing at the moment? he wondered.

Stop it! he told himself.

Stop it!

He had done all he could to protect and save her, and now he must banish her from his mind and concentrate all his efforts on his own survival.

ELEVEN

8 October 1974

The village of Upper Penfold lies just inside the Cambridgeshire border. Though it differs in some ways from Kneebury Thrubwell – the church is English Renaissance rather than Norman, the manor house is not Tudor but Jacobean, and thatched roofs seem much less popular here than they were there – my overall impression is that I've driven from one sleepy English backwater to another.

I change costumes on the way, and when I get out of the van at the Three Fiddlers public house, I'm wearing a fussy black-and-white jacket and skirt, a starched white blouse and flat shoes. My hair is pulled back tightly, and tied in a strict – almost severe – ponytail.

Oh yes, Poppy James – the bubbly and enthusiastic amateur painter – is gone, and in her place is Linda Moore – a slightly round-shouldered introverted bookkeeper – who ninety-nine percent of the population would classify as a virgin the second they laid eyes on her.

I enter the pub, and look around with fake nervousness. It is one of those hostelries that the brewery has decided should turn its back on its honourable late nineteenth-century origins and, by the addition of a few fake beams and numerous horse brasses, it has assumed the unconvincing disguise of an eighteenth century coaching inn.

I walk up to the bar, and the man standing behind it smiles at me, and says, 'Good evening. What can I get you?'

The smile is genuinely friendly, and I appreciate the fact that he's been tactful enough not to call me 'Miss'. I'm sure he'll be more than willing to do all he can to help me, but given his age (he looks to be in his early forties) he's unlikely to be of any use.

I feel this strong temptation to ask for a double gin and tonic, but that doesn't go with the image I'm trying to project, and so I force myself to say, 'Do you have any bitter lemon?'

'Of course we do,' he says encouragingly, like the nice man he so obviously is.

As I'm reaching into my big black spinster's purse to pay for my drink, I say, 'I was wondering if you could help me.'

'If I can,' he promises.

'I'm looking for a man called James Makepeace,' I tell him.

'Would that be one of the Makepeace's from up at the hall?'

'Yes, I think so.'

'Well, let me see now, I know Jacob Makepeace, and I've met his brother, Clive . . .' He scans the bar, and his eyes come to rest on a group of four men in their fifties. 'Do any of you know a James Makepeace?' he calls out.

The men look at each other questioningly, then one of them

says, 'You're going back thirty-odd years when you ask a question like that.'

'Maybe I am, Walter,' the landlord agrees. 'I wouldn't know, being an offcomer, now would I?' He turns to me. 'I've only been here fifteen years, you see, and in this village, that's just like arriving yesterday.' He looks back at the group of men. 'So what's the answer?'

'We knew him,' Walter concedes, reluctantly.

'Go and join them,' the landlord says to me, encouragingly, and when I look dubious he adds, 'they won't mind – really they won't.'

Then, addressing the group at the table again, he says, 'You won't mind if this nice young lady joins you, will you now, lads?'

It has to be said that none of them look overly enthusiastic at the prospect, but it's a foolish customer who turns down a request from the man who he depends on to pull his beer for him, and so they indicated that yes, they supposed it would be all right, if I felt I absolutely must.

If I'd really been the character I was playing, I'd probably have taken the hint and drifted away, but the pushy Jennie Redhead who lurks beneath Linda Moore's self-effacing veneer chooses to take their nods and grunts as a real show of welcome.

I walk over to them, sit down, and do a panning smile around the table. None of them smile back, nor does Walter make any attempt to introduce me to the others. They're like a colony of seals, resentful that some other creature – possibly a mermaid? – has had the temerity to climb onto their rock.

'So what can all you fine gentlemen tell me about James Makepeace?' I ask brightly.

'He used to live here in the village, a long time ago, and now he don't,' replies one of the men.

'What do you want to know for, anyway?' asks another, in a tone which identifies him as the alpha male of this particular seal colony.

I had anticipated precisely this kind of reluctance to talk to outsiders, which is why I have come to this pub dressed as Linda. And now it's time to put Linda to work.

'My mother met James during the war,' I say. 'She told me he was a very nice man.'

The four men chuckle to themselves.

'Are you sure it was *James Makepeace* she met?' Walter asks.
'Because when I think about him, "nice" ain't the first word that
comes to mind.'

'Oh yes, it was him, all right,' I say. 'He showed my mother
both his identification card and his army pay book. Anyway,' and
here I lower my voice and look down at the table, to indicate how
difficult all this is for me, 'they became very friendly, and one
thing led to another . . .'

'Go on,' says one of the men – and whilst he doesn't actually
lick his lips in anticipation, it's a damned close run thing.

So *now*, realising they're having a real life soap opera played
out before them, they're interested!

'When James finished his training, he was posted somewhere
else,' I continue. 'My mother wrote to him – several times – but
she got no reply. And then . . . and then . . .' We are approaching
the dramatic climax of my tale now, and the audience is listening,
open-mouthed. '. . . And then she realised she was pregnant,' I
gasp, glad to finally get the words out.

'Pregnant? With you?' asks one of the men, and I can tell he's
doing his best not to sound as if he's getting salacious pleasure
from the whole narrative.

'That's right,' I admit. 'Pregnant with me.'

It is now that I notice the man sitting on the next table. I guess
that he is probably around the same age as my little group, but he
hasn't weathered half as well. It is not just that his clothes are so
obviously uncared for. His hair is unruly, he could really use a
shave (and quite possibly a wash) and his eyes have a blood-
shot sheen, which he must have worked at attaining. But the
important thing about him isn't what he's wearing or how he looks
– what bothers me is that he's been listening to what I said, and
is now slowly shaking his head from side to side in a meaningful
manner, which could well be signalling either wonder or despair
– but is probably just expressing disbelief.

I turn my attention back onto my captive audience, because
we're about to reach the dénouement of my tale thus far – and
I don't want to spoil it through lack of concentration.

'Two months ago, my mother learned she had cancer,' I say,
bravely suppressing a sob. 'She hasn't got much longer to live,
and her dearest wish is that I should find my father and make

friends with him. She says if I can just manage that, she can leave this world at peace with herself.'

I am great – and there's not a dry eye among my listeners. But soft, I deceive myself, for the man at the next table not only refrains from shedding tears of pity, he is actually smirking at me.

'So you can understand why it's vital that I find my father soon,' I say, the plaintive waif on turbo-drive.

The men all look at each other again.

'We'd like to help – we really would,' says Walter, much affected by my performance, 'but there's not much we know. Being from the big house, James Makepeace didn't mix much with us peasants from the village.'

'And when he did, he usually caused trouble – and made damn sure that we got the blame for it,' one of his friends adds.

'And then he went away to that fancy university, and never came back,' says a third.

'Never?' I repeat.

'Never,' they agree.

'Everybody round here watches everybody else,' Walter says, and then, as if he feels that is open to misinterpretation, he adds, 'they're not being nosey, mind you, they just like to know what's going on.'

'I'm sure they do,' I agree.

'So you can take it from me that if James Makepeace had been within ten miles of this place, we'd have known about it,' Walter says.

Well, that's not definite confirmation that the body in the cellar is James Makepeace's as such, but it's considerably better than nothing. I thank my colony of (now) trained seals, and am gratified when they tell me I'll be welcomed back any time.

It is only when I stand up that I notice that the cynic who had been sitting at the next table has already left.

He is waiting for me in the car park, leaning against my blue van, though whether that is a deliberately chosen pose of nonchalance, or a requirement if he is not to fall over, is far from clear.

'Can I help you?' I ask.

'Who are you, and what do you want?' he asks.

'I'm James Makepeace's daughter and . . .'

'No, you're not,' he says, and he speaks with such conviction that I know there's no point in sticking to the story.

'I'm a private investigator,' I tell him. 'My name's Jennie Redhead. And who are you?'

'Fossington Gore,' he says. 'Julian Fossington Gore.'

'As you've probably already gathered, Mr Fossington Gore, I'm trying to find out everything I can about James Makepeace,' I say.

'I can tell you a lot, but it will cost you,' he replies.

'How much?' I ask.

I can see it in his eyes that he is calculating what he thinks he can get away with asking for.

'Twenty pounds,' he says finally.

'Tell me what you know, and then I'll tell you if it's worth twenty pounds,' I say.

'Money first,' he insists.

What the hell, I think – St Luke's can afford twenty pounds.

I take the notes out of my purse, and hand them to him. He scrutinises them carefully, as if he suspects forgery.

'They're real enough,' I say.

He puts the notes in a pocket of his none-too-clean trousers.

'James and I were at prep school and Eton together,' he says. He pauses. 'It's true!'

'I never said it wasn't.'

'Looking at me now, you'd never guess it, but I come from a good family and I used to *be* somebody,' he says, piteously.

If I allow him to carry on whining, we'll never get anywhere.

'You haven't done an awful lot to earn your twenty pounds yet, Julian,' I tell him.

'So what!' he says, turning aggressive. 'I've got it now, haven't I? What are you going to do if I don't fulfil my part of the bargain? Try to take the money back off me?'

'Not *try*,' I say. 'I *will* take it off you.'

He laughs. 'Do you really think you could?'

I say nothing, but just take one small step forward.

'All right,' he says holding up his hands, palms outwards. 'I'll tell you everything I know.'

'Good idea,' I agree.

'James and I were thrown together for most our childhoods – if it wasn't school, it was house parties or shoots. Schools like ours breed a fair number of nasty characters, but James was in a class of his own.'

'In what way?'

'He was very vicious, and he was very selfish, and he invariably ran all the rackets.'

'What kind of rackets are talking about?'

'You name it, he did it. If you wanted an essay written, then James could arrange it – for a fee. If you wanted one of the younger boys to jerk you off, James would supply him. Special food, tobacco, alcohol – James could lay his hands on all of them. He ran a book on the horses, and when you'd lost more than you could afford, he lent you money – at an outrageous rate of interest – so you could pay him what you owed him. Two or three of the boys I knew were expelled for their part in the rackets, but even though they suspected he was behind it all, the beaks could never touch James.'

'What happened after you both left Eton College?' I ask. 'Did *you* go to Oxford too?'

He shakes his head.

'No, I . . . I'd started having my troubles by then. I wasn't at all well, you see, and it seemed as if certain drugs would at least help to . . .'

So it looks like twenty quid wasted, I think as I listen, but he's done his best, and it certainly seems as if he could use the money.

'Do you have any idea where he might be now?' I ask, taking a shot in the dark.

'Oh, he's dead,' Fossington Gore says airily.

'Who told you that?'

'Nobody – I just know.'

'How could you just know?'

'Because I know – or at least, *knew* – James. He conned me, back in 1943, into betting against him in a horse race. I think now that my horse was nobbled, but that's neither here nor there. I accepted the bet, and the honourable thing (I cared about doing the honourable thing in those days) was to pay up when I lost. The problem was, it was fifty pounds I owed him. That was a lot of money in those days, and I couldn't lay my hands on it immediately. But I promised him I'd raise the money and pay him the next time I saw him. And I did raise the money, and held onto it for years, but he never came to collect it.'

'And from that, you assume he's dead.'

'From that, I'm *sure* he's dead. As I said, you didn't know him like I do. James' guiding principle in life was never to give anything away. I can assure you, he'd have travelled halfway round the world – spending hundreds of pounds en route – to recover a mere sixpence that someone owed him. And I owed him fifty pounds! So when I say he's dead, believe me, he's dead.' He fingers the money in his pocket. 'Can I go now?'

'Yes,' I say. 'Thank you, you've been a great help.'

He hasn't actually – he's really told me no more than my trained seals inside did – but I feel so sorry for a man in his fifties who feels he has to ask *my* permission to leave, that I want to say something to make him feel a little better.

I watch him walking back towards the pub – where, I suspect, most of my twenty pounds will end up being spent – and suddenly remember there was something else I wanted to ask him.

'Wait a minute,' I call after him.

He stops, and turns around. 'Yes?'

'You were so sure I wasn't James Makepeace's daughter,' I say. 'How could you have been so certain?'

'James would never have seduced your mother and then abandoned her when she was pregnant.'

'I thought you said he was a bit of a shit.'

'He was a *lot* of a shit – a real king among the turds – but he wouldn't have needed to run away, because he would never have got your mother pregnant in the first place.'

'What do you mean? How can you be so sure?'

'James Makepeace would never have impregnated any woman, because he was as queer as Dickie's hat band.'

James Makepeace was gay!

James Makepeace was gay, and he was at St Luke's at the same time as Charlie Swift!

And Charlie Swift was at St Luke's at the time James Makepeace disappeared off the face of the earth!

What are the chances that Charlie's path never crossed that of another gay man in a college which was already, as a result of the war, down to only a few students?

None at all!

So Charlie knew Makepeace, knew he had disappeared, and didn't tell me.

And where does that leave me? It leaves me with the suspicion that I've been deliberately manipulated, that General Charlie has sent me – his poor bloody infantry – into battle without even telling me what the enemy looks like (and perhaps even going so far as to provide *them* with a disguise).

My heart is beating like a drum solo, my pulse is disturbingly rapid. It can't go on like this, I tell myself.

What are my alternatives? I ask my inner self in what I hope is a calm and moderate way.

Simple, comes the reply, to trust Charlie or not to trust Charlie.

The evidence would tend to point me towards the latter of those two choices, but I know I'm not prepared to accept any evidence, however damning it might be.

Charlie is my rock – my foundation. If I don't believe in him, then I don't believe in anything.

TWELVE

9 October 1974

'm tied to the clapper of what just has to be one bloody big bell. I have no idea how I got here, and now really does not seem to be the best time to speculate on that.

Now is not even the best time to think about how to escape from this predicament, because, given that the bell I'm inside is swinging through quite a deep arc, my immediate concern is to prevent myself from being battered to death.

The trick is to fight gravity – never a plan with a long-term prospect of success in my view, but then, when you are living from moment to moment, you do what you have to do. So, while the bell is swinging, I keep as still as possible (marshalling my strength) and it's only when it reaches one end of its arc (which is when the clapper and the inside of the bell interact) that I twist around so that it's the other side of the clapper that hits the side of the bell.

The sound of the bell – ring, ring, ring, ring – fills my ears, and clouds my mind.

Wait a minute!

Hold everything!

Ring, ring, ring, ring?

That can't be right.

Whatever happened to ding, dong, ding, dong – the sound that bells are *supposed* to produce?

I open my eyes (I haven't even been aware that they were closed until this point) and get my first blurry vision of the phone on my bedside table – the phone, it now turns out, which has been the source of all my confusion.

'You bastard!' I say to it.

It doesn't look ashamed. It doesn't even look apologetic. It just keeps on ringing.

Since there seems to be only one way to silence it, I go through the tedious procedure of lifting my arm, picking up the receiver, and mumbling, 'Jennifer Redhead,' into the mouthpiece.

'Where the hell were you all day yesterday, Jennie?' asks a gruff voice on the other end of the line. 'I called your bloody flat, I called your bloody office, I even made a tour of your favourite bloody boozers – and what a epic voyage that was – but there was no bloody sign of you.'

'I was out of town, George,' I say, as half of my brain curses Hobson for ringing me so early, and the other half worries that he considered it necessary to ring me so early.

'You were out of town!' he repeats, in a voice that suggests I may just have committed an illegal act. 'And what were you doing *out of town*?'

Oh no, George, you don't catch me as easy as that, even if I am only half-awake (at best).

'I was doing my job,' I say.

I'm expecting him to persist with this line of questioning, but what he actually says is, 'If I'm remembering it rightly, there's a cafe just at the end of your street, isn't there?'

'Yes,' I agree. 'It's called the Copper Kettle, but . . .'

'Be there in fifteen minutes.'

'If you wouldn't mind telling me what this is all about . . .'

'Just bloody be there!'

The Copper Kettle is one of those places that falls well short of living up to the gentility and refinement of its name. Its tablecloths are plastic, its mugs heavy and chipped, and its cutlery clearly sourced from dozens of different places. It is not the kind of establishment in which you ask for a napkin (even a paper one), and anyone requesting *brown* bread is automatically assumed to be a member of the aristocracy, who has drifted in there by accident.

George Hobson doesn't look as if he's drifted in by accident. As he lowers his body (with unnecessary force, I feel) into the seat opposite me, he looks like a man with a definite purpose.

'This new murder better not have anything to do with the case you're investigating, or I'll feed you – and your client – to the sharks,' he says, without preamble.

'What new murder?' I ask.

A look which is mid-way between astonishment and disbelief comes to his face.

'You haven't heard?' he says.

'I didn't get back until late, and then I went straight to bed,' I tell him. 'The next thing I knew, you were phoning me up.'

'The victim is one Leonard Moon,' he says heavily.

For a moment, I can't think who the devil he might be referring to, then I say, '*Lennie* Moon?'

'That's right.'

'But who would want to kill him?'

'A very good question – and if I knew the answer, I wouldn't be bothering to talk to you.'

'How did he die?' I ask.

'His neck was broken. The doc said it was a very clean break, and he probably died instantly.'

'Where was he killed? Was it at home or was it . . .?'

'Who's the police officer here?' George interrupts me.

'You are, but . . .'

'Then that must mean that I get to ask the questions and you get to answer them, mustn't it?'

There's really no arguing with that.

'You say you were away all day yesterday?' George continues.

'Yes, I was.'

'So you didn't search Lennie Moon's bedsit?'

'I don't even know where Lennie Moon's bedsit is.'

'The reason I ask is because *somebody* searched it – and that person, whoever he or *she* was, did it very thoroughly, but also very carefully, so as to leave no mess. My guess would be that he or she desperately wanted to find something, but he or she didn't want the police to know that he or she had been looking.'

Whoever it was had been a little bit unlucky that the investigation had landed on George's desk, because – as I'd seen with the Shivering Turn case – studying the mess (or lack of it) that an intruder left behind was one of his specialities, and once he's stopped fixating on the idea that it was me, he'll probably be able to build up a fairly accurate profile of who actually was responsible.

'It wasn't me,' I say, in an effort to speed the process up. 'If I'm lying, may my throat close up whenever I try to drink a gin and tonic.'

George subjects me to a hard stare for maybe ten seconds, then he smiles and says, 'OK, so it wasn't you.'

'Do you think they found what they were looking for?'

George shakes his head. 'I can't be sure, but I don't think so. As far as I can tell, they searched every inch of the bedsit, so either it was the very last place they looked, or they didn't find it at all.'

'So it's still there?'

'Or it was never there at all.'

'It's hard to imagine anything that Lennie Moon might have that anyone else would want,' I say.

It's a mistake – and I realise that the moment that the words are out of my mouth.

'You seem to know a lot about him,' George says, his voice larded with fresh suspicions.

'I don't know much about him at all,' I protest, as I inwardly curse my own stupidity. 'I saw him around, now and again, when I was a student, but I've only spoken to him once, and that was recently.'

'And what did you talk about?' George demands – and it is very much a demand, in a suspect-interrogator sort of way.

'He said that he'd lost the boat that Mr Jenkins made for him, that Mr Jenkins had been very brave in the war (it turns out he was) and that he's got a war medal of his own.'

'Has he?'

'Has he what?'

'Has he got a medal?'

'No, how could he have, when he was a porter at St Luke's throughout the war?'

'So he was making it up?'

'Yes.'

'Which probably means there's no point in looking for any such medal in his bedsit, wouldn't you say?'

'That would be my guess.'

Hobson leans forward – and I call him Hobson because my friend George left the café the moment I let slip that I knew more about Lennie than I could reasonably be supposed to know.

'I need to know all the details of the case you're currently working on,' he says, seriously.

'And you know that I can't give them to you,' I tell him.

'Then I need your assurance that whatever it is, it can't possibly have anything to do with the death of Lennie Moon.'

Albert Boulting disappeared in 1916, James Makepeace in 1943. Given that there were twenty-seven years between the two, it would be stretching things, without the evidence of the bodies in the air vent, to find any credible connection there. And, it should never be forgotten, the bodies in the vent may not even be Boulting and Makepeace, but could be someone else entirely.

Now add Lennie's death to the equation – thirty-one years later – and that credulity is stretched to breaking point.

For God's sake, Lennie Moon wasn't even born when Albert Boulting disappeared.

So it should be very easy for me to look my old friend George Hobson squarely in the eyes and say, 'There's no connection between my investigation and Lennie's death.'

And do you know what – I can't do it.

I can't do it because my gut is telling me that however incredible it might seem, all these things *are* connected.

'Well?' George says impatiently.

'I can't think of any way in which Lennie's death might be connected to my investigation,' I tell him.

'That's not good enough,' he says.

'It's all I can give you,' I counter.

'I've helped you in the past,' he says.

'I know you have,' I agree. 'I've really appreciated it.'

'I've even cut a couple of corners for you, corners which were – at best – of dubious legality.'

'I know that too,' I say, and the truth is, I'm almost in tears.

'And I've done it all through friendship,' he says.

'Yes.'

'But if you won't do or say anything to help me solve this murder, then that's it, as far as I'm concerned. There'll be no more cosy chats, no more juicy titbits. You're out there on your own.'

He'd probably be satisfied if I just gave him Charlie's name, I think. And why wouldn't I? After all, Charlie let me go to the police for information – thus marking myself out – when he could have easily given me the information himself. And now I *really* need to talk to him – and he must know I do – he's disappeared as mysteriously as Boulting and Makepeace did.

So go on – tell George. Give him Charlie's name!

'If I uncover any information that might help you and won't damage my client, I'll see you get it right away,' I hear myself say.

'Again, that's just not good enough,' George says.

No, I didn't think it would be.

He stands up. 'I hope you don't live to regret this.'

Well, *Jesus*, so do I!

It is as I am bicycling down the Broad towards St Luke's that the idea starts to take some sort of shape inside my head.

The one thing that connects everything that's happened – says the little pixie at the back of my mind, who is attempting to sort things into rinky-dink order – *is Mr Gough.*

Mr Gough, I repeat, incredulously.

Mr Gough, my pixie says, unperturbed. *Mr Gough – that towering figure without whom it is impossible to imagine* anything *happening in the college. He was there at St Luke's when Boulting went missing. He was there when Makepeace went missing.*

And he was around twenty years dead when Lennie Moon was killed, I point out.

Hold on, says the pixie, *I haven't finished yet. Would you accept that all Mr Gough cared about was the honour of the college?*

Yes, by all accounts that was his only motivating force.

So he might well have killed Boulting because, through his disgusting activities, he was about to disgrace the college?

Yes.

And Makepeace, too?

Well, George Hobson did say that Makepeace was in some kind of trouble with the police just before he disappeared.

What about Lennie? Might not Lennie have done something that would bring the college into disrepute?

That's harder to imagine.

But not impossible?

No, not impossible.

So, what if Mr Gough had foreseen that kind of situation arising, and had set up a clandestine cleansing unit to nip any scandals in the bud, even after he was no longer around?

And who would be running this unit?

Mr Jenkins?

It could be him – or it could be someone else entirely . . .

The more I think of it, the more it starts to make sense.

Kings are desperate to leave a legacy behind them. Take Henry VIII as an example. He was perfectly content with his wife – she had been his friend and counsellor for over twenty years. And if he ever felt like a nubile wench on the side – well, he was the king, and there were any number of young women more than willing to accommodate him. Yet, because he wanted a legitimate son to carry on his dynasty, he divorced his wife, which involved arguing with the pope and the Holy Roman Emperor and creating divisions in England that were not fully resolved for over two hundred years.

And if kings are permitted to have such vaunting ambitions, might not a college head porter be allowed to have some quite modest ones?

Mr Jenkins is wearing a black armband and a mournful expression.

'The wife and I helped to look after Lennie for all those years,' he tells me. 'He was almost like family to us.'

Yes, I'm sure it's all very difficult for you, but he's not my focus of interest at the moment, I think callously.

'Would you mind if we talked a little about Mr Gough?' I ask, doing my best to mask my impatience.

'I suppose not,' he says, giving me one of those sideways looks that people give other people, when they've not quite worked out what's going on.

'Did Mr Gough have any close friends – someone who he really trusted?' I ask.

The expression that comes to Mr Jenkins' face says, as clearly as a flashing neon sign, that I've offended him.

'I like to think Mr Gough trusted me,' he says.

This isn't going to be easy, I tell myself.

'How can I phrase this?' I say – and it really isn't a rhetorical question. 'I know . . . I know Mr Gough would have trusted you to do something that he knew was right, but would he also have trusted you do something which he knew was wrong – but still really wanted doing?'

'Mr Gough would never have wanted something doing that he knew was wrong,' Mr Jenkins says stonily.

'Let's go back to his friends,' I suggest, teetering on the edge of desperation. 'Were there any of them who . . .'

'Mr Gough didn't have friends,' Mr Jenkins interrupts. 'He was the head porter and he *couldn't* have friends, because there was the danger of people thinking he had favourites.'

'But you're a head porter now, and you have friends,' I say.

And the moment the words are out of my mouth, I think, how can you say that? You don't know for a fact he has friends – because you know virtually nothing about Mr Jenkins.

'I do have friends,' he agrees, 'but I could never be the kind of head porter he was. And times change,' he continues sadly. 'Conditions change and attitudes change, and I doubt if even Mr Gough could be the head porter that he used to be, if he was in charge today.'

'Do you know anything about his will?' I ask.

'No, I don't. It was none of my business and I had no interest in the matter.'

I have reached number nine on my personal desperation scale, and have only one notch left to go.

'When you went to his funeral,' I say, taking that one last shot at it, 'did you happen to notice anyone who seemed peculiar?'

'I didn't go to his funeral,' Mr Jenkins says.

'Oh?'

'I would have done, of course, if it had been held in Oxford, or even in some other part of Great Britain – but it wasn't.'

I don't know why the hairs on the back of my neck should have started to tingle, but the plain fact is that they have.

'So where was the funeral held?' I ask.

'In some village in Majorca,' Mr Jenkins says. Then, in case I need some clarification, he adds, 'It's a Spanish island stuck out in the middle of the Mediterranean.'

'Yes, I know that, but why was he . . .?'

'It's where he went to live when he retired. We were all surprised when he told us that him and his missus were moving there, because, as far as any of us knew, they'd never been abroad before.'

Suddenly, as if to supplement my tingling hair, my heart is beating a little bit faster.

And why?

Because what's just been described to me is all so convenient!

Think about it! A man in his early seventies, who everyone agrees is as strong as a horse, goes off to a Spanish island (having shown no interest in 'abroad' before), and is dead within the month. Now what does that tell you?

'Did Mrs Gough come back to England after her husband died?' I ask Mr Jenkins.

'I couldn't say for sure, but I don't think so, because I'm almost certain that if she had come back, she'd have paid us a visit.'

Excellent!

'How were you informed that he was dead?' I ask. 'Did the college get a letter from the government?'

'Oh, nothing as formal as that,' Mr Jenkins says. 'Somebody living on the island kindly sent us a press cutting. I think we've still got it.'

He opens one of the drawers in the desk, takes out a battered file, and extracts from it a piece of newspaper which has gone brown with age.

'You can look at it if you'd like to,' he says.

Majorca English News
College Ex-Head Porter Dies.

We are sad to report the death of Edwin Gough, which was due
to a heart attack. Mr Gough had been a part of our little community for less than a month. He leaves behind a widow, Martha.

There's more, but having got the gist, I turn the article over, and
see that on the other side are the Spanish football results from the
previous Saturday, which, if my suspicions prove correct, is a
really nice touch.

So what have we got here?

We've got an Englishman with no experience of life abroad,
who moves to Majorca, where, back in 1954, long before the
tourist boom, the island was still recovering from the Civil War
and life was quite primitive.

We have his widow, who decides that, even without his support,
she can make a life for herself in a society where women count
for so little that they have to get their husbands' permission to
study, work or even drive.

And we have a tiny English expatriate community that still
thinks it is worthwhile to produce a newspaper on a professional
printing press.

It doesn't take me long to get the confirmations I need to turn my
theory into a working hypothesis.

The first thing I do is to ring the Balearics office of the Spanish
Tourist Board. The very helpful young woman who deals with my
enquiry is adamant that there is not now, nor ever has been, a local
newspaper called the Majorca English News.

'In 1954 there were only a handful of English people livin' on
Majorca,' she tells me. 'For why would they need a newspaper?'

Quite!

The General Register Office for England and Wales is quite
sure that though Edwin Gough was both born and married (to one
Martha Green), there is no record of his death, and therefore, all
other things being equal, it can be assumed that he is still alive.

That's good enough for me. I make one more (pointless) attempt
to get in touch with Charlie Swift, then cycle down to Cornmarket
and book a seat on the first available flight to Majorca.

THIRTEEN

14 October 1974

As we were coming in to land, I looked down at Palma de Mallorca Airport and realised just what a bloody big place it was.

'*Well, of course it's bloody big*,' said the hugely scornful voice in my head which I immediately recognised as the goblin who only used to visit me occasionally, but now seems to have taken settled in permanently, and, furthermore, to have signed up as a partner to my benevolent pixie, thus forming a resident double act.

'*If the airport wasn't big*' the goblin continued, '*how do you think it would handle the five to six million visitors who come here each and every year?*'

It wasn't like this in 1954, when Mr Gough left his beloved job as head porter at St Luke's College and came to Majorca to 'die' I reminded myself. Back then, the airport only had one runway, and it wasn't until the summer of that year that the authorities decided it was actually worth the bother of asphalting it.

Back then, tourists were not the norm but a curiosity – individual free spirits breaking away from the pack, and looking for something different. Now, the individualists have moved on, and huge waves of conformists continually sweep across the island in the summer months, in search of pints of Watney's Red Barrel beer and proper English pork pies.

As we circled the airport prior to landing, I was already asking myself if this whole trip was anything but a huge mistake.

There were perhaps a dozen reasons why it might be.

Wasn't there, for example, a very good chance that when Mr Gough had done all that was necessary to establish his own demise, he would have got away from the island as quickly as he possibly could?

Yes, that was possible, I conceded, after thinking the matter over for a few minutes – but wasn't likely.

This was a man, remember, who had never left England before he came to Majorca. It must have taken considerable courage for him – at his age – to make the trip in the first place, and so was it at all likely that he and his wife would have found the extra courage to move a second time? Besides, from what I've learned of him, he struck me as the careful kind of man who would not just cover his tracks well, but would also stay around to make sure they remained covered.

I know, I know, I was arguing this way simply because I was desperate and I needed things to *be* this way.

Or, to put it even more succinctly – if I hadn't got this, I really hadn't got anything at all.

We landed – bumpily – and were shepherded into a bus, then driven to the customs and immigration post. Two *Guardia Civil* officers – olive green uniforms, black three-cornered hats, heavy sub-machine guns and thick, yardbrush-style moustaches – glared disapprovingly at me through their blue sunglasses, but then they glared disapprovingly at everybody, and they clearly didn't consider it worthwhile to subject me to any kind of interrogation.

Once in the main hall, I wandered over to the car rentals and hired myself a car. I chose a Seat 127, because even though the college was paying for it – and could undoubtedly afford better – I just couldn't persuade myself to be extravagant.

Jennie Redhead – your value-for-money PI!

Outside the terminal, the air was pleasantly mild, and, for a moment, it felt almost as if I was on holiday.

But you're not, are you? snapped the pixie and goblin partnership simultaneously. *You're here to catch a triple murderer.*

How over-dramatic that sounded – and yet, if I was right about Mr Gough, it was no more than a statement of the facts.

I located my hire car in the parking lot, climbed inside and turned my key in the ignition. The engine replied like an old man who had been wearing a wet vest for far too long, but eventually it did catch enough to ensure locomotion, and I pulled away from the parking area.

I was heading for Palma, the capital of the island, which was only eight kilometres down the road.

And what did I intend to do once I was there?

I intended to check in at the modest hotel that my Oxford travel agents had booked for me.

And did I have a plan beyond that? my goblin wondered.

Yes, as a matter of fact, I replied (perhaps a little snootily), I did have a plan.

Was it a good plan?

I *did* have a plan, I repeated, much more defensively. Hadn't I just said that?

This plan of mine was based on a reluctant acceptance of the fact that there are so many foreigners on the island it would take an army of investigators to find Mr Gough, and thus, to have any hope of success, I would have to approach the problem from a different angle. And the angle I had chosen was not to look for him at all, but only to ask questions which would make it *seem* as if I was looking for him.

Can you see where I'm going with this?

What would happen next, I argued to myself, was that word would get back to him, and because he would start to see me as an irritant (or even more likely, a danger), then *he* would find *me*.

And, whilst I'll admit there might be some degree of danger in this for me, too, I am a young woman trained in the martial arts, whilst he is now a very old man who probably finds it a strain to carry a paper bag full of groceries.

So I should be all right.

Shouldn't I?

That was then, when the search was just beginning, back when I felt vigorous and fresh. Now, four days later, I am standing on the sea front in Palma de Majorca, looking across at the marina and thinking about the fact that my spine is aching, my knees are on fire, and a furious squash match is being played out inside my head (probably by my goblin and my pixie).

I have spent these last four days blitzing the island, beginning with the earliest established tourist areas (that is, the ones that may have existed when Mr Gough first arrived here), and then gradually widening my search to include the more out-of-the-way places. And everywhere I've stopped, I have tried to create a spark, which will hopefully light a fire, which – if the age of miracles has finally come to pass – will smoke Mr Gough out of hiding.

The problem is, it's impossible to say whether or not I've made any progress – though I have a sinking feeling in my gut which tells me I haven't.

The average conversation ran something like this:

> Me: (showing the barman of some beach-side establishment the only photograph I have of Mr Gough) *This picture was taken nearly thirty years ago, so the man in it will be much older now, but do you think you recognise him?*
> Barman: *Is he some kind of policeman?*
> Me: *No.*
> Barman: *Then why is he wearing that peaked cap?*
> Me: *He's a porter.*
> Barman: *You mean like, on a railway station?*
> Me: *No, at a university college.*
> Barman: *A university college?*
> Me: (with growing impatience) *Do you think it's possible you might have seen him, or not?*
> Barman: (taking some glasses out of his neat little dishwasher and stacking them on one of the shelves behind him) *To be perfectly honest with you, Señorita, I could not tell you yes, and I could not tell you no. You must understand that I see a lot of people.*

But what was really going on during this exchange?

As he was speaking, was the barman perhaps thinking to himself, *Mr Gough has always warned me that this day would come. I'd better let him know about it as soon as I can.*

Or maybe he'd been thinking, *I don't know why this mad red-haired bint is bothering me with the picture of an old bloke. I wish she'd just piss off and leave me alone.*

Back in the present, I turn away from the sea, and towards the bars which line the promenade – and that's when I see him.

He is around twenty-five or twenty-six, I would guess, and the fact that he is wearing a suit identifies him immediately as a Spaniard (the foreigners are all wearing shorts – the Brits revealing their pasty white thighs to the world, the Germans displaying their carefully and scientifically bronzed ones). Additionally – if such an addition were necessary to confirm his nationality – he is carrying a smart leather briefcase which fastens with old-fashioned brass buckles.

He is standing as still as I am, and watching me with an intensity which (I think) goes beyond a casual ogle. When he sees me looking at him, he quickly turns away.

I walk across to one of the cafés and sit down. He does, too. I sit there for perhaps a minute, then, when I see a waiter approaching, I stand up and move on to the next café.

And guess what!

I order a gin and tonic, and while I sip at it, I watch him trying to avoid watching me.

What's his game, I wonder.

He's too smartly dressed to be a pickpocket or a mugger, and I have too much respect for myself to think I'd ever look desperate enough to attract the attention of a gigolo. So maybe the simplest explanation is the right one – he's never been to bed with a redhead before, and he's wondering what it would be like.

Well, there's only one way to find out, I think, as I realise that all the aches and pains I was experiencing earlier have magically melted away.

I stand up and walk across to his table. When I sit down opposite him, he looks so startled that, for a minute, I think he's going to run away. Then he calms down, smiles, and says, 'Good evening, Señorita.'

'Why are you following me?' I ask.

He's thinking of denying it – I can see that in his eyes – then he changes his mind.

'I . . . I like to talk to British people, so that I can practice my English on them,' he says.

'How do you know I'm English?' I ask. 'With my red hair, most Spaniards think I'm a German.'

'But sometimes they do not like me approaching them,' he continues, as if I've never spoken, 'which is why I study them first – to see what kind of people they are.'

What an absolute load of bollocks!

'My hotel's just around the corner,' I say. 'Would you like to come up to my room?'

'For what reason?' he asks.

'For what reason do you think?' I reply.

He nods. 'Yes, I would like that very much.'

We don't even touch until we're in my modest hotel room, and then – in the great tradition of casual affairs – we throw ourselves into a passionate embrace.

Do you know something – he's not half bad.

When we finally both come up for air, he says, 'My name is Juan, and I am training to be a law . . .'

I place my index finger against his lips and say, 'Shh.'

'I don't understand,' he tells me.

'You want sex, I want sex,' I tell him. 'That's it. I know your name is Juan, since you've just told me, but I don't actually have to know it, because if I need to call out any name during what's about to happen – and I really hope I do – that name will probably be Jesus Christ, with an exclamation mark added for good measure.'

'I am not sure I understand,' he says.

'This is a one-night stand,' I tell him. 'I hope you can accept that, because if you can't, we stop right now.'

'It's fine with me,' he says.

So now we have an understanding.

Let the games begin!

When I wake up, I immediately look at my watch, and see it has just turned a quarter past seven.

Juan is lying next to me. He is resting on his right elbow, and gently stroking my hair with his left hand.

'Please don't do that,' I say.

'Do what?'

'Stroke my hair.'

'Don't you like it?'

No, I don't – and the reason I don't like it is because it blurs the boundary between sex and intimacy, and intimacy doesn't interest me.

'I'm just not in the mood,' I say.

He shrugs, and swings his legs off the bed and stands up.

Though I know it's a mistake, I find myself admiring him. And there is much to admire. He has the broad shoulders and thick arms of a strong swimmer, a flat stomach and powerful thighs.

What lies between the two (the stomach and the thighs) is also more than satisfactory.

He notices I'm looking at him, and can't prevent a little smirk from flashing across his face.

'I am busy for most of the day, but I am free in the evening, and I will take you round the tapas bars,' he says.

I shake my head. 'No thanks.'

'What do you mean?'

'What I say.'

'If you are occupied this evening, then perhaps we can leave it until the following . . .'

'This is it, Juan,' I say, and since he doesn't seem to be getting it, I try a little amplification. 'It's the end,' I tell him. 'It's finished. It's all over. We've reached the end of the road, and it's time to go our separate ways.' I pause, and scour my basic Spanish vocabulary. 'It's more a case of *adiós* than it is *hasta la vista*.'

Now he understands – and looks hurt.

'Didn't we have a good time last night?' he asks plaintively.

'We had an excellent time last night,' I assure him, and because I know men like to hear that kind of thing, I add, 'You were absolutely amazing.'

'Then I do not see why we must stop.'

I sigh. 'It's just that I don't want a boyfriend,' I tell him.

'Is it because I'm a foreigner?' he demands. 'Is that what it is? Do you look down on me?'

'I think you'd better get dressed and leave,' I say.

'Oh, I will do that,' he tells to me. 'Don' you worry 'bout that.'

He dresses at speed, as if now he knows he's going, he can hardly wait to be gone.

He stops in the doorway, and reaches into his leather briefcase.

'This is for you,' he says, holding out an envelope.

'Juan, I really don't want it, whatever it is,' I say.

'It is not from me,' he tells me. 'I was paid to give it to you. That is why I was following you – because I was waiting for the right opportunity.'

'What do you mean – the right opportunity?'

'I was told only to present the letter to you when I was certain no other person could see me doing it.' He pauses. 'You surely do not think I was following you because I found you attractive, do you?'

'No, of course not.'

He drops the envelope on the floor.

'*Puta!*' he says.

And then he is gone.

I wait until I can hear his footsteps on the stairs, then I cross the room and pick up the envelope. There is nothing written on the envelope itself, but there is a sheet of paper inside it. I pull the sheet out and note – automatically – that the handwriting on it is both clear and old-fashioned.

The note reads:

> Sóller Cemetery, noon tomorrow. Tell no one and come alone. If you're late, I won't be there.

There is no signature.

There doesn't need to be.

And tomorrow is now today, so if I'm to reach the other end of the island by noon, I'm really going to have to shift some.

FOURTEEN

15 October 1974

The guidebook informs me that Sóller is a town of fourteen thousand people, located in a large bowl-shaped valley in the north-west corner of Majorca. The book goes on to claim that the houses on the Gran Vía (which were built in the French Art Nouveau style by returning emigrants who had made their fortunes abroad) and the Church of Sant Bartomeu are both well worth a visit, and while I have no time for such matters today, even a cursory glance as I pass through the town is enough to convince me that they are.

The guidebook's other claim is that the cemetery, located just above the railway station, is of especial historic interest, and in this, too, it seems to have stuck on the right side of exaggeration.

It is certainly not like any cemetery I've ever seen before. For a start, it is on several levels, connected by terraced pathways. Secondly, it looks less like a graveyard than a garden or park, to which gravestones, tombs and small chapels have been added. There are mimosa trees, palm trees and rose bushes, as well as countless plants in pots at the foot of the graves. And beyond the walls, forming a perfect backdrop, are the wooded hills and low mountains.

I follow the path to the part of the cemetery reserved for non-Catholics. Here, on the stones, I can see English names and Dutch names and French names. And there is one name in particular, on a plain white stone now partially over-run with moss, which is extremely interesting.

Edwin Gough
1880–1954
He gave his life to service,
and died without regrets.

'At least half of that is true now, and the rest very soon will be,' says a voice from just behind my left shoulder.

I turn around. The speaker is very tall, very thin and – though he carries a walking stick with him – very erect. His nose is aquiline, his mouth broad, and his eyes – though watery with age – still show signs of both a considerable intelligence and considerable determination. After living on this sunny island for over twenty years, his skin is like cracked leather.

And, by God, he can move quietly when he wants to!

I know who he is, and he knows I know, so there is no point in either of us going through the farce of pretending.

'I came alone, as you asked me to,' I say.

'I know,' he replies.

There is just a hint of complacency in his voice which annoys me, and it is this annoyance which makes me say, 'Of course, I might have a back-up team of half dozen people back in the town.'

He shakes his head. 'You have no back-up team. If you had, this meeting wouldn't be taking place.' He pauses for a second, which may be because he's old, but I'm also certain is just for effect. 'You've been asking questions about me all over the island, young lady,' he continues.

I don't know if this comment is specifically designed to make me feel uneasy, but it has that effect anyway, because he's not just saying I've been asking questions about him in his local bar, or the village where he lives, he's saying he's aware that I've been doing it 'all over the island' – which is another way of telling me that his reach extends a long, long way.

'Yes, I have been making inquiries,' I agree.

'Making inquiries,' he repeats. 'That's an interesting way to express it. Are you with the police?'

'No, not now.'

'Not now,' he muses. 'Well then, if you're not a copper, who the devil *are* you?'

'My name's Jennie Redhead, and I'm a private investigator – working for the college,' I tell him.

I don't say which college, because that's another thing that's totally unnecessary.

He takes a careful old-person's step back, so he can examine me more thoroughly.

'Are you an alumnus yourself?' he asks.

'Yes.'

He nods, with some satisfaction. 'I can always tell. St Luke's leaves its mark on you, whether you want it to or not.'

'Did you really think you could get away with pretending to be dead forever, Mr Gough?' I ask.

'No,' he replies, 'but I hoped I could get away with it for long enough – and I have.'

'What do you mean – you've got away with it for long enough?'

Instead of answering, he gestures that I should just follow him.

He walks stiffly – but with assurance – on a crooked path through the gravestones, until we reach one which says:

Martha Tate
1882-1973
She lived a virtuous life, and
is gone to collect her reward.

'God will forgive her for entering His kingdom with a name which is not her own,' he says.

'Her real name was Martha Gough,' I guess.

'It was.' He pauses. 'A few months before we came out here, Martha felt a lump in her left breast. As it turned out, the tumour was benign, but it got me thinking.'

'Oh yes,' I say, noncommittally.

'I loved the college and I'd dedicated my life to it, but since she didn't feel about it as I did, it could be said that *she'd* sacrificed her life to St Luke's. It had taken me nearly fifty years to reach that realisation, but once I had – once I'd come to understand just how much I loved her – I resigned from the job that had been my *raison d'être*, and from then on, until she died, devoted my entire life to making my Martha happy.'

I raise my hands in the air and clap them slowly together . . . once . . . twice . . . three times.

I hear the sound being echoed back to me, after it strikes the bleached gravestones.

'What's that suppose to mean?' Gough demands angrily.

'It means that my bullshit detection meter has just suffered an overload, Mr Gough,' I tell him.

'A lady should not talk like that,' he says sternly.

'Then maybe it's just as well I'm not one,' I counter. 'Look, Mr Gough, I'm not saying that your wife *wasn't* a factor in your decision to resign as head porter, but she came third in your list of reasons – at best.'

'So what were those first two reasons?' he asks, his voice suddenly quieter and calmer – his overwhelming emotion, curiosity.

'The first was that while you still held the power, you wanted to use that power to put a worthy successor in place.'

'Harold Jenkins is a solid, respectable, hard-working man,' Gough says gravely. 'I don't think he'll have done as good a job as I did, but then what monarch ever thinks his successor will measure up to him?'

I have thought of him in terms of a monarch myself, but – somehow – hearing the words coming from his own mouth, is a little bit of a shock.

'Your second reason is that you didn't know how long your luck was going to hold out. You knew the bodies in the air shaft would be found eventually, and before that happened, you needed to make yourself safe by putting a fair distance between yourself and Oxford – a big enough distance, in fact, for you to be able to fake your own death.'

'What makes you think I know anything about any bodies hidden in some air shaft, Miss Redhead?' he asks.

'Not *any* bodies – the bodies of Albert Boulting and James Makepeace,' I say. 'Not any old air shaft, either, but the one in the cellar under the De Courcey Quad. And as far as your not knowing about them goes – how could you *not* have known about them, when you placed them in there yourself?'

'How can you be so sure that it was me who placed them in there?' he wonders.

We could continue lobbing questions back and forth forever, I suppose, just as if we were a couple of demented tennis players, but it's really time that someone broke the serve, and I volunteer me.

'I'll tell you how I knew it was you who disposed of the bodies, if you'll tell me how you faked your own death.'

'All right,' he agrees. 'You go first.'

I shake my head. 'Oh no, no, Mr Gough, the way it works is that *you* go first.'

'Don't you trust me, Miss Redhead?' he asks – and I'll swear he sounds just a little hurt.

'Don't you trust me?' I repeat, mockingly. 'That's the kind of thing that teenage boys say to teenage girls when they're trying to talk their way into their knickers.' I pause, to let that sink in. 'This is business, Mr Gough.' I continue. 'It seems almost like magic to you that I've found out some of the things I have, and you won't be able to rest until you know how I've done it. That's my main bargaining chip in this little negotiation of ours, and once I've explained away the magic, I'll have nothing.'

Actually, I'm bullshitting now, almost as much as he did earlier. The simple truth is that in terms of information, I don't care which of us talks first, but in terms of the power dynamic that's building up between us, I need to establish my predominance by making him back down.

Mr Gough thinks it over for a second or two, then slowly nods his head in agreement.

'It wasn't hard to die,' he says. 'It only took money – and not a lot of that, because, at the time, the island was poor. I put the whole matter in the hands of the local chief of police, who instructed the doctor to make a death certificate and the undertaker to put several sacks of sand into a coffin and then bury the coffin here. Once that was done, the chief got me a fake identity card in the name of Tate. He couldn't manage a false passport, but, as he pointed out, why would I need one? I haven't left Majorca since the day I first landed.'

'Why not register the death with the British Consulate?'

'My friend, the chief of police, thought that was just one step too far,' Gough says. 'The island was his own little kingdom, and he could pretty much control events in any way he wanted to, but bring a foreign government into the picture, and things would start getting very complicated. And why run the risk anyway? It seemed so unnecessary. My death was registered here – who would want to check if it was registered anywhere else?'

'Me?' I suggest.

'Yes, you,' he agrees. 'And now it's your turn. How did you know it was me who walled those two men up?'

'I know it was you because you used lime mortar,' I say.

'What do you mean?' he asks – but I can tell from the look on his face that he already knows what I'm talking about.

'Most people would have used Portland cement to wall up the bodies,' I say. 'It's much quicker – always an important factor when you're dabbling in homicide – and it's also a lot easier for the layman to use. But its big drawback is that it's not as kind to the building, because the building needs to shift a little, now and again, and to do that, it needs a mortar which is flexible – which bends to its will, if you like. Lime mortar will do that, but Portland is very rigid, so using Portland is almost like putting someone in a plaster cast, when all they need is an elasticised bandage. You used lime mortar because you loved the college and wanted it to be as comfortable as it possibly could be.'

'I certainly loved St Luke's at the time,' he admits, 'but time passes and memory fades, and I'm not sure I feel it as intensely as I used to.'

'But you felt it intensely back then, didn't you?'

'Oh yes, I certainly did.'

The conversation has started flowing amiably, but now it really is time to introduce a jarring note.

'Was it for love of St Luke's that you killed those two men, Mr Gough?' I ask.

'I've never killed anybody,' he says, steadily.

'Oh, come on!' I protest.

'Never!' he insists.

'Are you trying to tell me that you concealed the bodies from the police – which is a serious offence, and could have meant you went to prison – for the benefit of someone else?'

'Yes. In fact, it was for several "someone elses' benefits,"' he says, 'as well as for the college.'

'Of course, for the college,' I say, with a sigh.

'There's a nice little bar just the other side of that wall,' he tells me, pointing with his walking stick. 'If you'd care to come with me, I'd be more than happy to buy you a coffee.'

The bar Mr Gough leads me to is a low building with thick stone walls. It squats – toad-like – at the edge of the road, just beyond the railway station. It does not look particularly inviting from the outside – the only indications that it even *is* a bar are a few rusting metal advertisements for beer ('*¡Bebe Estrella!*') and tobacco ('*¡Viva Celtas!*') that have been nailed roughly to the wall – but inside it is pleasantly cool, if smelling slightly of cow shit.

There are four or five customers in the bar, and they all greet Mr Gough like a long-lost brother.

'*Hola, hombre!*'

'*Qué pasa, coño?*'

And now it's starting to get scary, because this is not neutral ground that he's arranged to meet me on – somewhere he can slip away from at a moment's notice – but his home patch.

This is where he lives, this man who – despite his denials – may well be responsible for three murders! And now *I* know where he lives! So there are two questions I would very much like to know the answer to – why have *I* been *allowed* to find out, and now that I have found out, what plans does he have for me?

Gough leads me to a rough wooden table, and indicates that I should sit down on the bench next to it. When I have done so, he sits down on a bench at the other side of the table.

'What would you like to drink?' he asks.

The words that come automatically into my mind are, *anything that won't poison me*, but I suspect that would not be well received.

I look across at the barman, who has the kind of lumpy face that would seem more at home in a medieval painting than it does behind a modern bar counter, and say, 'Could he manage a gin and tonic?'

'Certainly he can,' Gough says.

And then he addresses the barman in rapid Spanish, the only two words I can isolate from the stream being *Larios* and *tónica*, which may be ingredients, but could also be part of an instruction to the boys to get ready to dump a troublesome redhead into the sea.

'When I first came here, the Spanish Civil War had already been over for nearly twenty years, but the country was still suffering so much that it might only have finished the day before I arrived,' he tells me. 'Everybody was poor – and I mean, *desperately* poor. I mean *famine* poor! And then, slowly, we started getting tourists, and a bit of money began to trickle in. Now, most of us are doing quite nicely, thank you.'

I notice how closely he's identifying with Majorca – and I don't think he's just putting it on for my benefit.

'How do you, personally, manage to keep afloat?' I ask. 'I mean, you can't be living off your pension, can you, because dead men don't get pensions.'

'I built up a nice little nest egg when I was working at St Luke's,' he says. 'It wasn't that the pay was startlingly wonderful, but if you don't spend much of it – and I didn't have *time* to spend much of it, working at the college as I did – it soon builds up.'

'Even so . . .' I say.

'Even so,' he agrees, 'I'd be struggling to get by if it wasn't for my work as an advisor.'

'As an advisor?' I repeat. 'An advisor on what?'

'On whatever anyone around here needs advice on,' Gough says. 'If you can not only organise a St Luke's May Ball, but also do it in such a way that the student committee think they're the ones who have organised it, then advising people here on how to run a small business, or plan a wedding or a first communion party, is an absolute doddle.'

The barman brings the drinks over to our table. In what I've learned is the Spanish habit, he does not pour the gin into my glass until I can see him doing it, thus nipping in the bud any unworthy thoughts on my part that he might be fobbing me off with an inferior (and possibly potentially lethal) brand. When he's served me, he opens a bottle of Veterano, and fills the brandy glass far fuller than the measuring ring running round it indicates that he should fill it.

The commercial part of the process completed, the barman and Gough exchange a few sentences.

'*I'll need something to weigh her down once we've put her in the water,*' Gough says.

'*I can lay my hands on a couple of old tractor wheels that would just do the trick,*' the barman answers.

'*That'll do nicely,*' Gough agrees.

It's probably not what they're saying at all – but I have no way of knowing that for certain.

Does all this sound as if I'm not very worried? Trust me, worried is what I am.

And though I may be describing it in humorous tones, I am really finding it much less than funny.

I think back to what Juan, the trainee lawyer with the big libido, said – '*I was told only to present the letter to you when I was certain no other person could see me doing it.*'

Now why would Gough have told him that?

Simple! If I chose not to bring the letter with me – as I hadn't – then the police investigating my disappearance would have found it in my room. Then, if they could find a witness who saw Juan handing me the letter, they could tie the disappearance to him, and he could tie the disappearance to Gough – and Gough had taken great pains to make sure the chain didn't lead back to *his* front door!

'I didn't come here to find my real self, but that's exactly what happened,' Gough says, as he takes a swig of his brandy. 'I became a new man here on the island – a man I never even dreamed existed when I was back in Oxford. I've been very happy here, and so was Martha.'

'Is this new man you've become so different to the old man in Oxford that he himself would never have killed and walled up his victims?' I ask, because there is no point now in pussyfooting now.

Gough smiles, almost indulgently. 'That really is a very crude trick, you know,' he says.

'What is?'

'The new man I became would not have killed them, but then neither did the old man who I shed like an unwanted skin.'

'All right,' I say, 'maybe the new man wouldn't have killed them, but would he have walled them up?'

'I'd like to think he would – because it was always the right thing to do,' Gough says. 'But I can't be certain he would.'

'So you didn't kill Albert Boulting and you didn't kill James Makepeace,' I say.

'That's correct,' he agrees.

'But you know who did kill them?'

'Yes.'

'And are you willing to tell me about it?'

Mr Gough shrugs.

'Why not?'

Exactly! Why not?

What does it matter what he tells me when he has no intention of my being around to pass it on to someone else?

FIFTEEN

12 February 1916

With every step he took up the staircase that led to his rooms, Albert Boulting became a little more frightened.

He *was* being watched – he was sure of it – and, since no watcher ever had a benevolent intent, his wisest course (as he had already told himself a dozen times) was to flee Oxford, without returning to his rooms. Yet, though his fear was turning his stomach to water, his lust was still in control of most of his body, and it was his lust that was imperiously commanding his legs to mount the stairs.

When he reached his own landing, he came to a halt.

It was not too late, he argued.

He could still turn around and walk rapidly away.

But that would mean abandoning his photographs, lovingly collected (and at great expense) over the years. And he knew that without his pictures of sweet little girls gratifying themselves with big men (and sometimes, even, with animals), life would be complete misery.

He knew something was wrong the moment he opened his door and saw that the fire – which, when he had left that morning, had been nothing more than smouldering ashes – was now blazing merrily away in the grate and casting dancing shadows on the wall.

He tried to turn – and found he couldn't, because both his elbows were suddenly being gripped tightly by strong pairs of hands. And then he felt himself being flung forward into the room, and though he tried to keep his balance, it was an impossible task, and he ended up sprawling on the rug.

From where he had landed, he could see three sets of booted legs – two pairs under his table, and one pair next to it, which, added to the two men who had been hiding on the landing, meant there were five intruders in total.

'Don't just lie there like a dog, get up,' said a voice which managed to simultaneously sound young and yet carry with it ages of despair.

Boulting got to his feet and looked around him. The man standing next to the table was Hector Judd, the ex-soldier with one arm. The other four – the two at the table and the two blocking the doorway – were all wearing the uniforms of second lieutenants.

'You know who we are, of course,' said one of the two officers sitting at the table.

As a matter of fact, he did.

'Yes,' he said, 'you're all St Luke's men.'

But by God, how they'd all changed! He remembered them on bright summer days, playing cricket in the University Parks, and accepting either victory or defeat with equanimity, like the sporting gentlemen they were. He remembered them on winter mornings, returning to college just as he was getting up, after a rousing hour rowing on the river. How fresh and young they'd seemed only a year earlier – their bodies glowing with health, their optimism about life's challenges there in their bright eyes for all to see.

Now, there was barely a trace of the bright young men they had so recently been. Their eyes had become deeper and almost feverish, and their features coarsened. Even their chins had lost their distinctive manliness and determination, and now hung – so it seemed to an increasingly worried Boulting – like great lead weights attempting to drag the rest of their faces into the bottomless pit of hell.

Surprise had temporarily numbed Boulting's instincts, but now they were back up again, working at full throttle. And what his instincts said to him was that if you went into your room and found five uninvited guests there – guests who, moreover, didn't seem to be feeling the least bit awkward about the situation – then what you should do is get the hell out of there, as quickly as you possibly could.

He turned to the door. The two officers who'd thrust him into the room were standing firmly in front of it, legs spread and anchored to the ground, eyes watchful, hands one muscular process away from forming fists.

He turned back again, and noticed, for the first time, that a ceremonial sword had been laid diagonally across the table and had its tip pointing neutrally towards the corner of the room.

He almost laughed out loud, but then decided that the worst way you could insult a serious man was by not taking him seriously.

Instead, he contented himself with saying, 'You appear to have organised a court martial!'

'That's right,' one of the young men at the table agreed.

Downes! Boulting remembered now – his name was Downes!

'But you can't do that, Downes, old chap!' he said, and now he could see how ludicrous the whole thing was, he was starting to find it rather amusing. 'A court martial can only be conducted by high-ranking officers, and you, my friend, are no more than a second lieutenant.'

'I am *not* your friend,' Downes told him. 'And as far as the court martial goes, I have my standing orders to guide me. And what do they say?'

'I wouldn't know.'

'They say that if, for any reason, a military court needs to be convened, then it may be convened by the highest ranking officer available at the time, and that – if only by seniority of service – is me.'

'And why should one need to be convened?'

'It needs to be convened to try you, Boulting, for conduct unbecoming an officer and a gentleman.'

'But I'm not a soldier,' Boulting pointed out. 'So even if you are entitled to conduct a court martial, you have no jurisdiction over me.'

'Don't lie,' Downes said, in a tone which suggested that Boulting's words had caused him actual physical pain. 'Do you think we don't know what you did this morning?'

The girl! Boulting thought in a panic.

No, wait a minute, he hadn't touched the girl, and anyway, that had been in the afternoon.

'I've no idea what you're talking about,' he said.

'This morning, you were commissioned as a second lieutenant in the Welsh Engineers,' Downes said.

'How do you know about that?' Boulting gasped.

'If it's the truth – and it is – then it doesn't really matter how we know, does it?' Downes asked.

The captain! Boulting thought – the sneering, supercilious captain at the recruitment office, who'd taken a personal and unreasonable dislike to him, had probably tipped them off.

'This is ludicrous!' he said. 'You're not children playing in the garden. This is real life, and if you think I'm going to take this kangaroo court seriously, then you must be completely out of your minds.'

'Perhaps we *are* out of our minds,' Downes said seriously. 'When you've been to the front – as we all have – and seen men, who've been your friends all your life, blown into a dozen pieces, as if they were of absolutely no consequence, then perhaps you do become unhinged. But I don't think you ever lose your sense of what is right and what is wrong.'

'Listen . . .' Boulting began.

'And as far as taking us seriously,' Downes continued, opening his holster and placing his service revolver on the table, 'I would advise you to take us very seriously indeed.' He paused. 'During these proceedings, Lieutenant Springer will present the case for the prosecution, and Lieutenant Cole will act as your defence counsel. Lieutenant Matlock and I will be the judges.' He turned to the men standing at the door. 'Are you ready, gentlemen?'

'We're ready,' they replied.

'Then present your evidence, Lieutenant Springer.'

The lieutenant stepped forward – but not so far forward that he was no longer a barrier to Boulting making an escape.

'I call Hector Judd,' he said.

Judd looked around the room, as if searching for the spot on which he should be standing.

'You're fine where you are, Private Judd,' Springer said.

'Thank you, sir,' Judd replied.

'Would you care to give your evidence?' Springer asked.

Judd cleared his throat. 'In October last year, I was Parliamentary Recruitment Committee canvasser, and in that capacity I went to see this man,' Judd said.

'You must name him,' Springer said.

'Boulting – Albert Boulting.'

'And why did you go to see him?'

'I had to present him with a letter from the Earl of Derby, asking him to join the army.'

'And did you give him the letter?'

'Yes, sir.'

'And you saw him read it?'

'Yes, sir.'

'And what did he say when he'd finished reading the letter?'

'He said he'd think about it.' Judd paused for a moment. 'He also mocked me for having only one arm.'

'I did *not* mock him,' Boulting protested. 'I sang a popular and patriotic song to him. I thought it would amuse him.'

'Do you deny you refused to join the army?' Downes asked.

'No, I don't deny it,' Boulting said, with some bravado. 'It's not a crime, is it?'

'No,' Downes agreed. 'It's not a crime. My own personal feeling is that it should be on a par with desertion – and if you refused to join the army you should be shot – but we are working within the existing laws here.'

No, they weren't, Boulting thought – they were making it up as they went along.

'Well, now that's settled, I'd appreciate it if you'd all leave my room,' he said.

'Is there more, Lieutenant Springer?' Downes asked.

'Yes, sir,'

'Then, by all means, let's hear it.'

'Lieutenant Boulting is a well-known and notorious paedophile, sir,' Springer said.

'Aren't you going to object?' Boulting asked Lieutenant Cole, his supposed defence counsel.

Lieutenant Cole shrugged. 'So far, I've heard nothing to object to.'

'Then *I'll* object,' Boulting said. 'What gives you the right to call me a paedophile, Lieutenant Springer?'

'It's a well-known fact. Everybody in college knows.'

'What people *think* is proof of nothing,' Boulting said. 'To successfully make your case, you need either eye witnesses or strong physical evidence – and preferably, both.'

And then, as Lieutenant Springer reached into his uniform pocket, Boulting felt his heart sink.

What Springer had removed was a worn envelope – an envelope that was very familiar to Boulting.

'In this envelope are pictures of young girls photographed in the most disgusting and degrading positions,' Springer said. 'I have sisters of my own, so those pictures made me almost physically ill.'

'They're not mine,' Boulting said. 'Someone must have planted them in my underwear drawer.'

He realised his mistake the moment he had spoken, and could only hope that none of the others would spot it.

'If they are not yours, how do you know that they were in your underwear drawer?' Springer asked.

'If I was trying to frame someone, that's just where I'd put them,' Boulting said.

'So, they are not yours,' Springer said. 'In that case, you will have no objection to us burning them, will you?'

It felt to Boulting as if an ice pick had been driven into his heart. It had taken time and money – and yes, love! – to build up the collection, and it was his most precious possession. On the other hand, it was always possible he could build up another collection, whereas if he lost his life – and that was looking more and more likely – it was gone for good.

'No, I have no objection to you burning them,' he said, and

then, because he couldn't stop himself, he added, 'Might I see exactly what it is that you're burning, before you commit them to the flames?'

Springer gave him a look which said he was beyond contempt, and walked over to the fireplace. He took one photograph out, held it up to the flame and watched it burn. Then, when the flame had almost reached his fingers, he held what was left of the picture over the fire, and let the updraft take charge of it. The process completed, he extracted another photograph from the envelope.

He could have burned them all at once, Boulting thought, but he wants to see me suffer – they *all* want to see me suffer.

He turned his attention back onto Downes.

'Apart from a few rumours – which I unequivocally deny – and an envelope of photographs, which I have never seen before, you have no evidence. All you *do* have is supposition – and both you know and I know – full well – that in no court in the land could you ever get me convicted on anything so flimsy.'

Downes shook his head gravely. 'What you say might well be the case if this trial were being held in a civilian court, but the standard of proof in a military court is nothing like as rigorous as that required elsewhere. In a military court, we have leave to use our own powers of judgement.'

Boulting was a good amateur psychologist – any man who wished to exploit the weaknesses and uncertainties of children for his own benefit had to be – and he was finally starting to understand what was driving these men, and what they wanted. And with that understanding, real deep fear – stomach-churning fear, screaming-from the-bottom-of-his-lungs fear – came at last.

The story of the evil dragon threatening the kingdom might be no more than mythology, but its symbolism had been burned deep into the souls of these intense young men, he thought. The German army *was* the evil dragon, as far as they were concerned, and they had gone off like knights in shining armour to slay it. But once they were abroad, they had soon discovered that virtue was not enough – that evil, if it was well armed and well trained, had just as much of a chance of triumphing as good did. And so they had scaled back their ambitions. If they couldn't kill a full-sized dragon, then they would look for a baby one – a slice of evil small enough for them to deal with themselves.

I'm that slice of evil, Boulting told himself, *and there's not one chance in a million that they're going to let me get away.*

And at that, his bowels opened, and the room was filled with the unpleasant smell of fear and desperation.

A look of disgust appeared on the faces of the other men in the room, and then, as quickly as it had appeared, it was gone, and had been replaced with the most neutral – clearly artificial – of expressions.

They're pretending not to notice because it will embarrass me, Boulting thought. They're going to propose some horrible punishment for me, but it would still be bad form to increase my embarrassment.

It *was* ludicrous! The whole thing was insane. But wrapped up in their blankets of earnestness and self-righteousness, these four young soldiers – battle-hardened at the age of twenty – would never see it.

Matlock and Downes exchanged a brief glance which said that they, as the judges in the case, had heard enough, and had already reached a verdict. Matlock swivelled around the sword on the table, so that its point was no longer directed at the corner, but instead singled out Boulting.

Lieutenant Downes reached into his jacket pocket, and produced a silver cigarette case.

'Would you like a gasper, old chap?' he asked Boulting, in the friendliest possible tones.

Boulting took the cigarette between trembling fingers. Downes struck a match and held it out, but Boulting seemed incapable of homing in on it, and every time Downes moved the match to accommodate him, Boulting's hands seemed to decide to move in the opposite direction. Finally, when the match had burned down so far down that it was almost at Lieutenant Downes' fingertips, Lieutenant Matlock stood up and cupped his own hands around Boulting's to steady them, so that the operation could be completed.

Downes waited patiently until Boulting had sucked greedily on the cigarette a couple of times.

Then he said, 'It pains me to say this to a fellow member of St Luke's, but you have no self-discipline, nor self-restraint. You have dishonoured this college, and though you have not even begun to serve with them in any formal sense, you have dishonoured the

Welsh Engineers. I could pass sentence now, but such a formality could be set aside if you were prepared, voluntarily, to take the opportunity of personally redeeming at least a little of your honour.'

'Pass sentence! Redeem myself!' Boulting asked, in a voice in which it was hard to separate the anger from the fear. 'What do you plan on doing with me if I don't agree to do something to redeem myself? Will you march me out in front of a firing squad?'

'For all sorts of reasons, most of which should be obvious even to you, that is the one option we are hoping to avoid if we possibly can,' Downes said, with all the deadly seriousness and gravity of a high court judge. 'But *only* if we possibly can,' he added, ominously.

And as Matlock removed the sword from the table, Downes reached into a bag which had been resting at his feet, and took out a crystal tumbler and a bottle of whisky. He placed both the tumbler and bottle on the table, next to the service revolver.

'Are you suggesting that I kill myself?' asked Boulting, who had anticipated *being* killed, but never this.

'I would recommend that you drink only one or two glasses of whisky – which should be just enough to give you sufficient courage,' Downes said. 'Take more, and there is a real danger of either undermining your purpose or of becoming maudlin.'

'You really do expect me to go through with this, don't you?' Boulting demanded.

'I appreciate the fact that a man of your predilections may have no experience of using small arms,' Downes said, standing up, 'but this pistol is simplicity itself. I have already cocked it, so all you need to do is to place the barrel against your forehead and pull the trigger.'

And then, whilst not exactly melting into the night, Boulting's visitors were gone.

But they hadn't gone far. He heard the door click behind them, but not the sound of their footsteps going down the stairs.

They were waiting on the landing, he told himself – maintaining a silent vigil until he decided to do the right thing.

As calmly as he could, he considered his options.

They had left him with a loaded weapon, which, with a lot of men, would have been a big mistake to make. But it wasn't a mistake with him – they had assessed the situation accurately, and knew that he did not have the stomach for shooting his way out. Besides, even if they'd got that wrong, they had three guns to his one.

So what would happen if he simply called their bluff?

That wouldn't work, because after the crushing disillusionment of their experiences in France, they had their hearts set on getting a little of what *they* saw as justice in England – and they would not be denied it. If he would not kill himself, then they would have absolutely no qualms about doing it.

There was only one option – and that was escape.

Boulting opened the window, and looked down. In the light of a pale moon he examined the three-floor drop to the quad below, and quickly decided it was far too far to jump.

But he didn't have to jump, because growing up the stone wall was an ivy plant which had probably been there when King Charles I lost the Civil War (and then his head), and was as much a part of the building as the oak doors and mullioned windows.

He stepped onto the ledge, and grabbed hold of what felt like a very strong strand of ivy. Then he turned – awkwardly, because of the restricted space – until his back was to the outside world.

He lowered one foot off the ledge, while keeping the other firmly in place. But that served no useful purpose, because he couldn't test the strength of the ivy until it was holding all his weight.

He took a very deep breath, and launched his other foot away from the safety of the window ledge.

He had been squashed up on the ledge, but once his feet had nothing but air under them, he began to fall – and continued to fall until his body was stretched to the limit.

The whole process could not have taken more than a split second, but it had felt like hours. The muscles in his arms burned from taking on such unaccustomed – and unexpected – weight, but his grip was firm, and the ivy was holding.

His next step was to release the grip he had with his left hand and establish another grip, closer to the ground. This meant that instead of being vertical, his body was at an angle, but when he repeated the manoeuvre with his right hand, this was corrected.

He would have to go through all this at least ten or twelve times before he reached the ground, he calculated, and he could only pray that the self-righteous maniacs who were waiting on the landing would not lose patience, and go back into his room to find out why it was taking him so long to do what they considered to be the 'right' thing.

He had no immediate plan of what to do once he reached the ground, he suddenly realised.

What *should* he do?

Should he throw himself under the dean's protection, in the belief that however mad the four young officers were, they still had enough of a sense of tradition to respect the man's authority?

But that assumed the dean *would* protect him, didn't it – and who could say, on an evening in which the whole world seemed to have gone mad, that that was still the case?

It might just be best to make a run for it while he could. But dare he risk taking a train – which was the first place that his tormentors would probably look for him?

Perhaps, at this stage in his escape, he should not have allowed himself to think about such considerations as what would happen when he was safely on the ground, because, distracted as he was, he accepted his next right handhold as safe without testing it properly, and when he put all his weight on it, he felt it coming away from the wall.

Oh my God, he thought. *Oh my God, oh my God, ohmygod . . .!*

He tried to free himself from this useless piece of ivy, and instead get a grip on a much firmer one, but he had already swung out so far that his trunk was over the quad, and his right arm, even stretched out to its full extent, still could not touch the wall.

He needed to swing back against the wall, he told himself, but his right foot had already decided that since the centre of gravity had shifted, its best plan was to break free.

And suddenly he was upside-down.

He did not know how it had happened – he did not *care* how it had happened – but he wished to God it hadn't happened at all.

He mustn't panic, he told himself. Panicking was actually the worst thing he should do.

Could he right himself, he wondered. No, he didn't think he had the nerve. But even if he could summon up the courage from some-where, it probably wouldn't be a good idea, because all the extra strain inherent in the manoeuvre might induce the ivy to snap.

Yet he couldn't just hang there forever, could he?

And then he realised that he *wasn't* going to hang there forever, because even as he was thinking through his situation, his hand was slowly moving down the vine, stripping away the shiny leaves as it went.

Then even that strand was gone, and he knew – in what would be the last second of his life – that his head was about to hit the paving stones with some force.

SIXTEEN

15 October 1974

M r Gough is a natural storyteller, and I know this for a fact, because although I am sitting in this quiet Spanish bar on this benevolently warm autumn day, the dull thud of Boulting's head smashing against the paving stones still rings in my ears, and I can feel the icy fingers of winter caressing my bare knees.

'So what you'd got was a corpse lying stone dead in the quad,' I say. 'What happened next?'

'What do you think happened next?' asks Gough, and the disdain in his voice suggests that I should already know the answer, because all this occurred within the grounds of *his* college, and there is, therefore, only one thing that *could have* happened.

'I don't know,' I say, declining the invitation to acknowledge him as a combination of wise man and superhero. And then, just so he doesn't start to feel *too* much in control, I even decide to prod him a little. 'Actually, I do know what probably happened,' I continue. 'Someone informed the dean about what had occurred, and he decided that the way to handle it was . . .'

'The dean knew nothing,' Gough interrupts me, clearly annoyed. 'The dean was *told* nothing because he could have *done* nothing. He went to his grave in total ignorance of the events of that night.'

'So then, if it wasn't the dean, perhaps the bursar . . .'

'They brought the body to *me*.'

'*Who* brought the body to you?'

'Who do you think? The four young soldiers who'd been in Boulting's rooms with him! Two of them had gone downstairs before he fell – they wanted to get some fresh air – and they were standing in the archway at the bottom of the staircase when Boulting hit the ground. He practically landed at their feet.'

'Did no one else see him fall?'

'No one at all.'

'I find that strange,' I confess.

'You shouldn't. It was a dark cold night in February, remember, when most people prefer to be indoors. Besides, almost all the accommodation in that quad had been allocated to a military training school, and all the students were out on night manoeuvres that particular evening.'

'So the four young lieutenants brought Boulting's body to the porters' lodge, did they?'

'Yes.'

'Was there much bleeding?'

'Surprisingly little.'

'And you were the one who decided to wall up Boulting in the old air vent, were you?'

'Yes.'

'It was *entirely* your decision?'

'No one's but mine.'

'So *why* did you decide to do it?'

'Why?' Gough repeats. He takes a generous slug of his brandy. 'I decided to do it because it was the right thing to do.'

'Right for whom?'

'Right for everybody.'

'Everybody with the possible exception of the dead man,' I say.

'Yes, everybody with the possible exception of the dead man,' he agrees. 'But then Boulting was an abuser of children, and it could be argued that he got a far quicker death than he deserved.' He takes another slug of the Veterano. 'If I hadn't made him disappear, there would have been an inquiry into his death. And that inquiry would have been bound to reveal that the college had been sheltering the disgusting creature under its roof for nearly two years. The same inquiry would also have prevented those four brave young soldiers – who would have been called as witnesses

– from returning to France, where their country badly needed them to fight against the Hun.'

'So you decided to cover up a murder,' I say.

'There was no murder,' Gough replies scornfully. 'Perhaps Boulting fell from the wall. Or perhaps he was so overcome with shame in the middle of his escape that he simply decided to let go of the ivy. Whichever it was – suicide or accident – no crime was committed.'

'Except he would never have been out there at all if he hadn't been terrified of what the young soldiers might do to him,' I say. 'By the way, what happened to them? Do you know?'

'Of course I know,' Gough says, in his I-was-the-head-porter-and-I-knew-everything voice. 'Lieutenants Springer and Matlock were killed at the second Battle of the Somme. Cole died at Wipers, and Downes went missing at Cambrai. Judd went back as an assistant to the padre. He had his legs blown off two days before the armistice. They put him on a hospital ship, but by then he'd lost so much blood that it was impossible to save him.'

Do you know something – I'm inclined to believe this whole story!

And that's not only because it has the ring of truth about it, but also because I don't think Mr Gough, whatever his other talents, has the imagination to fill in the background with so many intricate details. So, as I see it, whilst he might have made some rather dubious ethical choices at the time, he's pretty much off the hook for the first – and *only* the first – of the killings.

But I also think that what happened in the aftermath of Boulting's death might well help to explain some of the circumstances surrounding Makepeace's death, nearly thirty years later – because having once had the experience of playing God, it wouldn't surprise me if Mr Gough hadn't developed a craving for an encore.

'Tell me about what happened to James Makepeace,' I suggest. 'Did he fall off a wall as well?'

'Now you're just being sarcastic, Miss Redhead,' Mr Gough says, sounding offended.

He's right, I was being sarcastic – and that was a big mistake, because whilst, amongst my generation, sarcasm is pretty much a main strand of the communication process, it's much more alien to a man who was born when Queen Victoria still had almost another quarter century of ruling to do. And this is something I need to bear in mind all the time I'm talking to him – *he's a very old man, and he doesn't see the world in anything like the same way I do.*

'I'm sorry,' I say, swallowing some richly deserved humble pie. 'It won't happen again.'

'What actually happened to Makepeace was that he was struck from behind, in the courtyard, and staggered into the closest place where he thought he might find help, which happened to be the porters' lodge,' Gough says in a tone which indicates that he's prepared to let bygones be bygones.

'What time of day did this happen?' I ask.

'It was night.'

'So it was dark?'

'Yes.'

'And I expect that, just as in the case of Boulting, the weather was awful, and there was no one around.'

'That's right.'

Now how convenient was *that*?

'So James Makepeace staggered into the porters' lodge,' I say. 'What did he do after that?'

'As soon as he was inside, he collapsed onto the floor. I bent down beside him, to see what I could do to help. His mouth was opening and closing, like he was trying to say something. "What's that, sir?" I asked, to encourage him. "The Americans," he managed to gasp. "It was the Americans what did for me." And no sooner had he got the words out of his mouth than he died.'

Again, incredibly convenient!

'Do you know what he meant by saying the Americans had done for him?' I ask.

'He meant they'd killed him.'

'And why would they have done that?'

'They'd done it in revenge – because they thought that he'd killed one of theirs.'

'And had he?'

'I can't say.'

'I thought you had your ear to the ground at all times,' I say, risking taunting him slightly. 'I thought there was nothing that went on in the college that you didn't know about.'

'In the college,' he agrees. 'But I can't be expected to know about everything that happens in the whole of Oxford and district.'

'You must know something – or you wouldn't have said that the motive for the murder was probably revenge,' I point out.

He shrugs. 'All I do know, is that the people I talked to from the American camp just outside Oxford, were convinced that Makepeace had murdered one of their regimental supply sergeants – a man called Comstock.'

'What did they base this belief of theirs on?'

'I think they based it on the fact that Makepeace was a queer.'

'I beg your pardon,' I say.

'A queer,' he repeats, and then, as if in an effort to make things clearer, he adds, 'a brown hatter, a bum bandit, a nancy boy.'

'Like Charlie Swift?' I suggest.

Gough stiffens in his seat. 'When you say Charlie Swift, are you perhaps referring to *Lord* Charles Swift?' he asks in a voice that carries with it all the chill of an Arctic gale.

'Yes,' I agree. 'I am.'

'Lord Swift is not a queer,' he says, with great dignity.

'Then what is he?'

'Lord Swift is a homosexual.'

I want to laugh, but I know it would be a mistake.

Lord Swift is not a queer, he is a homosexual!

In this modern world of ours, I've noticed that the owner of a large company can never be a fraudster or an embezzler – such low terms are reserved for men who run much smaller companies – and he must, instead, be considered the victim of creative account-ancy gone wrong.

And so it is with the English class system – Charlie, with a long and distinguished family history behind him, cannot be consid-ered a queer, but must instead be seen as a *homosexual*, which – if it is pronounced with a certain gravitas – almost sounds like it refers to a moderately high ranking member of the Church of England (say someone between provost and canon).

'So James Makepeace was a queer,' I say, doing my best to hide my distaste for a word which seems to come so naturally to Gough. 'I still fail to see how that ties in with him killing a US sergeant.'

'Sergeant Comstock was also a queer, though they don't call

them queers over there – they call them fags. He'd been seeing a lot of Makepeace, but then they had a row which led to a fight in one of the pubs. It was just across the river from Magdalen College and it was called the Crossed Keys then, though it's probably changed its name by now. Billy Bones, who was the landlord, has long since gone up to that great wrestling ring in the sky, but there might still be some of the regulars around who remember it, if you want to check.'

'I'll bear that in mind,' I say.

'Anyway, a day after the fight, Comstock's body was found down by the river. That bit is in the police files, if you're interested.'

I'm fairly sure that part of his story is true, and, in all probability, there are other parts of it which are, too. But taken as a whole, it doesn't add up.

How likely was it, for example, that anybody planning to kill James Makepeace would have attacked him just outside the porters' lodge, rather than waiting for the chance to murder him somewhere there was less likelihood of a witness suddenly appearing?

What were the chances that the assassin could deliver a blow which was hard enough to kill him, but not immediately – a blow that left him just enough time to stagger into the porters' lodge and blame his death on the Yanks?

Still, the best way to sort out the wheat from the chaff is to pretend to accept it all at face value initially, and then gently lead the discussion into areas Gough might be a little less comfortable in.

'I can understand why you hid Albert Boulting's body,' I say, and then, stretching the truth a little, I add, 'I even think, on reflection, that it was the right thing for you to do.'

'Thank you,' Gough says. 'I do not need your approval, but it is nice to know that I have it.'

Well, screw you! I think. But aloud, I say, 'What's got me really puzzled is why you decided to do the same thing with Makepeace's corpse.'

'I decided to hide that for exactly the same reason I decided to hide Boulting's,' Gough says. 'Look, I could have informed the Thames Valley police force, but there would have been no point, because they were never going to catch the murderer.'

'Weren't they?'

'Of course they weren't. All the Americans would have given each other alibis, and there would have been no way to break any of them. Besides, the police were already stretched, with so many of their officers gone to serve in the armed forces, so the investigation would just have made life even more difficult for them. So nothing would have come of my reporting it, except that it would have damaged the college's reputation.'

'Why would it have damaged the college's reputation – just because Makepeace was a homosexual?'

'No, because Makepeace wasn't *just* a homosexual – he was like a dog on heat. I don't want to shock you, but . . .'

'I'm not easily shocked,' I tell him.

'No, most women are not easily shocked these days,' he says, regretfully. 'Things are changing even here, on Majorca. Modesty and femininity seem to have gone completely out of fashion.'

'You were just telling me that Makepeace was "like a dog on heat,"' I remind him.

'And so he was. If it moves and it's got testicles, impale it – that was his motto. And I didn't want to see the newspapers filled with accounts of scruffy young tramps and layabouts describing in lurid detail exactly what they'd allowed a St Luke's man to do to them for a few pennies.'

Again, it's a question of degree, I think. If the young tramps he's picturing had been, instead, the younger sons of the aristocracy, and if, instead of buggering them in a convenient dark alley, he'd flown them out to a luxury villa in the South of France before having his way with them, then, somehow, that wouldn't have seemed quite so bad.

But even allowing for moral relativism, Gough's story still has its weaknesses.

'A queer is not as bad as a child molester,' I say, putting it, not without a certain degree of revulsion, in his terms. 'The college must have had a fair number of queers over the years – and its reputation is still intact.'

A rare look of indecision crosses Gough's face.

'The college's reputation might have survived, but I'm not sure that Lord Swift's reputation would have,' he says finally.

'You mean . . .'

'James Makepeace and Lord Swift spent a considerable amount of time together – naked.'

I'd learned over the previous few days that Makepeace had been at the college at the same time as Charlie, and that he was gay, but it had never occurred to me (or perhaps, in hindsight, it was more a case of I'd never *dared* let it occur to me) that they had been lovers.

Oh Charlie, you bloody fool, I think. Why did you have to hide that particular part of the story from me, your best friend – you insensitive, mistrustful, stupid, lying bastard?

But I mustn't be distracted . . . I mustn't be distracted.

I came here with the idea that Mr Gough was the mastermind behind the killings – a sociopath megalomaniac who was only truly alive when exercising the power of life or death over others. And though he's spent the last hour attempting to either charm, intimidate or confuse me – and sometimes all three at once – nothing he has done or said has made me abandon that original idea.

OK, maybe he didn't kill Albert Boulting (or even cause him to be killed) and maybe he didn't kill (or cause to be killed) James Makepeace, but over the forty-odd years he was in the college, there must – given his nature – have been other deaths he was implicated in, and there must be other bodies – perhaps a good few of them – stuffed away in quiet corners of St Luke's.

How do I know this?

I don't know it with certainty – but consider the logic. Gough has not set foot in the college himself for over twenty years, yet he still has enough power and influence in Oxford to compel someone else to kill Lennie Moon. And that's no small thing – that isn't a 'listen, I lent you a cup of sugar once and now I want you to do something for me,' type favour.

And surely, the only thing that would compel anyone to commit a murder would be the knowledge that if they didn't, other murders they had been involved in would be revealed.

Very clever, you're thinking to yourself, but what I haven't explained is why Mr Gough would want to have Lennie killed in the first place.

To which I counter – why would *anybody else* want Lennie killed?

Lennie was a sweet man-child who liked to play on the river

with the boats that Mr Jenkins had made for him. He offended no one. He wouldn't even have known where to begin.

Ah, but it may not be a case of what he *did*, but more of what he *knew*. He had been around for a long time and must have seen a great deal. And he couldn't be trusted to keep quiet about what he knew, especially once the college was swarming with police officers, as it would be once they learned about the two bodies.

'So you feel no guilt over anything you've ever done?' I ask Mr Gough.

'No guilt at all, in any way, shape or form,' he says, with what sounds like absolute conviction.

'I can understand that absence of guilt in the case of Boulting,' I say. 'I can even understand it in the case of Makepeace. But what about Lennie, Mr Gough? What about poor innocent Lennie?'

I am watching his eyes closely as I speak, and what I'm expecting to see is a flicker of guilt or concern cross them, before the iceman within him manages to reassert himself.

But that is not what I see at all!

What I do see is puzzlement, which is rapidly replaced by concern – and possibly even *fear*.

'Lennie?' he says tentatively, as if treading on treacherous ground which he suspects might give way at any time. 'Lennie Moon?'

'Yes.'

'What's happened to him?'

'Don't give me that, Mr Gough! You must know – even if you had nothing to do with it yourself! It was in all the English papers.'

'I haven't looked at an English paper in years.' His jaw quivers slightly. 'Please tell me what happened to him.'

'He's dead!'

'Was it . . . was it his heart? Or was it perhaps an accident?'

'It was neither of those. He was murdered!'

I'm still watching the eyes, and what I read there is horror – but also a sudden understanding of what must have happened.

'You didn't have him killed, did you?' I ask – and even if he confessed now, I wouldn't believe him.

'No, of course I didn't have him killed,' Gough says, in a cracked voice. 'He was very special to me.' He pauses, before continuing, 'How was he killed? Was his neck broken?'

Ask most people to describe a way of murdering someone, and

they'll come up with stabbing, shooting, poisoning, strangling and the proverbial blunt instrument. Push them a little more, and they may suggest drowning, running the victim over, and possibly hanging.

That the victim had his neck broken would occur to very few people, but Mr Gough came up with the possibility immediately – and there can be only one explanation of that.

'You know who killed him, don't you?' I demand. 'And if you know that, you probably also know *why* he was killed.'

'We've . . . we've always tried our best to protect him,' Gough mumbles.

'Who is "we"?'

'We've done all we could for over thirty years, but we should have known it would always end this way,' Gough says. 'Given what Lennie was like, how could it have ended any *other* way?'

'What are you talking about?' I ask.

'I'm glad that he's dead – it would be so much worse if he wasn't,' Gough says.

When I first met him, just over an hour ago, I thought he had all the vigour of a fit man of sixty, but as he raises himself to his feet, I realise I am watching an old, old creature who is barely alive.

'I have to go,' he says.

He staggers over to the doorway, opens the door, and is gone.

I notice that I have been running the flats of my hands across the table with some force, and when I lift them, I can see that I have collected several prize splinters in my fingers and palms.

I've been a complete fool, I tell myself – a fool who first built up a noir fantasyland, and then bought into it completely.

Did Mr Gough kill Albert Boulting?

No, of course he didn't.

Did he kill James Makepeace?

Absolutely not – though I don't, for a minute, believe his story about the Americans doing it.

Did he arrange to have Lennie killed?

No, he would never have done that, but I have no doubt that he knows who the killer is.

He is not a criminal mastermind – the leader of a death cult which has operated in St Luke's, undetected, for over half a century. He is a decent man who never initiated *anything*, but simply reacted in the way he thought would minimise the damage.

And when I was warning myself that I'd be lucky to walk away from here alive, I was merely creating a melodrama in which I – naturally enough – was cast as the tragic heroine, whereas the truth was, Mr Gough was doing his best to protect himself, but never intended me any harm at all.

I take a deep, wounded slug of my G and T.

Still, even though I'm a deluded fool, the trip hasn't been a complete waste of time, I tell myself bitterly.

I've learned, for example, that I can't trust my best friend in the whole world – and that has to be worth something.

SEVENTEEN

23 October 1943

It was late afternoon. Charlie Swift was in his rooms at St Luke's, savouring his afternoon tea – a pot of Earl Grey, hot buttered scones and a raspberry tartlet – when his door was flung unceremoniously open, and James Makepeace stormed in.

Makepeace was in a real state, Charlie thought – in fact, he looked even worse than he had the previous evening, when he'd realised that Sergeant Comstock had cut him.

'What's happened?' Charlie asked.

'I was walking along the river towards Sandford-on-Thames—' Makepeace began.

'Why were you doing that?' Charlie interrupted, incredulous. 'You hate walking. You *never* walk anywhere unless you absolutely have to – and I can't think of a single reason why you'd choose to walk as far as Sandford.'

'I was on my way to have a pint at the King's Head in Sandford, if you must know *all* the tedious details,' Makepeace said – and even delivered in a desperate angry voice, it still sounded like a very weak explanation.

'But why Sandford? Have you suddenly gone off all the pubs in Oxford?' Charlie asked.

'For God's sake, shut up and listen to me,' Makepeace said, in a voice that was bordering on a scream.

'All right,' Charlie agreed, speaking soothingly and at the same time making calming, conciliatory gestures with his hands. 'I'm listening, and what you need to do is to calm down and tell me exactly what the problem is.'

'I was walking down by the river, and I'd got nearly as far as Sandford when I saw a man lying in the grass just beyond the path,' Makepeace said. 'He was wearing some kind of uniform, and he wasn't moving. He might just have been sleeping, of course, but he was in such an awkward position that I thought he must have passed out, either due to drink or because of some medical condition. It must have been around half past three by then, and I knew it would be important to wake him before darkness fell, and the real cold set in.'

Nobody went from near hysteria to producing logical, balanced sentences as quickly as Makepeace had just done, Charlie Swift thought. This whole performance was just that – an act which had been as carefully worked out as any he might see on the stage.

Still, now it had begun, he might as well see the rest of the show.

'Go on,' he said.

'It was only when I knelt down beside him that I realised it was . . . that I realised it was . . .'

'Sergeant Comstock?' Charlie Swift suggested.

'How did you know it was him?' Makepeace asked.

'Just a lucky guess,' Charlie said, though, given the events of the previous evening, it had been an *informed* lucky guess. 'And which of them was he?' he continued.

Makepeace looked confused. 'I'm sorry, you've lost me.'

'Was he drunk, or was he ill?'

'He was neither. He was dead!'

But of course he was, Charlie thought.

'What caused his death?' he asked.

'I don't know, exactly,' Makepeace said, 'but there was a lot of blood on the back of his head.'

'So it looked almost as though he had arranged to meet

somebody, and that somebody had sneaked up behind him and hit him with some kind of weapon, wouldn't you say?' Charlie Swift speculated.

'Maybe,' Makepeace said weakly. 'I honestly don't know. I didn't stop to think about it.'

'Had he been dead long?'

'How should I know? I'm not a doctor.'

'Take a guess – just to please me.'

'No, I don't think he'd been dead long.'

'So it was quite a coincidence wasn't it?'

'Coincidence?'

'The fact that you happened to be walking along the riverbank, something you never do, just after he'd been killed.'

'Yes . . . no . . . I don't know. For God's sake, Charlie, maybe it was fate or something.'

'And was there anyone else around when you discovered the body?' Swift asked.

'No, there wasn't anybody – not a soul.'

'You'll have to report it to the police, you know,' Charlie said. 'You should have done it already.'

'Are you mad?' Makepeace exploded. 'Have you gone completely off your head? If I report it, they're bound to suspect that I killed him – especially after what happened in that pub last night.'

'After what happened in that pub last night, they'll suspect you whether you report it or not,' Charlie Swift pointed out. 'By reporting it yourself, you'll at least raise an element of doubt.'

'Raise an element of doubt! I have absolutely no idea what you're talking about.'

'The police might ask themselves why a guilty man would report the murder, rather than seizing his opportunity to run away while he still had it.'

'But that's exactly why I'm here,' Makepeace said.

'To ask me to go with you to the police station?'

'To ask you for some money, to help me get away.'

'Why me?' Charlie wondered.

'Isn't it obvious?'

'No.'

'I came to you because you're my friend and my lover.'

'Your friend and lover,' Charlie mused. 'I'm a good friend and lover who, if things had gone according to plan – which is to say if Comstock hadn't been murdered – would have woken up the day after tomorrow to discover that you'd been posted and – seemingly without any regret on your part – had completely disappeared from my life forever.'

'It wasn't like that,' Makepeace said.

'Then how was it?' Charlie wondered.

There was no satisfactory answer to the question, and Makepeace didn't waste his time trying to find one.

'The other reason that I've come to you is because I know you're a rich man,' he said. 'You should have no difficulty in raising a couple of thousand pounds before they find the body.'

'Finding the body might not take them long at all. Didn't you tell me it's just off the path, where anybody could see it?'

'What I said was that it *was* just off the path when I first noticed it. But it isn't there now, because I've moved it into some thick bushes.'

'So you're asking me to raise a couple of grand to help you – a murderer – escape?' Charlie Swift asked.

'But I'm not a murderer,' Makepeace protested. 'I keep telling you I'm not, but you won't listen.'

'You've told me, but I don't believe you,' Charlie said. 'Listen, even though it will look bad that you hit him from behind, you still might be able to plead self-defence. You could say that you thought it was the only way that you could protect yourself after he launched an unprovoked attack on you last night.'

'I'm not going to jail, not even for a single night,' Makepeace said, reverting to his normal arrogant self, now that all other ploys had clearly failed. 'You're going to give me two thousand pounds to help me make my escape with, and when I'm safely established somewhere that the law can't reach me, I'll send a message to you that I want another two thousand pounds.'

'And on and on, forever and ever, amen?' Charlie asked.

'No, of course not,' Makepeace protested, realising – belatedly – that it might have been wiser to have left the last part of his statement unsaid. 'Once I've got the four thousand pounds, that will be the end of it, and I'll never bother you again.'

'Even though we're such friends and lovers?'

'It would hurt me not to see you again, of course, but I'd be doing it for your sake.'

'I don't believe any of it,' Charlie said. 'Apart from the fact that you want my money, I don't believe a single word you've said.'

Makepeace grinned. 'Well, to be honest, Charlie, I can't say I blame you,' he replied. 'If I were in your shoes, I wouldn't believe me either.'

'So can you give me one good reason why I should do as you ask?' Charlie inquired.

'I can give you a very good reason,' Makepeace said. 'If I'm caught and charged with murdering a Yank, the Americans will probably demand that I'm hanged for it, and if that's what they want, that's probably what they'll get, because we certainly can't afford to piss off our American cousins at the moment.'

'I have faith in British justice,' Charlie said. 'I don't think it will give way to expediency.'

'Then you're a fool,' Makepeace told him. 'They'll sentence me to death, all right, and when they do, I'll confess to being a homo and having an affair with you. Why wouldn't I? I'd have nothing to lose, because there'd be no point in sentencing a man to two years imprisonment if they were going to hang him the following week. But it would be different for you, wouldn't it? They'd try you, and sentence you, and bang you up for at least a couple of years – maybe more, taking into consideration the sort of company you've been keeping. And you really wouldn't like that, would you, Charlie?'

'No,' Charlie Swift admitted, 'I wouldn't.'

Makepeace laughed triumphantly. 'There you are, you see,' he said. 'Short of killing me, you have no choice but to give in to my demands.'

EIGHTEEN

16 October 1974

A s I didn't know where Charlie Swift was, I couldn't have told him that I would be flying back in England this afternoon even if I'd wanted to, but I wouldn't have, anyway. I want no more to do with Charlie. No, it's even stronger than just 'want' – if I wish to maintain my sanity I can't *allow* myself to have anything to do with him – because even now, as I watch all the suitcases going round and round on the luggage carousel and wait for my own to appear, just the thought of Charlie is almost enough to make me break down.

I pick up my bag and head for customs and excise. There are no heavily moustachioed, gun-toting policemen here, just a few officials who seem either tired or bored, and barely give me a glance.

There is a metal barrier in the arrivals' hall, and a fair number of people are standing behind it. Some of them are obviously waiting for family members, and have looks of excited anticipation on their faces. Others, equally obviously, have been sent to pick up people they have never met before, and hold signs in front of them with the stranger's name written on them. And then there is one man who bridges the two groups. He is both emotional *and* holding a sign.

And what he has written on the sign is 'Carrot Top'.

A few days ago – maybe even as late as yesterday – the sign would have simultaneously amused and infuriated me. Now it seems like nothing more than a desperate, pathetic attempt on his part to recapture what we once had – and that simply isn't going to happen.

He tries to kiss me on the cheek, and when I turn away, he pretends not to notice.

He reaches out for my suitcase, and when I don't hand it over, he shrugs, as if that means nothing at all.

I break away from the crowd that has gathered to greet returning friends and relatives – oh, how I wish some of them had been waiting for me – and make my way towards the car rental desks.

Charlie tags along beside me.

'Aren't you surprised I managed to track you down?' he asks. 'I think I'd make a pretty good detective myself.'

I say nothing, but just keep walking.

'So did you learn anything useful while you were in Majorca, or were you just having a cosy holiday at the college's expense?' he asks – his voice kept light, to demonstrate that he knows I'm no slacker and it's just a joke.

I maintain my silence, but it's getting harder all the time.

'Oh, come on, Jennie, say something,' he urges.

So I do.

'You know you've made a complete bloody fool out of me, don't you, you bastard?' I say.

'Aren't you blowing this out of proportion?' he asks, still trying to be reasonable, but obviously hurt. 'It's true I didn't tell you that I knew James Makepeace, but . . .'

I come to a sudden halt, drop my suitcase on the floor, and swing round to face him.

'You didn't tell me you *knew* him!' I scream. 'You did more than bloody *know* him, didn't you? You were screwing the bloody arse off him!'

Lots of people stop to see what the commotion is all about – perhaps even to revel in this unexpected street entertainment – but I've reached the point at which I don't give a damn who hears me.

'Jennie,' Charlie says, softly and urgently, 'please just listen to what I have to say.'

'All right,' I agree.

He draws me away from the small crowd that has gathered, and even though they're all bursting to hear the next thrilling instalment, none of them has the nerve to follow us.

'First of all,' Charlie says, when he judges we've put a big enough distance between ourselves and the rubberneckers, 'I didn't know it was James Makepeace's body in the old vent.'

I'm not letting him get away with that.

'You didn't know for *certain*,' I correct him. 'But after all the trouble with the American in the pub, you must have considered it a strong possibility.'

'Ah, you've found out about that,' he says.

'Did you think I wouldn't?' I wonder.

'I didn't know whether you would or not,' he confesses. 'But it's true that the need to find out is the reason I hired you.'

'Is that supposed to make sense?' I ask.

'You were quite right just now, when you said that I suspected one of the bodies might have been James,' Charlie said, 'and if it did turn out to be him, I was afraid the police might suspect me of murdering him.'

'And why would they have done that?'

Charlie shrugs. 'Well, you know . . .'

'Because he was your lover?'

'Yes, and . . . and there might have been other things as well.'

'Such as?'

'They might have suspected that he was blackmailing me.'

'And was there any reason they might have had that suspicion?'

Another shrug. 'They'd know that Makepeace would have needed to get away in a hurry after Comstock was murdered.' He pauses. 'You know who Comstock was, don't you?'

'Yes, I know who Comstock was,' I confirm.

'They might have thought that he'd threatened to reveal our relationship if I didn't give him money. And that's why I didn't tell you all about it from the start – because I wanted to see if you could find it out by yourself.'

'You mean that if a smart girl like me couldn't find out, it was very unlikely that the police would?'

'Exactly,' he says, gratefully.

'And it didn't matter what happened to me, did it? It didn't matter that you'd put me at risk, and that I could have gone to jail – could *still* go to jail – for concealing evidence!'

'If I'd thought for a second that I was putting you at risk, I'd never have done it,' he says. 'But I didn't think *at all*. I was so panicked that I never considered any of the implications.'

I pick up my suitcase, and head straight towards the car rental booths.

'There's no need for that. I'll drive you wherever it is that you want to go,' Charlie says.

'I don't want you to do anything for me, ever again,' I tell him – and I'm breaking my heart anew even as I say the words.

We stop arguing when we reach the rental desk, and Charlie doesn't say another word until the girl behind the desk has the distraction of ringing the garage to order up my vehicle.

And even then, he speaks in little more than a whisper.

'Are you still on the case?' he asks.

Yes, I'm still on the case. I'm on it because I still have some of the generous retainer left – and now, of course, I know *why* it was so generous – and I'm damned if I'm giving it back to Charlie.

I'm on it because I'm that kind of person – because I don't like to walk away and leave unanswered questions behind me.

And I'm on it because, deep down inside myself, I still think I might find a way to help Charlie.

No, that third reason's bullshit, I think, dismissing it.

It simply *has to be* bullshit!

'Are you still on the case?' Charlie repeats.

'Yes, I'm still on the bloody case!'

'Then I might have a lead for you.'

'A lead!' I say dismissively. 'Oh, come on, Charlie – you might think that finding out when I was landing makes you some kind of super sleuth, but you're just deluding yourself!'

But then I think about it, and I decide that however preposterous his lead might be, it still has be a prizewinner in comparison to the leads I've got – which are approximately none – so I add, 'All right, let's hear it.'

'At the time Comstock was killed, he was being investigated by an American military policeman called Donald Dickerson,' Charlie says.

'Who told you that?'

'James Makepeace.'

'Oh, well, if it comes from such an impeccable source as your piece-of-shit ex-lover . . .'

'Just listen,' Charlie says. 'When the war ended, Dickerson didn't go back to the States. He stayed on in England – in Oxfordshire – because he'd married a local girl.' He hands me a piece of paper. 'This is his address and telephone number.'

I put it in my bag. 'Right, you've done what you came here to do, so there's no absolutely point in you hanging around and getting in my way any longer, Charlie,' I say.

He looks at me through eyes which are deep pools of misery.

'I know I've screwed up badly, but isn't there anything I can do or say . . .?' he begins.

'Nothing comes to mind,' I interrupt him.

I watch him walk away. He is doing a fair impersonation of a broken man. Well, that's what comes of unscrupulously using other people, and I've no sympathy for him.

In fact, now that I've seen the real Charlie for myself, I'm amazed that I ever even liked him, let alone felt any real affection for him. And if I'm certain of one thing, it's that I feel absolutely nothing for him now.

I sign the appropriate forms, and the girl behind the desk gives me the set of car keys.

'Normally, you'd have to take the shuttle bus to our lot,' she says, 'but we're having a quiet day, and in order to save you time, I've had someone from the garage drive it right up to the terminal.'.

'You're very kind,' I tell her – and I feel so grateful for that kindness that for one mad moment, I contemplate becoming a lesbian and doing all I can to win her love.

She reels off a registration number.

'Would you like me to write it down for you?' she asks.

She is so very, very kind, I think emotionally, and I wonder what I can possibly do in return.

'Shall I write it down?' she asks.

I detect impatience in her voice. There's no more than a tiny sliver of it, but it is enough for her to cease to be – in my eyes – a paragon of all that is virtuous and good, and to shrink her down to the pleasant, helpful, but totally unexceptional woman that she obviously is.

'No, there's no need to write it down – I'll remember it,' I say, and reel off the numbers myself, before she has a chance to ask me if I'm sure.

The car she's promised me – a nice new electric blue Ford Escort – is waiting there for me just where she said it would be.

I climb in, and insert the ignition key. I'm intending to drive away, but instead I just sit there and sob my heart out.

I don't know why – I just do.

NINETEEN

The man who answers the front door of the chocolate-box-pretty thatched cottage, just outside Abingdon, is in his late fifties. He is balding, and slightly overweight, though he seems quite comfortable with both these signs of aging. But looking him up and down (surreptitiously, of course, which is something we private eyes learn to do) I feel as if I can detect an entirely different man beneath the surface; this one young and eager and earnest and slim, with a crew-cut that declares proudly that he is an American – and couldn't possibly be anything else.

'Captain Dickerson?' I ask, out of politeness.

He grins. 'I was Captain Dickerson once upon a time, little lady, but that was before you were born,' he says. 'Now, I'm just plain old Donald T Dickerson, taxi driver of this parish.'

His accent is a melange of southern-fried American and mid-Oxfordshire educated-yokel English, and he has just been very disingenuous – or possibly merely modest – about his occupation, because I've been checking up on him, and he owns a small fleet of taxis and minibuses.

'Come inside,' he says. 'My wife isn't here at the moment, but I'm one of those liberated guys who can not only find his own way to the kettle, but can actually switch it on, so with a little bit of luck, I just might be able to produce a passable cup of tea.'

I like the man, and – much more to the point – I'm on the verge of trusting him.

He leads me into a large kitchen with an oak-beamed ceiling. There is an inglenook fireplace taking up most of one wall, and in the centre of the fireplace sits a wood-burning stove, surrounded by drying logs.

'Take a seat,' Dickerson says, indicating a large scrubbed table that I guess is used both for preparing the food and for dining at.

'This place is pretty English, hey?' he asks me.

'So English, Mr Dickerson, that most English people probably wouldn't recognise it,' I tell him.

'Call me Don,' he says. He grins again – it seems to come naturally to him. 'Yeah, I guess you're right about it being ultra-English. That's the trouble with us converts – we go way over the top.'

He crosses over the kitchen to the sink, and fills the kettle.

'If you'd told me before the war that I'd end up living in a country so small that you could slip it into one corner of Texas without it even being noticed, I'd have said you were crazy,' he tells me.

When the kettle boils, he warms the pot and measures out the tea from a swirling-patterned tea caddy.

No tea bags for this man – he is, as he has already acknowledged himself, as traditionally English as only a foreigner could be.

'Yep, I'd have said you were crazy, if you'd said that,' he repeats. 'And then I met my Susan at a dance at the base, our eyes met, we whirled around the floor to the music of Glenn Miller, and my fate was sealed.'

'That's a nice story,' I say.

'And what's even nicer is that it happens to be true,' he counters.

He brings the teapot, cups and saucers, milk jug, sugar bowl, sieve, spoons – and, of course, a packet of biscuits (ginger nuts) – over to the table.

A look of mild horror comes to his face, because – I guess – he's made the connection between my hair and the biscuits.

'I didn't mean to . . .' he says. 'It's not as if . . . it's just that ginger nuts are my favourites.'

'They're my favourites, too,' I say, which is diplomatic, if not entirely accurate.

He nods gratefully, then performs the tea ceremony (three spoons of sugar for him, none for me). He takes a sip of his own tea, and sighs in approval.

'I think I'm finally getting the hang of this,' he says.

'I think you're far too modest,' I tell him.

We both laugh, then his face grows more serious.

'When you rang me, you told me you wanted to talk about Sergeant Comstock,' he says.

'That's right,' I agree.

'Comstock was one of those guys who would have sold his own grandma if the price had been right,' Dickerson says. 'Hell, he'd have sold her to five or six different guys at the same time, if he'd thought he could get away with it. He was what you'd call a wheeler-dealer from way back, and he saw his time in England as an opportunity to make a real killing on the black market.'

This isn't really pertinent to my investigation, but the man has given up his own time to see me – not to mention providing me with a very nice cup of tea and some ginger nut biscuits – so the least I can do is show a little interest. And perhaps there's a reason he's dealing with this side of Comstock's life first – perhaps he's building up the nerve which he feels will be necessary if he's to talk about homosexuality in front of a 'little lady'.

'Yes, he saw it just like that – a way to make a real killing,' Dickerson says, then falls silent.

And it occurs to me that he's expecting me to take a more active part in this conversation.

'So what was it he decided to sell?' I ask. 'Was it petrol?'

For a moment, it seems as if he's no idea what I'm talking about, and then he grins again.

'I've lived in this country for over thirty years, yet when I fill up my car, I still think of it as gas – not petrol – I'm putting into the tank,' he says. He shakes his head in answer to my question. 'No, it wasn't that. The problem with gas – with petrol – is that while it might have been easy enough to siphon off from the big old tank on the base, it was too easily traceable on the outside.'

'What do you mean?' I ask.

'See, petrol was subject to the strictest sort of rationing. Everybody got the same number of eggs (damn few!) no matter who they were, but you only got petrol if you could prove that you needed it for essential war work. So if you were stopped at a roadblock, and had no documentation which stated you'd been allowed extra fuel by this ministry or that ministry, then the authorities knew straight away that you'd obtained it illegally. And there was only one place you could have got it from – the military base. So it wasn't a giant step from that to working out which particular soldier had sold it to you, which meant that those soldiers who might have thought about it – Sergeant Comstock amongst them – soon decided it just wasn't worth the risk.'

'So what *was* safer for them to deal in, Don?' I ask. 'Was it perhaps cigarettes?'

'Yeah, there was certainly a market in cigarettes – but it wasn't a big one,' Dickerson says. 'Nearly everything was rationed, you know – even bread went on the ration card at one point. But there were two things – and two things only – that the British government made sure were *never* rationed. The first was beer, and the second was cigarettes. And strange as it may seem to you, some Brits preferred their own tiny cigarettes (like Woodbines) to jumbo smokes like Pall Mall and Camel.'

'There's no accounting for taste,' I say, and all the time – because he's challenged me to find an answer, and I hate to give up – I'm thinking about what the Yanks might have been bloody selling.

And then it comes to me.

'What he was selling was nylon stockings, wasn't it?' I say.

'Do you know how nylon got its name?' he asks.

I groan inwardly, because this is going to be one of those fascinating facts that I so rarely find fascinating – but, like I said, he provided the tea and biscuits, and it seems only polite to go along with him.

'Isn't it because it was developed in laboratories in New York and London?' I ask, assuming that's the answer he wants me to give.

He beams with pleasure that I've not just got it wrong, but got it wrong in precisely the right way.

'That's a mistake that a lot of people make,' he says. 'It's certainly a very neat and tidy explanation, but, sad to say, it's a load of horsefeathers. It was, in fact, developed exclusively at DuPont Chemicals lab in Delaware – nothing at all to do with New York or London. They were originally going to call this marvellous new product "no run", but the problem with that was that it *did* run. So they played around with a few letters until they came up with a word which sounded about right – and that word was nylon.'

'So it *was* nylon stockings that Comstock was selling?' I say, as a gentle reminder that I haven't come here to be given a short history of the American petro-chemical industry.

'That's right,' he agrees. 'Comstock had cut a deal with one of the pilots who was flying in what were regarded as essential supplies for our boys – peanut butter, jello and the like. He must have brought in thousands of pairs before we had a clue what was going on. It was with the arrival of the stockings, of course, that James Makepeace comes into the picture.'

'So there was a business relationship between them before it became a sexual relationship, was there?' I ask, trying to make it easier for him to approach the almost-taboo subject by making him aware that I already know all about it.

'A sexual relationship?' Don Dickerson repeats. And we're both surprised – him by my statement, me by his reaction to it. 'Whatever are you talking about, my dear?'

'They were both homosexual, weren't they?' I ask.

'Makepeace might have been a faggot for all I know, but Comstock was about as hetero as they come. He didn't have much time for the niceties of the male-female relationship, mind you

– flowers and chocolates just weren't his things – he was more of a "wham, bam, thank you, ma'am" kind of guy – except that, a lot of the time, he missed out the "thank you" part.'

'Are you sure about this?' I ask him.

'I'm absolutely certain. There are a couple of ex-whores living not more than a couple of miles from here, who regarded servicing Sergeant Comstock as almost a full-time job. Incidentally, one of them is now a justice of the peace, but I suppose that's neither here nor there.'

So why had Mr Gough claimed that Comstock was homosexual when he clearly wasn't? And why *hadn't* he mentioned that Makepeace had been assisting Comstock in his black market activities?

It seems to me that there's only one possible explanation – he was laying down smokescreens to confuse me.

And why would he do that?

Again, there is only one possible explanation – he must have done it because he was trying to protect someone!

'You see, what Comstock needed was someone on the outside for distribution purposes, and Makepeace just fitted the bill perfectly,' Dickerson says. 'He was exactly the right man for the job, as he proved with the distribution plan that he came up with, which was so simple that it was almost genius.'

'What was it?'

'He got on well with women. I know that for a fact, because, a couple of times, I watched him in action. They found him charming. I believe a lot of women find faggots charming.'

I think about Charlie Swift – my own dear Charlie – though not in the present, where there are problems, but in the past, when there weren't.

'Yes,' I agree, 'they can be quite charming.'

'So Makepeace made friends with a couple of dozen working girls – and by that, I don't mean the kind of working girls who Comstock got his rocks off with, just the other side of the wire. What I'm talking about here are women who made things or grew things.'

'I understand,' I say.

'So he chats all these women up, and then he says to them, hey, if you sell these stockings in your factory or on that big farm you're working on, you can keep ten percent of everything you make. So, at bargain rates, he's got a dedicated sales force – and, for a while, it works like a charm.'

'So what went wrong?'

'You know that Makepeace had done officer training at Eton, and that made it more than likely he'd be called up, long before the invasion of France.'

'Yes, I understand how it worked,' I say.

'Well, he learned that he was about be posted away, and since there wasn't much chance he'd ever come back to Oxford – at least not while Comstock was still around – he decided that it would be pointless to share the last couple of weeks' profits with the sergeant. The only problem was that Comstock found out all about it, and when he ran across Makepeace in a pub in Oxford, they had an argument that soon turned to violence.'

'How do you know all this?' I ask.

'Comstock was with his two minders – and one of them, unbeknownst to him, was one of my people, who had been collecting evidence for weeks.'

'When did Comstock turn up dead?'

'It was less than twenty-fours later. The killer had hidden him in the bushes near the river, but a dog sniffed him out, and the dog's owner rang the police straight away.'

'And was it Makepeace who killed him?'

'Almost definitely.'

'And the police knew this?'

'Sure, we told them everything, because we'd had it clearly pointed out to us that once we left the base, it was their world we were operating in, and they were entitled to whatever we had.'

'So why wasn't Makepeace arrested immediately? And why is there nothing about this in police records?'

'The answer to both those questions is that the whole affair was more about politics than it was about justice,' Dickerson says.

'What do you mean?'

'There was already some friction between the base and some of the civilian population. Naturally enough, the young men (who saw all the prettiest girls from their village going around with GIs) and the mothers and fathers of those girls (who feared their daughters would be deflowered by one of these gum-chewing barbarians) were the most vehement, but they were by no means the only ones who resented the Yanks. Arresting Makepeace would only have inflamed the situation further.'

'Yes, I imagine it would have,' I agree.

'The Yanks would have demanded instant frontier justice. It would have been naïve of them to expect to see Makepeace hanging over the camp's main gate, but then a lot of these boys came from the backwoods, and they *were* naïve. And as for the Brits – there were a good number of them who would have objected to an English gentleman being arrested for killing a mere colonial barrow boy.'

'So you did nothing?'

'So we passed the problem right up the chain of command, and waited for the powers-that-be, on both sides of the pond, to decide whether justice should be done, or whether – in the interest of the greater good – justice should be ignored. And while we were waiting for their decision, Makepeace disappeared, so the whole problem went away.'

'What would you say if I told you that he was discovered dying in one of St Luke's quads, and that his last words, spoken to the head porter, were that the Yanks had done for him?'

'I'd say it's perfectly possible that Corporal Hicks – he was the Comstock minder who *wasn't* working for me – managed to track Makepeace down and do just what you say Makepeace possibly accused him of doing,' Dickerson replies. 'On the other hand, it's equally possible that Makepeace never said that at all, and that the head porter put those words in his mouth to protect one of your own.'

'What do you mean by that?'

'I mean that maybe Makepeace identified someone from St Luke's as the killer.'

'Like who, for example?' I force myself to ask

'Like the boyfriend he had with him on the night of the fight with Comstock.'

'Charlie Swift,' I say, with my gut sinking further with each word.

'I didn't know his name,' Dickerson tells me, 'but say this Swift gets worried that if Makepeace is arrested, it will come out about them being all queers together. Maybe he decides that would ruin him, and that the only solution is to kill Makepeace.'

Yes, maybe that was it, I think miserably. That's almost exactly what Charlie said the police would think – and maybe, too, it's exactly what *did* happen.

TWENTY

16 October 1974

I find Detective Inspector George Hobson sitting on the stairs outside my office. The pose seems reminiscent of something, but I'm not sure what, until I remember those old black-and-white American films, in which the angry cop pays the free-spirited private eye a visit. Actually, now I've got the context, I can see it's a pretty good *hommage* he's put on, though it would have been better still if he'd been wearing a heavy raincoat (rather than a Millet's anorak) and had had a fedora hat pulled down over his eyes.

Pen in hand, he's studying his newspaper, and though he looks up briefly when I reach the foot of the stairs, he goes back to the paper, as if I'm of no further interest to him.

As I get closer, I can see that what he's working on is a monster crossword puzzle, and that its almost entirely filled in, but when I attempt to take a better look at it, he quickly closes the paper, which suggests to me that the puzzle is no more than a prop, and the squares are filled with random letters.

I step around him, take out my keys, and unlock the office door. He makes no move to follow me.

'All right, so you're the roughest, toughest cop ever to have walked the mean streets of South Oxford – and I'm impressed,' I tell him over my shoulder. 'Now are you going to come into my office or not?'

He says nothing.

Well, screw him!

I open the office door, and step over the threshold.

'What do you know about the two bodies that were found in the ventilation shaft in St Luke's College?' he asks.

I freeze. 'I'm not sure I . . .' I begin.

'And before you say something that you might later regret, I should inform you that Lord Swift says you know nothing about them at all.'

'If he says that, then it must be true, mustn't it?' I ask. 'After all, if you can't trust a member of the British aristocracy, who can you trust?'

'You're playing games with me, aren't you, Jennie?' he asks harshly. 'You have been for days.'

'*You're* playing games with me,' I counter. 'You're even talking out of the corner of your mouth, like a poor man's Humphrey Bogart.'

He laughs loudly – as if to acknowledge that I've just caught him out fair and square.

'I'll tell you what I think,' he says, more seriously. 'I think you've known about these two dead bodies for quite a while, and that when you had the opportunity to tell me about them, you didn't take it. In other words, you have lied to the police, and are guilty of obstruction of justice.'

It's worse than that – I didn't just lie to the police, I lied to a friend. But the problem was, I thought I had another friend – an even closer friend – who needed me to do just that.

'It was this clash of loyalties . . .' I begin.

I know that I sound totally inadequate, but it's hard not to when you *are* inadequate.

'I must admit I was a little hurt at first – maybe even a little betrayed,' Hobson says.

'It wasn't about you,' I protest. 'It was about . . .'

'But I've got over that,' Hobson interrupts. 'And do you know *why* I've got over it?'

He falls silent, and it's clear that he's not going to speak again until I've forced myself to say something.

'No,' I say in a mechanical voice which is floating on an underlay of dread. 'No, I don't know why you've got over it.'

'I've got over it because this very afternoon, something exceptional happened. I – Detective Inspector George Hobson – have personally closed up not just one murder case, but two,' he says.

My mouth is dry, my head is pounding. I know that this is going to be just awful.

'The first murder was of James Makepeace,' he continues. 'Remember him, Jennie? I think we were discussing his disappearance in the Bulldog, only a few days ago.'

'Yes, we were,' I say.

'And the second is the murder of Lennie Moon.' He makes a great show of lighting up a cigarette. 'Now I'd like to say the case was solved by brilliant deduction on my part, but the truth of the matter is, the murderer just marched into the station this afternoon, and confessed.'

'It wasn't . . .' I gasp.

But it was – it *had* to be!

'That's right, the murderer is none other than Lord Charles Edward George Withington Danby Swift,' George Hobson says.

'It can't be him. That just isn't possible,' I argue.

But hasn't it already crossed my mind that Charlie might have killed Makepeace, so is it that much of a stretch to accept that he could have killed Lennie Moon as well?

Yes, it *is* too big a bloody stretch! A younger Charlie might have panicked and murdered Makepeace if he'd been threatened, but – though I've been wrong on so many other things about him – I'm still convinced that the Charlie I know would never have killed a holy innocent like Lennie.

'Well, you may think he didn't do it, but as well as me, two detective constables and one other detective inspector have heard what he's had to say, and we're convinced he's our man.'

'He's conned you,' I say. 'I don't know why he should want to do it, but that's what he's done.'

'The one thing he's *yet* to do is sign a confession,' George continues, as if I've never spoken, 'and he's more than willing to do that if I'll just bend the rules a little for him. Now normally, as you know, I wouldn't bend the rules for anyone, except possibly you – and that's all in the past – but since Lord Swift has been so very co-operative . . .'

I've been wondering why George has taken the trouble to come to my office and explain all this to me, and now I know.

'He wants to talk to me, doesn't he?' I say.

'Yes, that's right,' George agrees. 'He wants to talk to you.'

Even the thought of seeing him in those circumstances is enough to fill me with an unhappiness that is almost too much to bear. If

I thought I could persuade him to change his story, I'd endure even that, but my gut, my heart and my brain all tell me I couldn't.

I can't see him!

I won't see him!

'I don't want to talk to Charlie,' I tell George Hobson.

'I can well believe that,' George replies, 'but after the way we both know you've betrayed our friendship, I think you owe me at least that.'

He's right.

I do.

The interview room is on the first floor of the police station. It is painted in dark brown to waist height, and from there to the ceiling it is a sickly cream which, to me, says lamb's vomit, (though I must confess to never having actually seen a lamb throw up). The table is wooden, and wobbles, unless a doubled-up empty cigarette packet is placed carefully under the front left leg. The seats are of the folding metal variety, and are sprayed in olive green. The only source of natural light comes from a window set high in the wall opposite the door.

This is not the first time I've been in this room, not by a long chalk. In my brief career as a detective constable – which ended, ingloriously, in my enforced resignation – I conducted at least a dozen interviews in here. And, much more recently, during the Shivering Turn investigation, it began to seem as though I would never leave the place.

And here I am again – alone and waiting.

The door swings open, and Charlie is escorted into the room by two police constables. One of them must just have scraped the minimum height qualification – the other is so large he could almost scrape the ceiling. Giant-constable points Charlie towards the table, then watches him sit down opposite me. Mini-constable positions himself in the corner closest to the door. Once Charlie is seated, giant-constable takes his leave.

I look hopefully across at mini-constable.

'Sorry, ma'am, I have to stay,' he says, reading my mind, 'but I promise I won't be listening.'

Is there anything more depressing than being called 'ma'am' by a very small policeman?

Yes – and you have to trust me on this – it is much more depressing to look across the table at a man who has just confessed to two murders, and happens to be your best friend.

I had planned on a calm, reasoned approach to this meeting, but it doesn't quite work out that way, because my first words are, 'For Christ's sake, what do you think you're doing, you *bloody moron!*'

'I'm so ashamed of myself,' Charlie says. 'You told me I was putting you at risk with my cowardly behaviour, and you were quite right. Well, you're not at risk any more. Detective Inspector Hobson has assured me of that. That's one of the two reasons I asked to see you – to let you know you'll be all right.'

'And what was the other one?'

'We'll never meet again, Jennie, and I just wanted you to know that you are very dear to me – dearer than anyone else I have ever known.'

I can cry – or I can be the hard-boiled private eye.

I choose the latter, and I don't think I've ever put as much effort into anything as I'm putting into being the private eye right now.

'Let's go back to your first reason,' I say. 'Are you seriously claiming that the only reason that you confessed was because there was a possibility that if you didn't, I might get a prison sentence?'

'No, no, of course not,' Charlie says, glancing nervously at mini-cop. 'I confessed to the murder of James Makepeace because I was the person who killed him.'

'Why did you kill him?' I ask.

'You must surely have been able to work that out for yourself by now,' he says. 'The police were on his tail, and he needed money in a hurry, so he could make his getaway. He threatened me that if I didn't give it to him, he'd reveal that we were lovers, and I'd go to jail.'

'But he'd have gone to jail himself.'

'True, but by that point, he didn't have much to lose.'

'So you killed him?'

'Yes. I had no choice in the matter. Once I'd given in to his blackmail, I'd never have been free of him.'

'And Mr Gough helped you to get rid of the body?'

'That's right.'

'Why did you kill Lennie?'

'He was right there in the college, the night that I killed James Makepeace. We – that is, Mr Gough and I – persuaded him to keep quiet, but I knew that once the discovery of the bodies became public knowledge, he'd go into a panic. I couldn't let him talk about it, so I went to his bedsit, and I killed him.'

'Why do that, if you were going to confess anyway?'

'At the time, I didn't *know* I was going to confess. I only made up my mind after I'd met you off the plane.'

'So you killed Lennie needlessly.'

'I suppose so.'

'You *suppose* so. Is that all you can say?'

'What else can I say?'

'And don't you feel guilty about it?'

'Yes, I suppose I do.'

But he *doesn't* feel guilty – and that's not because he's incapable of feeling guilt, it's because he has nothing to feel guilty about.

'So you broke his neck,' I say.

'Yes.'

'Just like that?

'Just like that.'

'Breaking a neck is not as easy as most people seem to think it is,' I say. 'You have to get the right angle on it for a start, and you have to exert just the right pressure on just the right points at just the right time. It's a skilled job, especially when the person whose neck you're breaking is as big and strong as Lennie Moon was.'

'Stop this, Jennie,' Charlie hisses, glancing nervously at mini-constable. 'Stop it before you ruin everything.'

'By which you mean, before I persuade the police that you couldn't have done it.'

'I killed James Makepeace and I killed Lennie Moon,' Charlie says stubbornly.

'Who are you trying to protect, Charlie?' I demand. 'And why would you even want to protect the bastard who killed poor harmless Lennie?'

Charlie stands up.

'I want to go back to the cells,' he says to the mini-cop. 'I want to go right now!'

TWENTY-ONE

W hen I was growing up, people in Whitebridge used to say, 'Is it cold, or is it just me?' and that's exactly what I ask myself as I step out of the police station and onto St Aldate's.

It certainly *feels* cold to me, but then I've just come back from five days on the temperate island of Majorca, haven't I?

And maybe it *feels* cold to me because I'm in a state of shock – because my best friend has just told me that we'll never see each other again.

I hear a voice shouting, 'Extra, extra, latest edition!' and when I instinctively turn round to face him, I see the newspaper seller is wrapped-up from head to foot against the cold.

So it isn't just me who's feeling it, I think, starting to feel better.

And then I see the placard in front of him, and I instantly start to feel worse again.

OXFORD MAN COMES BACK FROM THE DEAD – AND DIES AGAIN.

The headline is self-explanatory – at least to me – but I buy the newspaper anyway.

The article isn't on the front page, but it takes up three of the inside ones, because the picture editor has obviously seen this as an excuse to pull a couple of standard shots out of his Spanish collection. Thus, there is a picture of a beach which at the opposite end of the island to the place where I met Mr Gough, and a picture of a cliff which I'm almost sure is on the island of Menorca. But there are also some more domestic shots – the modest bungalow where Mr Gough and his wife appear to have lived, and the beaten up Seat 500 which seems to have been his main transportation around the island.

I scan the article.

A man who committed suicide by gassing himself in his own garage in a small town on the Spanish island of

Majorca was known to all his neighbours as John Tate,
but documentation left on the passenger seat clearly
identified him as Edwin Gough, who was once the head
porter at St Luke's College, Oxford. Gough was believed
to have died over twenty years ago, and indeed has a
grave in Sóller Cemetery on that island. Mrs Joan
Maitland, who lived across the road from Tate/Gough,
said, 'He and his late wife were a quiet couple, but they
were always more than willing to help you out, if you
had a problem.'

Was Gough afraid of being dragged back to England to face
the consequences of his acts, I wonder.

I don't think so.

I think the whole process was just too much of an effort now
that he had lost his wife.

I think, in other words, that he simply couldn't be bothered,
and death was an easy – and not too upsetting – experience.

But how like him to have left all the documentation so easily
accessible, I tell myself. He was, I think, a man whose preference
was to have everything cut and dried, but who so often found
himself in a situation where, for the good of the college, cut and
dried simply wouldn't work.

I cross the road, and enter the Bulldog. By the time I reach the
bar, the barman has a glass hovering under the gin optic, and just
wants to know whether I'd like a single or a double.

What do you think I tell him?

I take my double gin and tonic over to one of the small tables
next to the window, and sit down.

It was from this very pub, I remember, that my last really insane
drinking jag began . . .

It had been a hell of a few days.

My father had died, and I was weighed down with guilt over
failing to do things for him that neither I – nor anyone else without
godly powers – could possibly have done.

The case against the Shivering Turn Society, into which I'd
invested my heart and soul, had all-but collapsed.

And somehow, the idea of ordering neat gin chasers to go with

G&Ts had seemed like not just a brilliant idea, but possibly *the* most brilliant idea of the twentieth century.

After the Bulldog, there had been the Red Lion and the Turl. By the time I'd reached the Eagle and Child, I'd probably been too drunk to even consider the possibility that I'd had more than enough.

I don't know how long I was in the Eagle – I was temporarily living in a special fuzzy time, in which minutes and hours played very little part – but I remember crashing my hip into a table occupied by two highly respectable couples out for a quiet drink.

And then, suddenly, Charlie (having been called by the pub landlord) was by my side, and ushering me to the door. The taxi he'd called didn't want to take me – the driver calculated, not unreasonably, that there was a very good chance I'd puke – but Charlie gave him two hundred pounds – then and there – to cover loss of earnings if I did spew up my load.

Once he'd got me home, he undressed me, and put me to bed. He tucked me in, too – he didn't make a particularly good job of it, but it's the thought that counts – and offered to spend the night on my incredibly uncomfortable sofa, if that was what I wanted.

And that's Charlie Swift for you – thoughtful, tolerant, and generous to a fault.

Charlie is simply not the kind of man who would rob someone else of his life (even someone as despicable as James Make-peace had probably been) in order to save himself serving prison time, I tell myself.

I know that now, and I'm very ashamed that I ever doubted it, even for a second.

And if he would never have killed James Makepeace, then he would never – *ever* – have killed Lennie Moon.

He needs me to get him out of this mess – there's simply no one else who can do it – and in order to achieve that, I've suddenly got to become a lot smarter than I seem to have been so far.

I order a second G&T, and think about what I do actually know.

I *know* that Mr Gough blamed Makepeace's murder on the Americans, and (conveniently) that was what Makepeace allegedly claimed himself, just before he died.

It could be the truth, or it could be a lie.

If it was a lie, Mr Gough's reason for telling it was obvious; it tied up all the loose ends, and pointed any future investigations up the most unpromising of blind alleys.

So I can understand that lie. What I *can't* understand is why he would lie about the *reason* for the murder – why he would give it a sexual spin when there clearly wasn't one – because, although Makepeace *was* homosexual, Comstock definitely *wasn't*.

Another question: why did Mr Gough choose to hide the existence of the black market operations from me, when they would have provided not only a *better* explanation of why Makepeace killed Comstock, and Comstock's associates killed Makepeace, but one which, if I chose to investigate it, I would find was actually grounded in fact?

There's only one answer possible – the reason Mr Gough didn't want me looking too closely at the black market racket was because there was something about it that would make me abandon the idea that one of Comstock's gang was the killer, and focus my attention on someone else.

But who could that someone else possibly be?

I really can't see Mr Gough being involved in the black market – it would have been a denial of everything he ever believed in.

I can't see Mr Jenkins becoming involved, either – for pretty much the same reason. Besides, he couldn't have killed Makepeace, because by the time the murder occurred, he was somewhere on the south coast, training to be part of the invasion force.

And what about Lennie Moon? It's inconceivable that the scheme could even have been explained to Lennie. He'd just never have got his head round how it was run.

OK, so I've reached the end of a blind alley, just as Mr Gough intended me to.

Keep calm!

Take a few steps backwards, and then try approaching things from a different angle.

When I told Mr Gough that Lennie had been murdered, his initial reaction was not so much shock as grief – as if he'd always known that Lennie *might* be killed. And that doesn't make sense either, because if you hear a gangster's been killed, you shrug your shoulders and say you suppose it's just an occupational hazard, and the same is pretty much true of a politician.

But a porter – a childlike man who divided his time between the college, his bedsit and the river, where he watched puppies playing and forgot about boats he'd put in the water?

Is there perhaps something – some small grain of truth – in Charlie's explanation of why Lennie had to die?

Charlie said that he'd had to kill Lennie because Lennie had seen him kill Makepeace, which was not true, but is it possible that Lennie saw someone else kill Makepeace?

Maybe, but if he had, then Mr Gough must have known about it, too – if only because Lennie would have found himself incapable of keeping it a secret from his boss.

And if Mr Gough knew, then he'd have been in much the same danger himself, yet he never even gave me so much as a hint that he thought he might be next on the killer's extermination list.

My thoughts are dashing round and round in circles, and if not I'm careful, I warn myself, my hippocampus will become one giant whirlpool, and the rest of my brain will be sucked into it, never to be heard from again.

I order a third gin and tonic – this is going to have to be my last if I'm going to be any good for anything – and turn my mind to my one and only close encounter with Lennie Moon:

'*Mr Jenkins isn't the only man to have a medal from the war,*' he'd said proudly. '*I've got one, too.*'

'*Is that right?*' I'd asked.

'*Yes, I got it when . . .*'

And it had been at that point that Mr Jenkins had intervened.

'*Lennie!*' he'd said, in a much harsher voice than I'd ever heard him use before.

Lennie had looked totally lost.

'*Remember what we said about that medal?*' Mr Jenkins had asked.

But poor Lennie hadn't, and Mr Jenkins had been forced to spell it out for him.

'*We . . . said . . . that . . . you . . . shouldn't . . . talk . . . about . . . the . . . medal . . . to . . . people . . . because . . . it . . . might . . .?*'

'*Because it might make them angry!*'

'*That's right, Lennie, it might make them angry.*'

And later, as we walked around the college together, Mr Jenkins had said to me, '*I hope I didn't sound too harsh back there, but*

people who've got medals can get quite offended when they hear
Lennie pretend to have one – I know they shouldn't, but they do
– and so, in order to avoid any unpleasantness, I've told him never
to talk about it.'

I'd accepted all this easily enough at the time, because Lennie
was merely background to the investigation – a bit player who
didn't merit serious consideration. But he isn't a bit player now
– he's very much centre stage – and the more I think about it, the
more it doesn't add up.

For a start, I don't think Lennie had the kind of imagination
that would have allowed him to conjure up a medal, and – more
specifically – a medal from the war. And Mr Jenkins didn't say
to Lennie that the medal *didn't exist*, nor did he tell me that it
didn't – at least, not as long as Lennie could still hear him. What
he did say to Lennie was that Lennie shouldn't talk about it.

So, given all that, the chances are that there is, in fact, a medal
– but that, for some reason, Mr Jenkins is eager that no one knows
about it.

Suddenly my instinct is getting very excited about the medal,
which means – if that instinct is right – that the medal is going
to be very important – perhaps even crucial – to the investigation.

That's why Lennie's bedsit was searched after his murder, I tell
myself – it was because the murderer was looking for the medal.

If he found it, then I'm left up another blind alley, banging my
head against yet another brick wall.

But if he *didn't* find it, then the chances are the police – who
had both the experience and the time to conduct a proper search
– did find it!

I have a strong urge to ring George Hobson now – to tell him
I demand to see this important medal of Lennie's, which will
explain everything, and will set Charlie Swift free.

I suppress the urge by reminding myself that I am not exactly
in George's good books at the moment, and that the only way I'm
ever going to get to see the medal is by being very persuasive (i.e.
sneaky).

I look at my watch. It is early evening, which means it will be
at least twelve hours before I can do anything positive.

I don't know if my nerves will survive it.

TWENTY-TWO

17 October 1974

George Hobson is a fussy eater. I'm not talking here about the quality of the food he eats – an alley cat would turn up its nose at some of the garbage he joyfully shovels down his gullet – but rather the fact that he likes to make an aesthetically pleasing pattern of his meal before he attacks it. And breakfast is no exception to this rule, I think, as I stand in the doorway of the Early Bird Café, watching him – three tables down – addressing his plate.

Stage one of the process is to cut up his sausage into four equal pieces, and then arrange the pieces around his fried egg, so that, from above, it might well suggest (to any observer) four fat little brown worshippers gathered at a giant monument to the god of the sun. Next, this Salvador Dali of the breakfast plate builds palisades of crispy bacon rashers, which run from one fried tomato minaret to another, around the entire sun temple complex.

I tell myself that the reason I'm blocking the entrance to the café is that I don't want to interrupt him while he's having so much fun, but I know – deep down – what the *real* reason I'm putting off talking to him is.

I know, too, why I'm choosing to frame my current thoughts in this flowery, frivolous, quasi-poetic manner – why I'm thinking of George as dipping one of his newly-cut sun worshippers into his golden lake, before opening his mouth to allow it to make the ultimate sacrifice, when all he's actually doing is swallowing a bit of sausage dipped in egg yolk.

Oh yes, I know what the game is all right!

The game is called put-off-the-moment or perhaps you-can't-face-reality-quite-yet.

But I *can't* put off the moment, and reality *does* have to be faced.

Looking around casually – as people sometimes do – George finally notices me standing in the doorway. His initial surprise lasts no more than a moment, and then he gestures, with a crook of his index finger, that I should join him. It is not perhaps the most welcoming gesture that's ever been aimed at me, but I suppose it's about as good as I'll get.

He waits until I've sat down, then says in a voice thickly coated with world-weariness, 'Why are you here, Jennie?'

'I'm here to stop you making a big mistake,' I tell him.

'Oh, so you're here purely for my benefit, are you?'

'Yes.'

George curls a rasher of bacon around a slice of fried tomato, spears them both with his fork, and pops them into his mouth.

He's making me wait, and he knows he can afford to – because he holds all the power.

'You're here for my benefit,' he repeats, 'and it has nothing at all to do with Charlie Swift?'

'I'm here for him, too.'

'You're just going to have to come to terms with the fact that he did what he said he's done,' Hobson says. 'Everyone else has.'

'It was a clean break, wasn't it?' I say.

'What was a clean break?' George asks, going for a sausage-fried tomato combo this time.

'Lennie's neck,' I say, trying to keep the exasperation out of my voice. 'His bloody neck!'

'Yes, it *was* a clean break, as a matter of fact,' George says – and now he's sounding just a little uncomfortable.

'The doc didn't use the term "professional break" by any chance, did he?' I ask.

George blinks. He only does it the once, but I don't miss it – because it's what I've been looking and hoping for.

'Charles Swift was in the army during the war,' he says, defensively. 'That's probably where he was taught to do it.'

'Taught to do it professionally,' I say, ramming the point home.

'Taught to do it professionally,' he concedes.

'You were in the army,' I say. 'Do you know how to break a man's neck *professionally*?'

'I wasn't in the army during the war,' he says. 'It was peacetime when I did my national service.'

'Ah, so in peacetime, the army doesn't see the need to teach you how to kill, so you all make daisy chains instead.'

'You're being frivolous now.'

'Charlie was a tank commander,' I say, 'and if Lennie had been run over by a tank, you'd get no argument from me if you arrested him. But Lennie wasn't run over by a tank, was he?'

'So you're sure Swift didn't do it?'

'Yes.'

'Then tell me who you think the real killer is, and I promise I'll give it my serious consideration,' George challenges. 'Unless, of course, you can't do that, because you have *no idea* who he is.'

He's expecting me to look down at the table, and mumble something about not knowing who the real killer is, but being certain it isn't Charlie.

But that wouldn't be true because I think I *do* know who killed Lennie. And how did I reach that conclusion? Well, if you rule out Charlie, there's really only one person it *could* be, just as there's only really one person (a different person) who – given all the kerfuffle that occurred after James Makepeace's death – could have killed Makepeace himself. What I still don't know for sure is what motivated Lennie's killer, but I'm starting to agree with Mr Gough that it may have been a mercy killing.

'Well?' George asks, slicing a bit off one of his eggs, and swishing it through the juice left by his tomato.

There's virtually no physical evidence in this case, so if I'm ever to get Charlie out of jail, the murderer is going to have to confess. And who is more likely to get that confession out of him – me or the fried egg monster?

'I can't give you a name at the moment,' I tell him, 'but if you were to answer a couple of my questions, I think that maybe I could.'

'Like what?' George asks.

'If I could look at the evidence that you collected from Lennie's bedsit—'

'That's not a question – that's a request to tamper with the evidence – and the answer's no!' George interrupts.

'You know I'm a good detective,' I say, trying to sound – unsuccessfully – as if I'm not pleading. 'You know that you'd never have cracked the Shivering Turn investigation without me.'

'That's true,' he concedes. 'In fact, there'd never have been an investigation at all, without your persistence.'

'Well, then . . .?' I ask hopefully.

'The answer's still no.'

'Don't let the fact that you hate me at the moment blind you to the need to do what's right,' I beg.

'I don't hate you,' he says sadly, 'it's just that you've turned out to be a big disappointment to me. But even if you hadn't, I wouldn't show you the evidence, because – and listen very carefully to this, to make sure you take it in – because you're *not a police officer.*'

Well, that's Plan A buggered, so we'll have to switch to Plan B – and given that Plan A was desperate, I don't hold out any great hopes for its successor.

But I have to try – for Charlie's sake, I have to try!

'If I talk about some of the things that might have been in Lennie's bedsit, will you confirm whether they were there or not?' I ask.

'I might,' George says.

'A television set? '

'Yes, there was a small colour television.'

'Pictures on the wall?'

'No, there weren't any of those.'

'How about a medal?'

'The last time we discussed medals, you said there was no point in looking for Lennie's medal, because it didn't exist,' George said. 'Was that just another one of your lies?'

'I've never lied to you,' I say. 'I may have avoided telling you the truth, but I've never lied to you.'

'So when you said there wasn't a medal, you really believed there wasn't one?'

'Yes.'

'But now you do believe there is one?'

'Yes.'

'What changed your mind?'

'It's the only thing that makes sense.'

'Well, I'm glad it makes sense to you, because it certainly doesn't make sense to me, and I am not prepared to either confirm or deny that a medal formed part of the evidence collected,' George says, stiffly.

But even if he doesn't realise it, he just has.

'You must have known it was significant the moment you found it, because it had been so carefully hidden,' I say.

'How did you know . . .?' George begins, before clamping his mouth tightly shut.

The answer is that, as with so many other aspects of this particular case, I *don't* know for sure. But if it hadn't been well hidden, then surely the killer would have found it.

The question of *why* it was hidden is much easier to explain – after Lennie told me about the medal, and Mr Jenkins was unusually sharp with him as a result, Lennie would have been living in fear that Mr Jenkins would take his precious medal away from him.

George Hobson has quite given up eating – maybe something I said took his appetite away – and is waiting for me to answer his question.

Well, screw that, I've a good few questions of my own that I need an answer to.

'It wasn't a real medal at all at all, was it?' I ask, taking a blind – if calculated – leap into the dark. 'It wasn't a Victoria Cross, or a DSM, was it? It wasn't even a civilian low-level one – like an Amateur Swimmers' Association proficiency medal.'

'No comment,' George says.

'You've looked it up in the text books, haven't you . . .?' I press on, and a slight flick of his eyebrow tells me I'm right about that, 'but you haven't found anything that even resembles it.'

'If you have any more information which is relevant to this case, I suggest you reveal it now,' George says.

He sounds rattled, but so might any man who's beginning to suspect that maybe his case against a double murderer isn't quite as solid as he thought it was when he got up that morning.

'Well?' George demands.

'The only information I have is that Lennie Moon once told me he had a medal, and Mr Jenkins, the head porter at St Luke's, told me that he didn't.'

'And what sense can you make out of that?'

For the first time in this conversation, I might just have the whip hand and I'm not about to squander it.

'Tell me about the medal,' I say.

George swallows hard, and for a moment I think he's about to tell me to go to hell, then he shakes his head – as if he's appalled at what he's about to do, but he's going to do it anyway.

'It's made out of some sort of alloy,' he says. 'I haven't had time to have it analysed yet.'

'Describe it to me,' I say.

'There's a soldier on the front – at least, he seems like a soldier at first glance, but when you look at him more carefully, you notice he's wearing a peaked cap like the one the porters at St Luke's wear. The only thing on the back of the medal is two words – "For Bravery".'

It's a simple message that even a simple person could understand – and be proud of. I'd been expecting something like that.

'And the medal's engraved, rather than moulded?' I ask.

'Yes, it is,' George agrees. 'So are you going to tell me what it means now?'

'I'm not sure what it means,' I say, and when I see he's getting angry, I hold up my hands to calm him down. 'I'm *really* not sure,' I insist, 'but I'd guess that the medal was made to reward Lennie for doing something, and also as a way of ensuring that he kept quiet about it.'

'When you talk about "something", are you talking about something directly connected with a murder?' Hobson asks bluntly.

'Yes,' I say. 'I rather think I am.'

TWENTY-THREE

17 October 1974

I find Mr Jenkins in the porters' lodge. He is sitting in one of the battered armchairs, and his wife, Lucy, is sitting next to him. They are holding hands, and they look up when I enter, as if they've been expecting me.

And maybe they have.

I walk straight over to the display cases on the far wall.

I don't exactly know why I do that – but if you put the

thumbscrews on me, I suspect I'd probably confess that it was a delaying tactic.

I look at the clipper – the Cutty Sark, isn't it? – and, for a second time, I experience an overwhelming admiration for the craftsman who painstaking constructed it.

Neither of the Jenkins' has yet said a word, but the sound of their silence fills my ears like a graveyard scream.

I turn around. Mr Jenkins has a stoical expression on his face – the look of a man who knows how the drama about to be played before him will end, but recognises that he must sit through the formalities anyway.

Mrs Jenkins is less stoical, like a woman waiting to be told that there is a great malignancy stealthily growing within her body.

'How many boats did you make for Lennie?' I ask Mr Jenkins.

He smiles a sad, weary smile.

'I lost count,' he admits. 'He didn't just lose them on the river, you know – he'd accidentally sit on them, or drop them in the road in front of an oncoming bus. But I still kept making them for him, because he was worth it.'

'And, of course, you made the medal for him,' I say.

Mrs Jenkins squeezes her husband's hand. 'Don't, Harold!' she pleads with him.

He squeezes back.

'It's too late now, love,' he tells her. 'It's far too late.' He turns back to me. 'Yes, I made it. I was part of the army of occupation in Germany at the time, but I sent it back to England, and Mr Gough presented it to him in a secret ceremony he probably made up as he went along. Still, Lennie liked it – Lennie was thrilled.'

'The police have it now, you know,' I tell him.

'Was it in his bedsit?'

'Yes.'

'Then it must have been well-hidden.'

'Are you saying that because you looked very hard, but still couldn't find it?' I ask him.

Lucy Jenkins squeezes her husband's hand again, but he merely pats her arm with his free hand.

'Yes, I'm saying that because I looked and didn't find it,' he agrees. 'Of course, I wasn't at my best when I was conducting the search. In fact, I was rather upset, because I was very fond of Lennie.'

'You'd looked after him for over twenty years,' I say.

'That's right,' he confirms.

'Would you mind if we rolled things back a little and talked about James Makepeace's death?' I ask.

Mr Jenkins shrugs. 'No, I wouldn't mind at all'

'Where were you when he was killed, Mr Jenkins?' I ask.

'I was undergoing a mock interrogation at a secret location on the south coast.'

'And why were you doing that?'

'So that I would know what to expect if I fell into the hands of the Gestapo.'

'Why did you need that special kind of training?'

'Because I belonged to a secret unit – it's *still* secret, as a matter of fact – and there was a very good chance I *would* fall into the hands of the Gestapo.'

'You weren't part of the D-Day Invasion of France at all, were you?' I ask.

'Officially, I was,' he says. 'If you check through the official records of 3rd Infantry Division, you'll find that Lance Corporal Harold Jenkins was in the first wave of troops to land on Sword Beach on the sixth of June 1944, and that's the story I'm supposed to tell anyone who asks.'

'But it isn't true?'

'No, it isn't. By the time the Allied troops landed, I'd already been in France for over six months.'

'So when did you learn that Makepeace had been killed?'

'Not until I was finally allowed to contact Lucy, which was towards the end of June.'

'And by then, he'd been walled up in the air vent for over nine months.'

'Yes, that's correct.'

'Don't you ever feel guilty about it?' I ask.

And this man, who I have known for ten years, does something I have never seen him do before, something – if I'm honest – that I didn't believe he was even capable of.

He loses his temper.

'Well, of course I feel guilty!' he says. 'There hasn't been a day since I learned about the killing that I *haven't* felt guilty. But it's only Lennie I've ever felt guilty about. I couldn't give a toss about what happened to that bastard James Makepeace.'

18 October 1943

For days, Harold Jenkins had been telling himself that every single man in the history of the world, who'd ever been called up to fight in a war, must have worried about leaving his wife behind.

It was only a natural reaction, and he was certain that if he'd discussed the matter with all the other soldiers getting ready to be shipped out, they would have confessed to having the same doubts and concerns that he had himself.

But the problem was that – whilst he might tell himself that he was sure that *was* the case, when it came right down to it – he was not *completely* sure.

What if he was wrong about it? What if they were as secure about leaving their wives while they went off to fight as they'd have been about leaving them while they went to the corner of the street, to buy a packet of cigarettes? What if they laughed at him, and pointed him out when he passed by them?

'There goes Harry Jenkins. He's worried that the moment he leaves, some other sod will be jumping into his bed. Well, he can't have been giving his wife much of a seeing-to if he thinks that as soon as he's gone, she'll be on the lookout for something better.'

And the problem was, he half-believed that himself. Not the bit about what went on in bed – he had no doubts about how good they were together in that particular area – but the part about her wanting something better, which had absolutely nothing at all to do with sex.

He was a college porter, as his father and grandfather had been before him. He liked the job – more than liked it, he regarded it almost as a sacred trust.

But Lucy didn't come from the service tradition. Her dad worked on the assembly line at the Morris car plant at Cowley.

'It's bloody awful repetitive work, and I bloody hate it,' his future father-in-law had once told Jenkins. *'Doing the same thing, day-in, day-out, it's enough to drive you round the bloody twist, but when I get that pay packet on Thursday, when I bounce it up*

*and down in the palm of my hand, and think about all them little
extras I can buy for my family, well then, I know it's all worth it.'*

And Lucy, though she maybe didn't even realise it, had brought
some of that same attitude with her to the marriage:

*'Why should we put up with the dowdy furniture the college
has given us, when there's a beautiful three-piece suite in the
window of Chetwind and Sparrow's high class furnishings?'* she'd
once asked.

'Because we'd be spending money we haven't got,' he'd argued,
*'and in another few years, the college will change the furniture
anyway.'*

'I don't want to wait,' she'd said angrily. *'I don't see why I
should have to wait.'*

The war had changed all that, of course. You couldn't buy
tempting consumer goods now, even if you had the money, because
there weren't any.

But the war wouldn't last forever, and when it ended – when
the shop windows once more started filling up with stuff – they'd
be faced with the same dilemma all over again.

Maybe Lucy was already thinking about that. Maybe she'd
decided her marriage had been a mistake, and had determined to
make a much better match the next time.

And the problem was, it must look to her as if there were so
many good matches around, especially now that, with the shortage
of male servants, she was helping out in the college.

Yes, she was suddenly surrounded by gentlemen who had
country estates and could take out their cheque books and buy a
dozen three-piece suites from Chetwind and Sparrow's, if that was
what they wanted to do.

Of course, none of the young gentlemen would ever seriously
contemplate marrying her. Even if their families would allow it
(and that was as likely as a three-legged pig winning the Grand
National), the young gentlemen themselves wouldn't want to spend
the rest of their lives saddled with someone who would be a
constant social embarrassment to them.

He knew that, because he knew *them* – had been studying them
since Mr Gough had introduced him into the porters' lodge as a
small child. He knew they had been brought up to believe that
they could have anything they wanted, and that included pretty

young serving girls – could have them, and then, once they were bored with them, could discard them without a second's thought.

Yes, *he* knew them – but *she* didn't! She might believe their stories about whisking her away to their castles. She might . . . she might open her legs for them as a down payment on a promise that would never be fulfilled.

And wasn't it already starting to happen – even while he was still there himself?

Hadn't he caught her huddled in corners with James Makepeace, giggling like a schoolgirl?

'*Stay away from Makepeace*,' he'd warned her.

'*Why should I?*' she'd countered. '*He's a real laugh.*'

'*He's only after one thing.*'

'*You may be right, but I haven't got the one thing he's after, because he's a nancy boy.*'

And she believed that!

She really didn't understand what kinds of games these unscrupulous men played! She had absolutely no idea what lies they'd tell a girl to get what they wanted from her!

How *was* he to protect her from them once he'd gone?

He needed help – a deputy – and he had no idea who he could ask.

His real father had died in the last war, and should he now go to his second father – Mr Gough – and admit that he was not sure that he could control his own woman? No, he could not do that – his pride simply would not let him.

His mother was dead, and he had no brothers. His whole life had been based on two pillars – his marriage and the college – and now the latter couldn't help him, and the former was the problem.

There had to be somebody who could help him, he told himself – there simply had to be.

When he did finally come up with a name, that name was Lennie Moon's – which only showed the true measure of his desperation.

19 October 1943

Harold Jenkins' plan was simple. He would set Lennie to watch Lucy, and if Lennie saw that things were going too far between Lucy and Makepeace, he would tell Jenkins' cousin, Mildred Drew, about it.

Then Mildred would get in touch with him. He didn't know how
that would work yet – he'd have to be in the training before he
could work out the details – but he would find a way because
he *had to* find a way.

If Mildred did get a message to him that something serious was
going on between Lucy and Makepeace, he would throw himself
on his commanding officer's mercy, admit that he had done wrong,
and say he was more than willing to accept any punishment inflicted
on him, but please – please – could he be granted compassionate
leave to see his wife before that punishment began.

But, though the plan was simple in itself, what was far from
simple was getting the idea across to Lennie.

'You want me to watch them?' Lennie asked, mystified, as he
and Jenkins shared a pot of tea in the local café.

'That's right, Lennie,' Jenkins said. 'I want you to see what
they do when they're alone together.'

'But if I'm with them, they won't be alone.'

'You have to arrange it so that you can see them, but they can't
see you. Can you can manage that?'

'Maybe,' said Lennie dubiously. He frowned. 'But I'm not sure
that I want to do it, Mr Harold.'

Jenkins felt a sense of outraged injustice rushing through his
entire body. *Don't you realise how much I do for you on a daily
basis?* he wanted to scream. *Don't you understand that I have
to take on extra work because you couldn't handle it – and that
I do it gladly? Yet when I ask you to do this one little thing for
me, you say you're not sure you want to.*

That was what he *wanted* to say, but he didn't, because he knew
that whenever anyone got angry with Lennie, Lennie would retreat
into his shell, and might stay there for hours.

So instead, keeping his voice level, calm and friendly, he said,
'Why don't you want to do it, Lennie?'

'Because my mum says you shouldn't stick your nose
into anybody else's business. She says that nobody likes a nosey
parker.'

'And she's right, most of the time, but this is different, because
I think Mrs Lucy might be having an affair,' Jenkins said.

Lennie looked back at him blankly. 'An affair?' he repeated. 'I
don't know what that means.'

It means sticking his tongue right down her throat, Jenkins thought.

It means bending her over, lifting her skirt over her head, and taking her from behind.

It means . . .

'Do you know what men and women do together, when they're in bed?' he asked.

Lennie grinned, now that he was back on more solid ground.

'They go to sleep,' he said.

'Don't they do anything else?'

Lennie frowned again. He thought he had delivered the perfect answer, but he'd clearly been wrong.

'Do they talk to each other?' he asked, tentatively. 'Do they play games like "I Spy"?'

Jenkins sighed. He'd never be able to explain it to Lennie, and for a moment he was tempted to drop the plan completely.

And then the images started flooding his brain again – Lucy on her back, her legs locked tight over Makepeace's arse; Lucy on her knees, reaching forward and unbuttoning Makepeace's trousers.

'The thing is – and I'm only telling you this because I know I can trust you – Mr Churchill thinks that Makepeace is a German spy,' he said, in a quieter, more confidential tone.

'A spy!' Lennie exclaimed.

'Hush now!' Jenkins said, 'you don't want everyone to hear, do you?'

'But a spy . . .' Lennie said.

'So you'll watch him, will you – you'll fulfil your patriotic duty?'

'I'll try my hardest.'

A more subtle mind than Lennie's might have wondered why, if Makepeace was a spy, it was only necessary to watch him when he was with Lucy Jenkins. But Lennie wasn't blessed with such a mind, and it was enough for him to know that he was helping Mr Churchill.

23 October 1943

James Makepeace was fourteen when his uncle had caught him in the stables with the new assistant groom, and had immediately hauled him up before his father – Colonel Sir Rupert Makepeace – for a swift and unequivocal judgement.

Sir Rupert had chosen to hand down this judgement from behind the mahogany desk in his study, a large room containing few books but many stuffed heads of animals he had slaughtered.

Standing in front of that desk, his hands linked behind his back in the approved manner, James had known that the wisest thing to do in that situation was to blame it all on the groom, who was a couple of years older than he was. And indeed, that had been precisely James' plan, because grooms were easily replaceable, especially in the middle of a depression, when nearly half the population hadn't been getting enough to eat.

Yes, that had been his intention, but as his father had droned on and on about how weak and easily led he had been, he felt something snap – and an anger like he had never known before had begun to burn inside him.

'It wasn't easy at all, you know,' he'd told his father – aware that daring to interrupt the old man was, in and of itself, almost a capital offence.

He'd been amazed that though he was so very angry, his voice sounded light and amused.

'No, it wasn't easy,' he'd repeated. 'In fact, it took rather a lot of skill, because, you see, that groom isn't naturally a homo at all.'

The colonel had suddenly turned a red which was almost scarlet, and a prominent vein had begun throbbing on his forehead.

'Am I to take . . . to take it . . . am I to take that to mean that rather than him seducing you, you seduced him?' he had demanded.

It was such a great relief to have finally come out in the open that James felt almost light-headed.

'Yes, I seduced him,' he had agreed, 'and he's only one of dozens of young men who've passed through my legs.'

'There must be institutions – medical centres – where you can be cured,' the colonel had said shakily.

'I'm sure there are,' James had agreed, 'but I certainly won't be going to any of them.'

'If you won't obey me, I'll cut you off without a penny,' the colonel had threatened.

'Then cut me off,' James had replied, with a recklessness born of newly discovered, wonderfully all-encompassing anger.

The colonel had not done quite that, because his wife – who had set great store by education – had made him promise to support his son until he graduated from university, but after that, the colonel said, whatever else happened, the disgusting little creature was on his own.

As much as he enjoyed the power that his anger released in him, Makepeace had been forced to acknowledge that it had, more often than not, got him into a situation that no sane man would ever wish to find himself in. But he had never imagined it would place him in such a perilous situation as he found himself in after his meeting with Comstock, that sunny October afternoon.

He had agreed to meet Sergeant Comstock by the river, on the day which – though neither of them knew it when the arrangement was being made – would be Comstock's last day on earth. As far as Makepeace was concerned, he had been caught out trying to pull a fast one, and since the game was now up, he had fully intended to comply with all the sergeant's demands. He'd taken with him the money he owed Comstock (though 'the money he had failed to cheat Comstock out of' would probably have been a better description) and had been ready to hand it over. If they had not parted as friends at the end of the transaction, then they could have at least have parted on a handshake.

But Comstock hadn't wanted it that way. What he'd wanted was to belittle the other man – to tell his version of events, in which James Makepeace was a man of little spirit, and was only handing over the money because he was too terrified to do anything else.

It was like being lectured to by his father all over again, Makepeace had thought, and when Comstock had turned his back on him – presumably to show that *he* was not a coward, and that he had nothing but contempt for his opponent – it had only been a moment's work to pick up a large stone off the ground and smash the back of his head in with it.

Makepeace was no fool, and he recognised that his actions would have consequences.

Comstock's gang would want him dead, the police would want him in custody (and, at some point in the future, executed).

Yes, there would be consequences, so the trick was not to be around when those consequences fell due.

He would have to run away, and when he finally stopped running and settled somewhere, it would be as someone else, because James Makepeace would have to disappear forever.

What he needed now was money – as much as possible. He had tried to blackmail Charlie Swift, but Swift had shown a strength of character he had previously kept well hidden, and had refused to help, whatever the consequences for himself.

So, if he could not get a lot of money from one person, he would have to get a little money from a lot of people, and the first of these people he had on his list was Lucy Jenkins.

The Master of St Luke's often took his dinner in his rooms, and that night, Lucy Jenkins had been assigned the task of taking it to him.

The journey from the kitchen to the Master's Quad could sometimes be difficult because of the blackout, but there was a full moon that night, and it was easy for Lucy to pick her way.

The return journey looked like being quite another matter. Thick black clouds had appeared from nowhere and covered the moon, thus plunging the college into darkness.

Standing in the archway at the foot of the Master's Staircase, Lucy wondered what she should do. There seemed to be only two alternatives. The first was to grope her way back to the kitchen. The second was to wait and see if the clouds drifted away again.

She had just decided on the latter course when a hand reached out to grab her arm, and a voice said, 'Don't scream, it's only me.'

'What do you want?' she asked.

'Money,' James Makepeace told her.

'But I've given you money. I've paid you everything I got for selling the stockings, once I'd taken my commission out of it,' Lucy protested.

'That's true enough, Lucy,' Makepeace agreed, 'but now I want your commission as well.'

'That isn't fair, I . . .'

'I haven't finished yet,' Makepeace said, squeezing her arm even tighter as he spoke. 'I want any other money you have, and anything of value that I might be able to sell. And if you don't give me all of that, I'll report you to the police, and then you'll go to prison for trading on the black market.'

The clouds drifted away from the moon, and they could see each other's pale, ghostly faces.

'Let go of my arm,' she said.

'What, and have you run away from me?' he asked, and he realised how much he was enjoying this small act of intimidation. 'No, I won't let go of you, my girl. I'm going to keep a firm grip on you until you've given me what I want.'

'You wouldn't dare behave like this if my husband, Harold, was here,' she told him.

'But he isn't here, is he?' Makepeace asked. 'He's off on the south coast somewhere, training to become cannon fodder.'

'I used to think you were a real gentleman,' she said. 'But you're not. You're nothing better than a guttersnipe.'

'And you, my dear, are just a brassy little whore who was lucky enough to find an idiot like Jenkins who would marry her,' he replied.

'Don't you dare call my husband an idiot, you swine,' Lucy hissed, like an angry cat.

'What should I call him, then?' Makepeace wondered 'A dupe? Or perhaps a cuckold?'

She didn't know what either of those words meant, but she was sure they were not very nice – and that was when she spat in his face.

'You little bitch!' he said.

And then, while keeping a firm hold on her arm with his left hand, he raised his right arm and slapped her as hard as he could across the face.

It was then that he heard the sound of heavy, awkward foot-steps behind him, and became aware of a voice which seemed to be shouting, 'Gemis-pie, Gemis-pie, Gemis-pie,' as if it were some manic chant.

He turned around to see that the big man was almost on him, and automatically pushed Lucy Jenkins roughly to one side, in order to make room to defend himself. But he had left it far too late – the angry giant slammed him against the wall by the Master's Staircase, and then grabbed his head and began to batter the masonry with it, all the time relentlessly sticking to his war cry . . . 'Gemis-pie, Gemis-pie, Gemis-pie . . .'

The first blow sent thousands of tiny pains shooting through Makepeace's head. The second was numbing, and almost pleasant. He could not have commented on the third blow, because by then he was already dead.

Lennie Moon released his grip and watched the other man's body slowly slide down the wall.

'German spy,' he said, in a much softer way now, 'German spy, German spy, German spy.'

It took Mr Gough the whole night to chip out the stones from the closed-off air vent, slide James Makepeace's body through the gap, and seal up the hole again.

He was not alone. In one corner of the cellar sat Lucy Jenkins, taking regular sips from a hip flask that Gough had provided her with. At some point during the night, she appeared to have soiled herself, but she did not seem to have noticed it, Gough was too busy to deal with it, and Lennie Moon (who had had similar accidents himself) was far too much of a gentleman to mention it.

Lennie tried, at several points, to assist Mr Gough, but there was not really enough time to allow him to help, and Gough worked on alone.

At about half past three, Lennie – who had obviously been giving the matter some thought – said, 'Shouldn't we tell Mr Churchill about this?'

'He's already been told,' Mr Gough said, 'but you do understand that nobody else can be told, don't you?'

'*Why* can't anybody else be told?' Lennie asked, in a voice that was a mixture of sulky and rebellious.

'Because Mr Churchill doesn't *want* anybody else to be told,' Gough said urgently. 'Because Mr Churchill – who is your Prime Minister and the most important man in England – wants it kept a *secret*. Do you understand that?'

'I suppose so,' Lennie agreed reluctantly.

Another half hour passed.

'Will I get a medal?' Lennie asked.

'A medal?' Gough repeated. 'Why should you get a medal?'

'I should get one for killing the German spy,' Lennie said, as if it was obvious.

'But why would you even want a medal?' Mr Gough asked, as he slid another brick in place. 'I know you killed the spy, Mrs Lucy knows you killed the spy, and Mr Churchill knows you killed the spy. And we're all grateful to you. Isn't that enough?'

'I've never won anything before,' Lennie said, sadly. 'All the time I was in school, I never got a prize. The other boys used to laugh at me. They called me Lennie No Win. So if Mr Churchill would just give me a medal . . .'

'I expect he will give you a medal,' Gough said, because he could see no way out of it. 'But it will have to be kept secret, just like killing the German spy will have to be kept secret. You do understand that, don't you?'

'Yes,' Lennie said, unenthusiastically.

'And you won't get it right away, because Mr Churchill is a busy man, so you're going to have to learn how to be patient.'

'I know,' Lennie said.

17 October 1974

'Mr Gough told me that, every morning for two years, Lennie went to his mailbox to see if the letter from Buckingham Palace had arrived,' Mr Jenkins tells me. 'But he'd promised to be patient, and he was, and when the medal did finally get here, he was as pleased as punch.' He pauses, and then clearly deciding that what needs to be said needs to be said now, he adds, 'I was never going to let Lord Swift go to jail, you know, however much he tried to persuade me that was just what I should do. All I wanted was a little more time with Lucy, before I gave myself up.'

'It was all my fault,' Lucy Jenkins says. 'Everything was my fault. If I hadn't got friendly with James Makepeace—'

'We all make mistakes,' her husband interrupts her. 'And we can't rewrite the past, so there's no point in trying.'

But she hasn't finished.

'If only I'd told you *why* I was seeing him,' she continues, 'but I knew you'd disapprove, because you're such an honest, decent man.'

'I should have trusted you,' he says. 'I should have known you'd never betray me with that man.'

There is passion and hurt behind their words, but for all that, it is plain they are simply rehashing the same dialogue which has dominated their lives for over a quarter of a century.

'Let's talk about Lennie,' I suggest.

'Once the bodies had been found in the shaft, I realised that there was no way I could keep Lennie out of prison,' Mr Jenkins says. 'But I couldn't let him go to prison, either, because that would have been a living hell for him.'

'So you decided to kill him?'

'I did.'

And this was exactly what Mr Gough had immediately understood in that run-down bar in Majorca. This was why Mr Gough had said he was glad that Lennie was dead.

'The doctor said it was a clean break,' I tell Mr Jenkins.

'Yes, it was,' he said, as if he needs no confirmation from me. 'We can never know what anyone suffers in that split second before death, but that's all it was – a split second. And he never suspected a thing, because . . .' he pauses and gulps, '. . . because I was his friend, Mr Harold.'

'You'd done it before, hadn't you?' I ask.

'More than a dozen times,' he confirms. 'When you're on the kind of mission I was on, you need to be able to kill quickly and silently.'

'You told Mr Gough about that part of your work, didn't you?' I ask.

He nods. 'We weren't supposed to, but you have to tell someone – you just have to, or it will fester inside you.'

'*How was he killed?*' Mr Gough had asked, '*Was his neck broken?*'

And, once I'd confirmed that it was, he'd known pretty much the whole story.

'The reason I lied to you about what I did in the war, Miss Redhead, was because that's what they ordered me to do,' Mr Jenkins says. 'I should still be lying, but I've told so *many* lies since I killed Lennie that I'm heartily sick of it.'

'Were you really awarded the Distinguished Service Medal?' I ask.

'Oh yes, but it was awarded for something that I didn't actually do, because they couldn't give it to me for what I *had* done.'

'You went through all that, and yet you still came back here,' I say, before I can stop myself.

'What do you mean?' he asks.

'You must have seen things I've never seen, and done things I've never done,' I tell him. 'You're much more of a grown-up than I'll ever be and yet, after all you'd seen and done, you still came back to your job in the porters' lodge.'

'What happened in the war has got nothing to do with real life,' he says. 'All I've ever wanted to be was the head porter at St Luke's College, and, you see, that's what I am.'

I find myself almost hating him for the decisions he has taken. Here is a man who is not only undoubtedly brave, but is also an artist, and yet he has chosen to fritter it away in order to follow a family tradition. It seems such a waste.

And though I love my college for the enlightenment and opportunities it has brought me, there are moments like this when I see it as an archaic impediment to progress, which should have been swept away years ago.

Am I confused?

You bet I am.

'Besides,' Mr Jenkins says, 'there was always Lennie to consider.'

Ah yes, there was always Lennie to consider.

I think of all the components that helped to make up this little tragedy, and realise that without them being interlocked in such a complex manner, it would never have happened.

If Lennie hadn't fallen off the ladder because the bursar wouldn't buy a new one . . .

If he'd taken the compensation he'd been offered, instead of accepting a job for life . . .

If Makepeace had gone to some other Oxford college, or chosen one in Cambridge instead . . .

If he hadn't met Comstock, and agreed to sell his black market nylon stockings for him . . .

If Lucy Jenkins hadn't been employed by the college as a result of a shortage of male servants . . .

If Lucy had been honest with her husband about what she was doing – or had not done it at all . . .

If Mr Jenkins had trusted his wife more . . .

If, instead of setting Lennie to watch her, Mr Jenkins had confided in Mr Gough . . .

If Makepeace hadn't killed Comstock . . .

Enough! More than enough! If I think about it any longer, I'll probably go completely out of my mind.

'When are you going to give yourself up to the police?' I ask Mr Jenkins.

'This afternoon,' he says.

'I'm sorry . . . really sorry . . . that things have worked out the way they have,' I tell him.

He nods. And in that nod I can see a man who has faced death and also caused it, and then chosen to return to Oxford to immerse himself entirely in that six-hundred-year-old organism which is St Luke's.

'I'm sorry, too,' he says. 'We're all sorry.'

TWENTY-FOUR

18 October 1974

A number of students are sitting at the terrace tables outside The Head of the River pub. I can understand why they're out there, braving the cold, because there's definitely something special about the River Isis at night – something which is intangible, yet still seems to promise perfect freedom and unlimited possibilities.

Once upon a time, I would have been sharing the magic with these young people, and so, I suspect, would my companion for the evening, Lord Charles Swift. But our undergraduate days are already becoming distant memories, and without even discussing the possibility of choosing the outside seating, we head for the warmer interior.

Since it's a celebration – of sorts – Charlie orders an uncommonly rare wine. One of the bar staff, unsure they have it in stock, goes to the cellar to look for it, and when he finally emerges with the prize – a good ten minutes later – he, and the rest of the people behind the bar, fuss over it as if it were a delicate chick that had just hatched or an exquisite Chinese ornament.

Meanwhile, creating absolutely no excitement at all, I have been sipping at my gin and tonic, a drink which is so *un*-uncommon that I'm surprised they don't keep a large zinc bucket full of it under the counter.

We take our drinks over to a table near the window, and once we're sitting down, I say, 'So what have the police told you?'

'That I'll almost definitely be prosecuted for wasting police time . . .'

'Which you did.'

'Which I did, I agree. But they also went on to say that unless I'm very unlucky, and get a magistrate in a bad mood because his wife has just run away with window cleaner – or maybe has decided *not* to run off with the window cleaner – I'll probably get off with a suspended sentence.'

'You bloody English aristocrats – you think you can get away with murder,' I tell him. And then it occurs to me that, given the circumstances, it was not the most tactful thing I could have said.

'This is *supposed* to be a fine wine, but I think I might have met the donkey that peed it,' Charlie says, in an attempt to lighten the mood.

Bless him!

But like it or not, there are matters that still need to be discussed.

'Why did you do it, Charlie?' I ask.

For a moment, I'm afraid he's going to say, 'Do what?' But then he shrugs, as if he'll go along with it just to humour me.

'You know why I confessed to James Makepeace's murder,' he says. 'It was to get you out of the mess that my own cowardice had dropped you into in the first place.'

'I don't mean that,' I say. 'I want to know why you confessed to Lennie Moon's murder.'

Another shrug. 'I did it to protect Jenkins.'

'How did you know it was Mr Jenkins who killed Lennie?'

'Maybe I worked it out. Maybe I'm getting to be as good at this detecting lark as you are.'

'*Charlie!*' I say sharply.

He grins, 'Jenkins came to see me. He assured me that though he wouldn't be around anymore, he had timetabled portering duties in such a way as to make sure the college would run smoothly for the next two weeks. He also gave me a shortlist of the people he would recommend to take over from him.'

'Oh God!' I hear myself moan.

'I asked him why he was talking all this nonsense about not being around,' Charlie continues, 'and he said he was about to turn himself in for Lennie Moon's murder. So I told him not to be so stupid, and pointed out that as I was planning to turn myself in for Makepeace's murder, I might as well follow the example of the supermarkets and give them one for the price of two.' He frowns. 'I think I may have got that a bit wrong.'

'You've just told me what you did, but not why you did it,' I point out.

'Why did I do it? I suppose it was because Jenkins has given his life to the college, and I felt it only right that the college – in the person of the bursar – should now offer him its protection.'

'Now we'll have your real reason,' I tell him.

He sighs. 'I didn't think I could bear the thought of Jenkins and his wife being separated,' he says. 'I thought it would be much easier for me, you see, because I don't have anybody.'

'You have *me*,' I say fiercely.

'Yes, for the moment,' he agrees. 'But when you find the love of your life, you will abandon me – quite rightly so, and I wouldn't want it any other way.' He sighs. 'That is, inevitably, the tragic fate of old queens.'

The thing is, I'm not sure I ever will find the love of my life in Charlie's meaning of the word. I think that being brought up in a home that was terribly civilised and terribly polite – but in which emotion was seen as a steel-jawed trap you should always tiptoe around – has made me immune to that kind of thing.

Far better, from my perspective, to have the occasional fling – like my night on Majorca with that Spanish boy whose name I've already forgotten.

And if I'm right about my never falling in love, what will happen to me in the future? Charlie is so much older than I am, you see, and – barring the very unexpected – is bound to shuffle off this mortal coil long before I do, thus leaving me to cope with life alone.

Maybe, when that happens, I could find a nice young homosexual to adopt – but even as I consider the idea, I recognise that, in practice, I would never contemplate such disloyalty.

Maybe I could get myself a crossbred dog with just a hint of King Charles spaniel in him, and tell everyone he was a Lord Charlie.

That's right, make a joke of it.

Way to go, Jennie!

I wonder if it will always be like this – the adrenalin rush when I'm wrapped up in an investigation, the feeling of let-down when it's all over.

'Life's the pits, isn't it, Charlie?' I say.

'Perhaps it is,' he agrees, 'but it's always better *living* in a pit than being *buried* in one.'

He's right, of course.

I really hate it when he's right!